HEA OR

D

AND H ELS

"A gift mes

"One of America's most endearing historical fiction authors."
—*RT Book Reviews*

"No one brings home small-town America in a more picturesque manner than bestselling author Dorothy Garlock."
—*Under the Covers Book Reviews*

STAY A LITTLE LONGER

"Heartwarming...love blooms."   —*Publishers Weekly*

"Touching...[a] poignant, engrossing story of life, death, and second chances...Well written and swiftly paced, this story brings to life a time period that is seldom-used in romance."
—*Library Journal*

"An emotional...profound Americana tale [with a] strong ensemble cast...fans will relish this terrific historical."
—GenreGoRoundReviews.com

"Garlock is so familiar with her time period that she makes writing it look easy. Her attention to detail is astounding, and she does an incredible job of putting you in both time and place."   —LikesBooks.com

"Vivid...Garlock weaves the tale expertly."
—*Waterloo-Cedar Falls Courier* (IA)

TRAIN FROM MARIETTA

"An enjoyable and relaxing curl-up read for a cozy Sunday afternoon!" —*Historical Novels Review*

"A sweet, satisfying romance." —*Publishers Weekly*

· RIVER RISING

"Once again, Garlock captivates." —*Historical Novels Review*

"Garlock does a terrific job...Fans will be delighted." —*Booklist*

SONG OF THE ROAD

"Outstanding." —*AromanceReview.com*

"This romance is a treat, buoyed by strong characters and Garlock's old-fashioned, no-nonsense storytelling." —*Publishers Weekly*

HOPE'S HIGHWAY

"An entertaining cavalcade of characters...heart-throbbing romance." —*Publishers Weekly*

"No one evokes the Depression like Garlock...A great, hopeful read." —*RT Book Reviews*

MOTHER ROAD

"Bestselling Garlock's endearing characters and vividly depicted milieu will enchant her legions of readers." —*Booklist*

"An engaging tale, spiced with Depression-era detail." —*Publishers Weekly*

DOROTHY GARLOCK

Keep a Little Secret

GRAND CENTRAL
PUBLISHING

NEW YORK   BOSTON

Grand Central Publishing
Hachette Book Group
237 Park Avenue
New York, NY 10017

www.HachetteBookGroup.com

Printed in the United States of America

First Edition: March 2011
10 9 8 7 6 5 4 3 2 1

Grand Central Publishing is a division of Hachette Book Group, Inc.
The Grand Central Publishing name and logo is a trademark of Hachette Book Group, Inc.

Library of Congress Cataloging-in-Publication Data
Garlock, Dorothy.
  Keep a little secret / Dorothy Garlock.
    p. cm.
  ISBN 978-0-446-54012-4 (hardcover)
  ISBN 978-0-446-54014-8 (trade)
  I. Title.
  PS3557.A71645K44 2010
  813'.54—dc22
                    2010008602

This book is dedicated to the Friday morning
coffee girls, Ann Doubler, Denise Hathaway-Easley,
Mary Ann Hendricks, Lindy Lemon, and Marge Theiss;
and good friends Michelle and Doug Klein, Jody
and Rex McChesney, and Lois Woiwood.

Thank you all for being my sounding board.

Keep a
Little Secret

Secrets

Oklahoma's so bright it hurts my eyes,
Yet when I squint I can see for miles.
In this clear light it's a grim surprise
That secrets so dark lie behind some smiles.

Does that kind man hide a cruel past?
Does this rude man have a tender heart?
Is this romance too fragile to last?
Will my brave new life soon be torn apart?

Is hatred the goad and vengeance the task?
In such evil soil, can true love grow?
These are painful questions I dare not ask.
They have answers I fear to know.

—F.S.I.

Prologue

Longbow, Colorado—December 1938

OWEN WALLACE STOOD ALONE on the ramshackle porch of his family's small house, staring absently into the falling snow. The storm had come on hard in the last hour and showed no sign of letting up. Before him, the hood of the doctor's automobile had already become covered, despite the heat of the rapidly cooling engine. A swirling, merciless wind cut sharply on the exposed skin of Owen's hands and face, but he paid it little heed.

Though the inside of the small house was warm, well heated by the wood-burning stove, Owen felt no need to head indoors in spite of the miserable weather. Outside, alone with the growing fury of the winter storm, he could pretend that his mother wasn't dying, if only for a short while.

Behind him, the door opened, then was quickly closed.

"I'm afraid there is nothing more that I can do for her, Owen," Walter Calloway, Longbow's doctor, said in a resigned tone of voice. "She never woke while I was examining her, but her sleep is far from peaceful."

Owen gave a slight nod in answer, still facing the falling snow.

"Though it greatly pains me to say it, I believe the day we've all been dreading has finally arrived."

"How much longer does she have?"

"It's all in the Lord's hands now," the doctor answered. "Hannah is doing her best to keep Caroline comfortable, but besides making sure that the fire remains fully stoked, all we can do now is wait."

Dr. Calloway's heavy-lidded eyes, hidden behind thick-framed glasses, gave ample evidence that his concern was genuine. He looked tired, worn beyond even the many years he had served the town, weighed down by the burden of an illness he couldn't hope to cure.

"Thank you for everything you've done for her," Owen offered.

"I only wish that I could have done more," Dr. Calloway answered, putting a hand on Owen's shoulder in condolence, before he trudged through the piling snow to his car and drove away.

For a few moments longer, Owen remained on the porch. Looking out into the distance, he could see only the faintest glimmer of light emanating from a weather-shrouded home; the homestead he shared with his mother and sister had few neighbors, and now, even in their greatest hour of need, no one offered to help. Whatever was to come they would face alone, as always.

Reluctantly, Owen went indoors. When he entered, Hannah didn't glance up from her duties. With determined diligence, his sister wiped away the beads of sweat that dampened their mother's brow. Caroline Wallace lay small in her bed, ravaged by her sickness, her teeth chattering and her tiny, fragile shoulders shaking as if they were leaves caught in the teeth of an April storm. What beauty she'd once possessed had been stripped away by illness, leaving behind dark and sunken eyes, cracked lips, and skin as pale as faded parchment.

Soon she would be dead.

Tenderly, Hannah swept back a stray strand of her mother's grey hair, tucking it behind the sick woman's ear. With a weak smile, Hannah whispered words of comfort to the restless woman, but Owen was too far away to hear them clearly. Caring for her night and day, Hannah did all that she could, although nothing seemed to lessen Caroline's suffering.

The small, three-room home Owen shared with his mother and sister was sparsely furnished; besides the bed in which his mother lay, the front room contained nothing except a rickety table, a pair of broken-down chairs, and the dilapidated wood-burning stove. Their lives had been full of little but struggle. Owen tossed a few more pieces of wood into the fire, following what little advice the doctor had been able to give.

Eventually, Hannah rose from her mother's bedside and joined Owen beside the stove. Both weariness and worry were etched across her face; caring for Caroline in her dying days was a burden they had both willingly shouldered, but a burden nonetheless.

"Dr. Calloway said that it's only a matter of time." Owen's words faltered.

"Don't say such things," Hannah whispered, her eyes darting to where her mother still fitfully slept. "She'll hear."

"She can't hear us now, Hannah."

"You don't know that for certain."

"Even if she knows what we're saying," he explained, "I don't reckon she'd fault us for seeing the obvious."

"It's just not something that I want to hear."

"But it's the truth."

Hannah's mouth opened as if she wanted to argue the point further, but instead her gaze wistfully settled upon their mother. For a long while, the room remained silent save for the crackling of the fire.

"She isn't going to be able to tell us now," Owen finally said. "Once she's gone, we'll never know."

"It's no longer important."

"The hell it isn't!" he snapped, the worry and anger he had been holding inside for days, months, and even years finally starting to erupt. "Are you saying that the knowledge we've waited our whole lives to learn can just die with her?"

"What are we supposed to do, Owen?" Hannah pleaded, her eyes growing wet with tears. "Do you want to rouse her and make her talk? Should I quit making her as comfortable as I can until her tongue finally loosens and she tells us who our father was?"

"But we just can't . . . we have to know . . ." he sputtered, knowing how difficult it had always been to put what he wanted into words. Frustration burned in his belly. "Goddamn it all!"

Hannah's hand found his and he turned to face her.

"We need to accept that we may never know," she said softly.

Owen fought against the meaning of his sister's words. All his life he had wondered about the man who had abandoned them when he and Hannah were still in their mother's womb, who had broken his mother's heart and left her to fend for herself and her children . . . the man who had forced them to accept charity and ridicule from neighbors and who now would not be there to watch Caroline Wallace breathe her last.

"I can't do that," Owen spat solemnly. "I can't accept it. I'll tear this place apart piece by piece if I have to. Mother may have wanted to keep her little secret, to try her damnedest to protect us, but for what that man has done to all of us, I swear that I will know his name."

And then that son of a bitch will pay!

Chapter One

Kansas City, Missouri—June 1939

WITH AN OPEN HAND, Charlotte Tucker slapped the well-dressed young man flush across his clean-shaven face, releasing a storm of shock and anger to darken his handsome features. While her blow clearly hadn't hurt him, her reaction to his forward and improper advances had undeniably taken him aback. The sound of her striking him, loud as a gunshot, hung in the air of the train depot.

All around them on the busy station platform, people had begun to gawk. In the instant after Charlotte struck the man, there had been a deafening silence, hushing the frantic hustle and bustle of travelers scurrying to their destinations. But that quiet was short-lived. Murmuring voices rose as faces turned, fingers pointing at the source of the commotion.

"How dare you say such things to me!" Charlotte shouted, ignoring the attention she was attracting. "Have you no shame!"

"Miss...I...I..." the man stammered. "I'm afraid that you must have misunderstood me..."

"How could I possibly have mistaken what you said?" she disagreed forcefully. "When a man approaches a young woman he doesn't know, has never so much as spoken to before, and asks if she would like to find a hotel room for the afternoon, what could his intentions possibly be?"

Color rose at the man's collar, a bright, obvious crimson of embarrassment, in stark contrast to the perfect white of his starched shirt. His discomfort was worsened by the snickers that rose among the crowd.

"But...but I never said such things!" he argued defensively.

"And now you go and make it worse by lying!" Charlotte accused. "How many other young women have you approached in such a scandalous way, scheming and lurking in the shadows until you found an easy mark?"

"Ne-never!"

"I suppose you imagined that I would go along with your ridiculous, insulting plans," she continued, not giving the man a moment's pause. "You never imagined you would be exposed, did you?"

"What kind of man says such a thing?" a voice asked from the crowd.

"Must be some kind'a pervert!" another added.

Quickly looking from side to side, the man was uncomfortably aware that he was drawing too much attention to himself. Dropping the façade of innocence, he stepped closer to Charlotte, reached out, and snatched her tightly and painfully by the wrist.

"You better keep that mouth of yours shut, bitch," the man threatened, "unless you're looking to get hurt!"

Instead of shrinking in fear from the man's threats, Charlotte rose to meet them defiantly, her gaze never wavering, even as she unsuccessfully tried to disentangle herself from his grip.

"Let go of me this instant!" she cried.

Before the sound of her angry voice could fade into the depot, the man suddenly raised his hand as if he meant to strike her, a blow that would have hurt more than the one she had struck. Still, Charlotte never flinched, facing her would-be attacker with steely determination. But before the man could follow through with his intentions, a voice cut through the relative quiet of the platform, startling all those who watched.

"Now what seems to be the matter here!" a deep baritone bellowed. "That ain't no way to treat a lady, fella!"

Charlotte turned to see a squat, frowning policeman waddle over menacingly to where she and the man stood, his watchman's stick clutched tightly between calloused, thick fingers. He looked ready to act and broach no disagreement. At the sight of him, the man released his grip on Charlotte and took two hesitant steps backward.

With his arrival, the crowd began shouting in explanation, a jumble of voices where only bits could be heard.

"...and then that man laid hands on her..."

"...was only defendin' herself!"

"...and it's just like she done said, 'cause I seen the whole darned thing!"

"Now, now, now, let's everybody quiet down!" the police officer shouted, putting a quick end to the rising chatter. Turning to Charlotte, he asked, "Is what these here people is sayin' true, miss? Was this chap botherin' you?"

Charlotte nodded, explaining the man's repugnant suggestion that they find a hotel room. "And that's when I slapped him," she added.

The police officer laughed heartily. "Can't say I blame ya for it!"

"But...but...but what she's saying isn't true, Officer," the man protested, assuming the innocent look he had unsuccessfully used just after Charlotte slapped him. "I'd never so much as spoken a word to her before she walked up and slapped—"

"Now why don't you and I head on back to the depot office," the officer said as he clamped a vicelike grip on the man's wrist while wiggling his watchman's stick threateningly. "That way we can have ourselves a little chat 'bout the whole thing.

"Sorry for the problem, miss," he added to Charlotte as he led the man away.

A small smile crept across Charlotte's lips at the

satisfaction of having the disgusting man led away to his just punishment, but just as she was feeling smug about her victory, she glanced up at the large clock at the far end of the depot, and realized that she was about to be late. Snatching up her bags, she turned on her heel and dashed toward her rail line.

She had a train to catch.

Settling breathlessly into her seat, Charlotte thanked her lucky stars that she hadn't missed her train. Out on the platform, the conductor shouted, "All aboard!" Moments later, the engine's shrill whistle pierced the air of the busy depot and the train began to pick up speed and head toward its destination.

"We're moving, Mommy! We're moving!" the little girl in the seat ahead said in excitement.

"Yes, dear, we sure are," her mother answered.

Charlotte smiled and settled into her seat.

Outside her window, the hustle and bustle of Kansas City, the cars and trucks and trolley cars, the buildings and construction that strained upward toward the summer sky, soon began to fall away, replaced first by houses and then by tall stalks of corn and endless fields of cattle as the city gave way to the countryside.

Removing her white hat, Charlotte pulled a small mirrored compact from her purse and began fixing her long, tousled blond curls. For a moment she paused, examining her bright blue eyes, high cheekbones, and pert nose.

Accepting compliments, welcome or otherwise, had always been difficult for Charlotte, even if she knew she had some beauty. All her life, she had been told that she was the image of her mother, Alice, who had died while giving birth to her.

With a sigh, Charlotte closed her compact, smoothed the soft fabric of her white blouse and dark blue skirt, and settled back into her seat, thankful that her ordeal on the platform was over.

I've come a long way from Minnesota…

In her purse, folded carefully, was the telegram sent to her from Sawyer, a small town out in northern Oklahoma, hiring her to teach in their school. Her hands had shaken, with equal parts of excitement and nervousness, when she stood in the telegraph office at Lancaster College to send her acceptance. From that moment to now, traveling to her brand-new job, she had walked on air.

All her life, Charlotte had wanted to get away, to see what the world had to offer her. Growing up in Carlson, Minnesota, little more than a hiccup of a town north of the Twin Cities, she'd spent her childhood days playing in the woods that lined the shores of Lake Washington. But even before she went away to teachers' college, she had yearned to see more of the world.

And that telegram from Oklahoma promised the opportunity to be independent in a new environment.

But excited as she was over what lay ahead, she knew

that there were things she'd miss about the life she was leaving behind.

Saying good-bye to her family, especially her parents, was hard. They were in tears the whole way to the depot. For Rachel, her mother's younger sister who had raised Charlotte and then married her father, the separation was particularly painful. Though there was no doubt that Rachel wanted her "daughter" to go out in the world and succeed, she still felt as if she were losing her little girl. Leaving her father, Mason, brought back some of Charlotte's earliest memories. For her first six years, she had believed, as had the rest of Carlson, that her father had perished on some unknown battlefield in France during the Great War. When he finally returned, his face terribly scarred by an exploding shell, Charlotte had been the one to find him, deathly sick in a shack in the woods. To have him returned to her life, to watch as he smiled over her accomplishments and he worried at her failures, was a greater joy than she could ever have imagined. Seeing him at the depot, his dark hair growing white at the temples, affection beaming from his face, was a memory that Charlotte would carry with her to Oklahoma.

Even her grandmother, Eliza, who had helped Rachel raise her, had come to the depot to see her off. She had often chastised Charlotte for the troubles she caused as a child, but Eliza was now proud at what her granddaughter had achieved.

The hardest person to say good-bye to had been her half sister, Christina, younger by seven years, and her closest friend. There were many differences between the two of them physically; Christina had black hair and piercing green eyes and an even temperament while Charlotte was far more prone to fly off the handle, but the bond between them had always been unshakeable. All the hours they spent together, talking about their dreams and hopes, seemed to have passed by in an instant. To watch her older sister set off on the course of her life had prompted Christina to count the days until she could do the same.

And so, two days earlier, the twenty-year-old Charlotte Tucker had waved farewell to all that she had known. Through tears, she imagined that those who had passed away from her life—her mother, old Uncle Otis who had died one night in his sleep with a beaming smile across his face, and even Jasper, the mangy mutt who used to follow Charlotte on her many adventures around Carlson—were all watching down approvingly from Heaven above.

What lay ahead Charlotte couldn't know, but she couldn't wait to get to Oklahoma and begin her new life. Whether it was teaching schoolchildren, seeing new sights, meeting new people, or even, as impossible as it was to imagine, falling in love, she was ready to enjoy every step of the way.

As the reddish yellow sun, as full as a saucer, began its descent on the far distant horizon and stars crowded the edges of the sky announcing the coming of the night,

Charlotte closed her eyes, relaxing with the gentle rocking and swaying of the train car, and slowly drifted to sleep.

One of the first days of the rest of her life was finally drawing to an end.

Charlotte awoke to bright rays of sunlight streaming through the window onto her face and the sounds of her few fellow passengers as they began to stir. Her sleep hadn't been peaceful; a man's snoring had wakened her and she had the vague memory of gazing out her window upon the shimmering surface of a slow-moving river silvered by moonlight. Fortunately, she'd been able to fall back to sleep. She rubbed at her neck, stiff from the discomfort of having to sleep sitting up.

Outside, the landscape had changed as the train sped through the night; gone were the gently rolling hills of prairie grass, replaced by a mostly flat scrabble occasionally spotted by squat, clumpy hills of much-redder soil than any she had ever seen before. Tufts of buffalo grass sprang up here and there, far taller than the rest of the short, parched-looking grass. Trees were few and far between, with bunches of scrub bushes scattered about.

Having grown up on the shores of a large lake, surrounded by majestic maple, elm, and pine trees and the thick woods full of wildlife, Charlotte found the many differences of the Oklahoma landscape startling, yet beautiful at the same time. She wondered whether the people she would meet in Sawyer would be so different from those at home.

Suddenly, Charlotte spotted one of them. Up on a rocky rise, sitting atop a tan and white horse, was a cowboy. When he caught sight of the passengers looking up at him, he took off his dusty hat and gave them a hearty wave. Charlotte managed to wave in return, but only after the train had moved on and the cowboy had fallen from sight.

At the front of the train car, the door opened and in walked the train's conductor, a portly man with a thick, bushy white mustache wider than the small hat sitting atop his head. Checking a pocket watch connected by a chain fob to his vest, he nodded to passengers as he made his way down the narrow aisle.

"How much longer until the train arrives in Sawyer?" Charlotte asked.

"Next stop." He thumbed in the direction the train was heading. "By my watch we should be there in just under twelve minutes."

The first signs of Sawyer soon began to come into view. There were ranches with enormous steers and dozens of horses all lazing behind sturdy fences. As the train passed by one ranch, a battered pickup truck pulled out and followed alongside Charlotte's car, its tires kicking up enormous plumes of dust, before finally turning away just short of town.

Craning her neck out the window to get a better view, Charlotte could see the center of town ahead. Except for its water tower, it didn't appear to be much different from Carlson. Businesses lined the main street, their signs and awnings announcing their wares, as people milled about on their daily business. On the far side of town rose a church spire, stark white against the brilliance of the blue sky. A group of children, with a yapping dog in tow, did their best to keep up with the train as it slowed. Near the small train depot, its iron wheels screamed against the iron tracks. With another blast of its whistle, it shuddered to a stop.

Gathering her things, Charlotte hurried into the aisle, scarcely able to contain the nervous excitement that coursed through her. Up ahead, a man groaned exhaustedly as he heaved himself out of his seat, planted his cowboy hat over his sun-burned head, and headed for the door, stopping when he saw Charlotte approach.

"Ma'am," he said with a nod of his hat, letting her go by.

"Thank you," she replied.

Once she had passed, Charlotte stifled a smile at the thought that the man looked as if he would have been much more comfortable on the back of a horse than inside the train. She wondered if he wasn't the source of the snoring that had woken her in the night!

Finally, she was before the door. Pausing until a box was placed beneath the steps, Charlotte took a deep breath, accepted the assisting hand of the conductor, and stepped out onto the platform.

Chapter Two

THE EARLY AFTERNOON summer sun felt warm upon Charlotte's skin as she futilely tried to shade her eyes from the bright glare. A sniffing wind swirled the scattered dust at her feet. The air felt dry and heavy, a far cry from the oppressive humidity of Minnesota, but no less hot.

Sawyer's train platform lacked the activity of the depot in Kansas City; besides the cowboy who had nodded to her, the only other passenger who disembarked was an older woman, her shoulders hunched low from the weight of the pair of heavy bags she carried.

At first glance, Charlotte saw no one waiting for her.

"Miss Tucker?" a loud voice asked, startling her.

Charlotte looked up as a middle-aged man, well-worn cowboy hat in his hand, strode toward her from deep shadows inside the depot. Trailing behind him was another man.

"Yes?" she replied cautiously.

Smiling broadly, the man stretched out his hand in greeting. "I'm John Grant. You'll be stayin' at my ranch while you're here in Sawyer."

Immediately, Charlotte felt at ease. She had received a letter weeks earlier from Mr. Grant, offering her a place in his home on a horse ranch. Apparently, he rented out a couple of rooms in much the same way her grandmother had at her boardinghouse in Carlson. Having grown up in such an environment, Charlotte had readily accepted his offer.

"It's a pleasure to meet you, Mr. Grant," she answered.

"Now, the only men I ever knew that went by 'Mr. Grant' was my pa and my grandpappy before him, and since I ain't half the man either one of them managed to be, it just don't seem right for me to be takin' their names. I'd like it best if you'd call me John."

"Only if you call me Charlotte," she replied, taking his offered hand.

"Then you got yourself a deal."

John Grant made a strong first impression with his neatly combed, snow-white hair, his deep-set, sparkling blue eyes, and his broad, welcoming smile. But the ruggedness of a rancher was hard to disguise. The many lines and wrinkles on his weathered face, his hands worn and calloused, and his bronzed skin were the result of his days spent working beneath the hot Oklahoma sun. With his shirt, pants, and boots caked with dust he would never be mistaken for a banker or lawyer.

"This is one of my men, Del Grissom," John explained, introducing Charlotte to the man who had followed him from the depot.

"Nice to meet you," Del offered with a tip of his dusty hat. He was much younger than his boss; his thick coal black hair fell from beneath the hat's brim and framed a worn, narrow face. Occasionally, his left eye gave a sort of nervous tic, all of its own accord. Still, he looked to Charlotte to be a hardworking, pleasant man.

"Your trip weren't too hard, I hope," John said.

"Not at all," she said. "It was wonderful to see a different landscape. It sure is a far cry from what we have in Minnesota."

"Even so, my thinkin' is that people who spend too much time in one of them iron contraptions," John said, nodding at the idling train, "find themselves needing a washbasin and a few hours of shut-eye. Once we're back on the ranch, you'll have a chance to have both."

When Charlotte's heavy black trunk in which she'd packed away all of the life she had known was unloaded from the train with a heavy thud, John and Del each grabbed an end and hoisted it up as if it were lighter than a bale of hay, and headed for the end of the platform.

Charlotte followed along behind, smiling with every step.

John Grant drove the old truck from the station and headed down Sawyer's main street with Charlotte in the passenger's seat. Del sat in the truck's bed, riding alongside her baggage. Glancing back, she saw that he seemed content to travel in the back, one arm resting upon the truck's railing as the afternoon sun shone brilliantly down.

As they drove, John pointed out all of the sights in town; from the post office, to the grocer's, and even to the theater, Charlotte felt dizzy with all of the information that was being sent her way. The streets were lively with people going into the stores and other places of business. John explained that they were trying to get their business done before the sun got to be too much to bear.

"Folks in these parts ain't too complicated, not like in a city," John explained, giving a wave out the window. "They go to church, look after their loved ones, and say, 'Howdy,' to their neighbors. They like things to be simple, but that doesn't mean they're simple folks, if you know what I mean."

"I do." Charlotte nodded. "Sawyer sounds a lot like where I come from."

"Good folks is good folks, no matter where they call home."

Occasionally, John would give the truck's horn a brief tap and yell out the window at someone he knew.

"There's Carlton Timmons' barber shop," John told her, pointing out the business as they passed. "Known Carl 'bout all my life, and except for one reservation, I can say he's as fine a man as this town's ever produced."

"What's that one thing?" Charlotte asked.

"He's one hell of a cheat at cards," John answered. "You ain't a fancier of poker, are you?"

"No, I can't say that I am. Are you?"

"Used to be, but I ain't no more on account of Carl!" John exclaimed.

Soon, the truck passed by the last business that lined Sawyer's Main Street and took a gentle turn alongside the dried-up remnants of a creek's bed. In an instant, the sights of the town had vanished, replaced by the same kind of scrabbly earth as she had seen from the train.

"Where's the school?" Charlotte asked, looking around, wondering just where it was that she would be spending her days.

"Back on the eastern side of town," John explained, thumbing over his shoulder back toward where they had come. "Since it's the opposite direction from the depot, I figured it'd be best to wait until the next visit into town 'fore givin' you a chance to become acquainted with it. School won't be startin' for a few more weeks, so there's plenty of time."

"Is the ranch far from Sawyer?" Even as she asked her questions, Charlotte wondered why she hadn't bothered to inquire about where she would be staying in all of the time she'd been corresponding with John Grant.

"Not far," the rancher answered. "'Bout two miles or so."

When John glanced over at Charlotte, he could clearly see the confusion written plainly across her face. To soothe her, he explained that although his ranch was a distance from town, he had long been a member of Sawyer's School Board, and that after she had agreed to come and teach at the school he had volunteered to provide her with lodging.

"You see, the truth of the matter," he explained a bit sheepishly, "is that...well, I was hopin' that maybe you'd be able to help me with a...a problem I've been havin' on the ranch. My askin' you to stay with us ain't without other motives."

"A problem? What sort of problem?" she asked, her interest rising.

"While I'd be happy to try explainin' it to you, it's really the sort of thing that's best seein', I reckon. Somehow, I ain't just sure that my words would explain."

For a long moment, Charlotte stared at John Grant as the truck continued on its way. On the one hand, she didn't like thinking that she had agreed to come all the way from Minnesota under false pretenses. But on the other hand, something in the old rancher's face made her believe she was not being maliciously manipulated.

"Will it interfere with my job at the school?" she asked.

"If it does, then I won't fault you for stoppin'."

Charlotte thought it over for a moment longer before saying, "I'm not agreeing to anything without knowing what it is exactly that you want me to do, but I'll do my best to go into it with an open mind. If it's something I feel

I can do without harming the reason I was brought here, then we might be able to manage to work something out."

"I couldn't expect you to be agreein' to more."

"But if I'm going to be living out on the ranch, how will I be getting back and forth to the school?"

"You mean to say you can't drive a truck?"

"Do you expect me to drive *this* every day?" Charlotte exclaimed, more than a bit surprised.

"Hell, ole Betsy here don't much like *me* drivin' her." John chuckled, patting the seat between them. "Some days gettin' her started is tougher then coaxin' a stubborn horse out of its stall, sometimes the damn steerin' wheel jerks to the left so hard it feels like it's tryin' to escape right on out the window, and I don't even want to warn you 'bout drivin' her in the rain."

"Then why did you ask?"

"Just an old rancher's sense of humor, is all."

"I can't say that I found it particularly funny," she admitted.

"Most folks don't," John snorted. "The truth is that one of the fellas that's workin' for me on the ranch heads into town pert near every day for some errand or other and I reckon catchin' a ride with him'll get you anywhere you'd want to go. Even if it's rainin', blowin' to beat the band, or even snowin', we'll manage to get you wherever it is you'd need to be."

"So this employee of yours has managed to tame Betsy,"

Charlotte teased, clearly liking the fact that John Grant was so quick to humor.

"This truck ain't all that different from the horses we got back on the ranch." He smiled knowingly. "With the really wild ones, the ones that would just as soon stomp you into a mud hole as let you put a saddle on 'em, you don't ever really break what spirit they got, not really. 'Bout as easy to tame as a spring storm that come rollin' in across the prairie. In the end, you just hope and pray that you ain't the one that ends up broken."

John Grant's horse ranch lay just across a worn and rickety bridge that spanned a wildflower-strewn creek; unlike the dried-up streambed that lay just outside of Sawyer, its rushing water gurgled across rocks below their passing wheels. An enormous pair of trees, sun dappling their breeze-blown leaves and branches, stood silent watch as the truck drove beneath.

"We're here," John said, nodding toward the house.

"It's . . . it's . . ." she began, but her words failed her.

The ranch house was much more than Charlotte had expected; two stories tall with a pair of porches on each floor that ran the length of the front of the building, decorated with four columns, the house showed that John Grant's enterprise had been successful. Painted a crisp white, it shone as majestically in the sunlight as a jewel. Surrounded by a white fence, the property was dotted with

young trees. High above them, a windmill churned lazily
in the soft breeze.

Farther back on the property, numerous small buildings lined a path that led from the ranch house to the
holding pens at the rear. A couple of larger barns, painted
dull red with white trim, had their doors flung open, and
men milled about, working on various chores. Laughter
and the sounds of labor, steel hammers colliding with
anvils, even the sawing of wood, rose above the sounds
of the truck. *There's so much activity!* Charlotte was even
pleasantly surprised to see a couple of men cultivating a
garden.

But what really caught her attention were the horses;
those who ran wildly about the pens, and others who
milled about next to the water trough, or were ridden by
men herding a small group of steers. All were captivating
to Charlotte: white, black, brown, and spotted colors in
between. With their upraised ears, large and expressive
eyes, and strong musculature, they were beautiful.

"Do you ride?" John asked.

Charlotte shook her head.

"That is somethin' we're gonna have to change," he
declared.

He drove the truck up the drive, shouting a bit of
encouragement to a pair of men who were working with an
unruly black and white stallion in a nearby corral. Turning
toward the house, he slowed the pickup directly before a
side door. Del leaped from the back of the truck before the

vehicle came to a full stop, his boots crunching loudly on the hardscrabble ground when he landed.

"Don't you worry yourself none 'bout your belongin's," John explained. "Del'll have one of the other fellas help him haul 'em up in a bit. In the meanwhile, why don't you let me show you your room."

Charlotte followed the rancher as he led the way through the side door, passed through the mudroom, and into a small foyer. Beside them, an entryway led into the kitchen, but she didn't get more than a quick look before John began to climb a nearby staircase toward the upper floor.

All along the length of the tall stairway were framed photographs, some so old that they were brown and mottled. Some were posed, bearded gentlemen with their impassively unsmiling wives standing beside them. But there were other images that were more captivating; one photograph was more than two feet wide, a panoramic view of the breadth of the ranch.

"That photo is from my pa's time," John explained, coming back down the steps to where Charlotte stood. "That's him standin' there at the front of the house," he said, pointing a worn finger to the small figure visible at the head of the walk, his thumbs hooked into his vest.

"He looks like a proud man," Charlotte remarked.

"As a peacock," John stated. "He was rightfully pleased with what he and his father before him built."

"Where are you in this picture?"

"More likely than not, I was runnin' around in my short pants as blind to what was happenin' as a baby bird just out its shell." He chuckled. "You know, for the longest time, I thought these pictures was nothin' but a waste of time, memories best forgotten, but now that I'm older, it's nice to be able to look back to what come before."

"I wish I had photographs to look back on in my family," Charlotte answered wistfully, "but most all of my family's history was lost in a fire when I was a little girl."

"I'm sorry to hear that."

Charlotte followed John up the remaining steps and down a darkened hallway to the last room on the right. After opening the door, he stood to the side, encouraging her to enter.

"It probably ain't what you're used to," he said, "but I hope that it'll do."

Sunlight streamed through the southern window, illuminating a room without much furniture. Beside the single bed, there was only the nightstand near the door and the dresser against the opposite wall. Light fell upon the washbasin atop the dresser, sending shimmering reflections dancing across the ceiling.

"It's perfect," she said.

"I'm happy you think so," he answered, "but if there's anything you need that you don't have, let us know."

"I will."

"You get yourself a bit of rest 'fore dinner and don't worry 'bout missin' it, 'cause there'll be more noise than if the circus come to town. A mess of hungry cowboys make more than a fair share of racket!"

As John shut the door behind him, Charlotte twirled about the room, so excited about her new life she had to release some energy. Still, John's advice was no doubt sound, and she lay back on the bed. It was hard to believe she was so far from Minnesota.

Closing her eyes, Charlotte found sleep as easily as if she had reached out and grabbed it.

Chapter Three

By the time Charlotte awakened, the sound of boisterous voices was rising up from the bottom of the stairs. Peeking out into the hall, she saw that Del had brought her belongings. After refreshing herself at the washbasin, she selected a fresh blouse, tied back her blond hair, and took a long look at herself in the mirror above the dresser.

Charlotte pulled at the thin chain around her neck and freed the locket that had been given to her by her father soon after his return to her life. Popping open the clasp that held it shut, she looked down upon the tiny photograph of her mother that had accompanied Mason Tucker across the battlefields of France. Though less faded and far better traveled than the images John Grant had hung along the stairway, the image of her mother, a woman she had never known, was her greatest treasure.

With a smile, she closed the locket, slid it safely back inside her blouse, and made her way down the stairs.

The dining room at the Grant Ranch was bustling with rowdy men who were finally finished with a long day's work. Their raucous, noisy laughter occasionally was punctuated by a shout and good-natured ribbing. To Charlotte, everything was a bit disorienting. She smiled and nodded here and there as she wove her way through the throng and over to where John waved at her, every step allowing her to hear snippets of the many conversations going on around her.

"—that dang bull is a heller, fer sure."

"—if'n we don't get rain soon, we're gonna get blowed clear down to Texas."

"—the way that son of a bitch was buckin' I thought I might get throwed all the way to the pearly gates."

"That's about the only way you'll get there!"

When Charlotte approached the long table in the center of the room, she was surprised to see several women racing back and forth from the kitchen carrying wide platters and deep bowls heaped high with food: huge portions of green beans, red potatoes, high-rising biscuits, and steaks. But when she inquired if she could help with the preparation of the meal or in setting the table, John shooed her away.

"You're a guest here and that means your only job is to sit down at the table and eat your fill."

"But surely I could help in some way?"

"It seems to me that you're the sort of gal who gets an idea in her head and can't let it go, no matter what argument is used 'gainst it." John chuckled. "After all the time you spent travelin', why don't you just let things be as they are, at least for tonight."

Reluctantly, Charlotte agreed.

Happy that he had persuaded her to see things his way, John began to introduce Charlotte to each of the men who worked for him. From Ken Caldwell on to Matthew Hoskins and then to Dave Powell and beyond, the list seemed endless, one weather-beaten, whiskered face replacing the one that came before, if only for an instant, over ten in all.

"Is it always this hectic at dinnertime?" she asked a cowboy she thought was named Will.

"Nope, it sure ain't," the man answered. "Some of our nights is spent sweatin' over our wood-burnin' stoves, cookin' up whatever grub we scrounge up from the general store Mr. Grant maintains. But tonight we was invited to the house for proper eatin' on account of you bein' here."

"All of this for me?" she said in surprise.

"With the look of this here food," he smiled, glancing over at the laden table, "there ain't a one of us who's gonna complain!"

Then John gently grabbed her by the elbow to introduce her to someone else. "This here is the part about John Grant that most people like best," he beamed proudly, "and

I can't say I blame them. Charlotte, I'd like you to meet my wife, Amelia."

With her thin, mousy auburn hair piled high atop her head in a haphazardly formed bun, soft and round greenish gold eyes that seemed mismatched above her high, rosy cheeks, and a thinly pursed mouth over a weak, dimpled chin, Amelia Grant struck Charlotte as an awkward match for her lively husband as she was shorter than John by nearly a foot. Amelia wiped her hands on her apron before offering them to her new guest; they felt warm and clammy to the touch.

"Welcome to our home," Amelia said softly.

"Thank you so much for having me here," Charlotte replied.

While her first assumption was that Amelia was as meek and timid as a church mouse, Charlotte couldn't help but notice the sweat that slicked the woman's brow and the steely strength readily apparent in her arms and hands. To think her unimportant would be to underestimate the burden she carried as a ranch owner's wife. Besides, the fact that John doted on her, singing her praises unabashedly, crowing about her as if she were blessed from on high, was another indication that there was more to Amelia Grant than what initially revealed itself.

Del came up beside her with his hat in his hand and a warm smile; though she had just met him earlier that day, Charlotte found herself happy to see a face she recognized. "Are you gettin' settled in all right?" he asked.

"I am, thank you."

"Arrivin' somewhere new can be a bit overwhelmin'." Del chuckled, nodding to all of the commotion around them.

"I'm finding that out."

"Give it time and I'm sure it'll start feelin' like home."

Suddenly, the rear door crashed open thunderously and a deep voice bellowed into the dining room, silencing all other talk.

"Thank goodness you didn't start without me! I'm so hungry my stomach is gnawing on my backbone!"

Squeezing through the door to the dining room, enthusiastically greeting his fellow ranch hands, was undoubtedly the largest man she had ever seen. Hugely proportioned, he was as impressive to behold as a prize ox at the fair; his broad shoulders looked wider than a pair of axe handles, and his taut, muscular arms strained against the fabric of his work shirt.

When the huge man made eye contact with John, he hurried over to where they stood with the enthusiasm of someone about to receive a gift.

"I reckon this must be our new schoolmarm!" he practically shouted, towering over Charlotte with such a presence that she found herself speechless.

Thankfully, John stepped into the silence by saying, "Charlotte, let me introduce you to one of the best hands a rancher could ever hope to have. This big fella is Hale McCoy."

"It's really nice to meet you," Hale said.

"I...I...why...yes, it is..." Charlotte stumbled.

"Let's hope she ain't gonna be this tongue-tied standin' up in front of the classroom." Hale laughed. "Or else I got the feelin' those little buggers are gonna have the run of the roost!"

"She ain't the first woman to trip over her words the first time she met you!" a voice shouted from the back of the room.

"I believe my mother was the first, startin' on the day I was born!" Hale boasted.

"That poor woman!" came another shout.

Though Charlotte was quite certain she was blushing a bit at the teasing, she could see that Hale McCoy, for all his size, clearly possessed a gentle soul. From the downy blond hair that stood up in a prominent cowlick to his mischievous, dancing light blue eyes, he was childlike and charming. She found him easy to like and began warming up to him even if she was the source of his amusement. She decided that she would deal with him the same way she had always dealt with those who were so overwhelming.

I'll give it back every bit as good as I get!

"I wasn't stumbling over my words because I was tongue-tied," Charlotte corrected, straightening her shoulders and raising her chin to meet Hale's questioning gaze. "I was only drawing in my breath in the hope that you would be able to hear me all the way up there."

Hale was momentarily taken aback, but his eyes lit up

and he finally exclaimed, "Oh, I like her! She's got spunk in spades!"

"And don't you forget it," she declared.

"I'm thinkin' you ain't," he said with a chuckle.

"Seems to me that you're gonna fit in just fine under this roof," John joined in.

Before any more teasing could ensue, the ranch owner called everyone to dinner, holding out a seat for Charlotte near the head of the table. Hale settled his massive bulk into the seat directly opposite her, clearly relishing the thought of more verbal jousting during the course of the meal. Amelia took the seat to Charlotte's immediate right. Every ranch hand looked up to where John stood, not a hat to be seen on a single head.

"Since we have the providence and good fortune to have a new face here among us," the older man began, looking over to where Charlotte sat," it only seems proper that she be allowed to say Grace."

Taken aback, Charlotte managed to sputter, "I...I... couldn't possibly know what to say..."

"Ain't nothin' to it with a mouth like yours," Hale teased.

Charlotte shot him a withering look but only managed to make him laugh harder.

"Just do the best you can," Amelia encouraged.

Nodding, Charlotte bowed her head and clasped her hands together in her lap. Saying a silent, private prayer before beginning, she said,

"Thank you, our Father in Heaven above, not just for

the large meal prepared for us and the wonderful company in which it will be shared, but also for bringing me safely from my family in Minnesota to be among such kind and," Charlotte paused for a moment, opening one eye to look at Hale before adding, "interesting people. May our time together continue to make us every bit as happy as I have been this day. Bless us and this house. Amen."

When she finished, Charlotte looked up cautiously, as if she expected someone to raise an objection to her words, but instead found that everyone at the table had already turned their attention to loading their plates with food. With a silent laugh at her unnecessary nervousness, she joined them.

Just as dinner was drawing to a close, silverware being set down on plates still containing the last bites of a deliciously rich apple pie, the back door beside the mudroom opened again. Before Charlotte could turn around to see whoever had just entered, she was struck by the clear, surprising strangeness of Hale's reaction.

All throughout the meal, the enormous ranch hand's mood and voice remained every bit as great as his size; every time she had ventured an opinion, Hale had been there with a contrary comment, his deep baritone drowning out every other voice at the table.

But now when he spoke, Charlotte was taken aback.

"Eve...evenin'," Hale sputtered, his voice only a fraction of what it had been only moments before.

Her curiosity completely getting the better of her, Charlotte turned and looked back over her chair; there, walking into the dining room, was a very pretty young woman. About the same age as Charlotte, with raven black hair that swept loosely across her narrow shoulders, green eyes that moved easily about the room, and features as delicate and dainty as a starlet on a Hollywood movie poster, she beamed at the group at the table. Still, beneath her smile a sad weariness flickered a moment, as if it were a candle's flame, before vanishing.

"I'm terribly sorry that we're so late in getting back, but I just couldn't manage to get away from my work at the office," she explained, her voice every bit as remarkable as her looks. "With all of the new cases Mr. Barnaby's law practice takes on, my day never seems to end!"

"That's quite all right, dear," Amelia answered. "It couldn't be helped."

"Have a seat," John invited.

"You mean Hale didn't eat every last morsel in sight?" she teased.

"I'd . . . I'd make sure there was some left for you, Hannah," he replied.

"I just bet!"

"As much as I like a good-natured ribbin', 'specially when it's at Hale's expense," John interrupted from his spot at the head of the table, "now seems 'bout as good a time as any to make us a few introductions. Hannah, this is Charlotte Tucker, the young lady who's to be our new teacher."

"It's so nice to meet you!" Hannah exclaimed as her gaze settled upon Charlotte for the first time, her eyes lighting up as she took the other woman's hand in her own. "It's so nice to meet you! Everyone here has been eagerly anticipating your arrival. I'm Hannah Williams," she said, tucking a stray strand of dark hair behind her ear. "I've only recently come to Sawyer myself, so I know what it's like to be the new face in town. If there's anything you need, anything at all, please don't hesitate to ask."

"I will," Charlotte answered, instantly warming to Hannah. "So far, everyone has been very helpful."

"Everyone?" Hannah asked with a sly curiosity.

"Of course," Charlotte answered, a bit confused.

"Are you sure Hale hasn't been giving you any trouble?" Hannah persisted, training her eyes upon the large man as if he were a small boy who had just been found by his mother to be up to mischief. "He's a bit of a scalawag who's been known to irritate if given the chance."

"I...I haven't, Hannah!" Hale protested. "Honest I haven't!"

"If you even suspect him of getting out of line," Hannah said, nodding to Charlotte with a wily smile, "you just tell me and I'll take care of it!"

"I will," Charlotte said with a laugh.

"Maybe we ought to get Hannah to come on out to the

corrals once in a while." A cowboy snickered at the far end of the table. "What with the way she gets that big ox to snap to attention, I reckon there ain't no wild horse that could ever stand a chance!"

"Shut up down there!" Hale thundered in answer, but his angry tone did nothing to quell the laughter that filled the room.

It was at that moment that Charlotte understood Hale's bizarre reaction to Hannah entering the room.

He was in love with her.

Even now that he was the butt of the joke, the object of ridicule from everyone in the room, Hale's eyes still occasionally darted toward Hannah, checking to see if she was watching him. Gone was the overpowering force of personality Charlotte had felt only an hour before, replaced by shyness and uncertainty.

Once the sound of laughter had finally died down, John turned to Hannah and said, "I imagine that Owen wasn't too pleased to wait for you."

"You know how Owen is," she answered, shrugging. "Nowadays, there isn't much that seems to make him happy."

As if in answer to the speculations, a man stalked into the dining room, the sound of his heavy footfalls echoing loudly.

"Speak of the devil." Hannah chuckled.

Owen only grunted in answer.

Charlotte was immediately struck by just how much

Owen resembled Hannah; he had the same dark, thick hair that curled slightly where it hung beneath the brim of his hat, his eyes were the same alluring green, and though stubbly whiskers covered his face, it was clear that his features were every bit as conversation stopping. While Owen wasn't anywhere near as large a man as Hale, he was nonetheless broad of shoulder. His bare forearms were marbled with the muscles of a man who was no stranger to hard work. Wispy dark hair peeked from the top of his unbuttoned work shirt.

"It was a long wait for you, Owen," John commented.

"Couldn't rightly make Hannah walk all the way from town," he grumbled. "If I had, I'd never have heard the end of it."

"And she wouldn't have been the only one saying so," Hale added.

Suddenly, what should have been clear to Charlotte from her physical observations was laid bare before her: Owen and Hannah were possibly twins. But though she had met Owen Williams only seconds before, she was struck by how utterly different his personality appeared to be; where his sister was openly friendly, Owen was rude and caustic.

"Grab yourself some food," John offered Owen.

"Maybe a bit later," he replied with a tip of his hat. "I still have some things to take care of 'fore the sun gets too far gone."

"Don't you want to at least meet Charlotte Tucker?"

Hannah offered, pulling the ranch's newest guest forward. "She's Sawyer's new teacher."

With an expression of both exasperation and boredom, Owen turned to Charlotte; but when their eyes met, something in his face changed. Only for an instant, his gaze widened and his mouth softened. If she hadn't been looking right at him she would undoubtedly have missed the change, but she couldn't help but wonder if it was comparable to her own surprise.

Unbidden, Charlotte's heart had begun to pound in her chest. Only a glance had passed between them, but she found him so devastatingly handsome, so rugged and strong, so different from the few other men who had entered her life. She couldn't help but wonder about him, if he possessed more than just his looks, and found herself hoping that if she got to know him a bit, she wouldn't be disappointed. Blinking, she looked away, startled at her emotional response, a bit flustered at how she, usually so confident and sure of herself, felt on slippery ground. She could only hope that he hadn't seen the foolishness of her thoughts written large on her face.

"Evenin'." He nodded. "Nice to meet you."

"Pleased to meet you, too," she answered.

Without another word, Owen turned on his heel and left the room, and all returned to their conversations. Still, Charlotte watched him go, wondering if she had imagined a connection between them, no matter how thin it might have been.

But just as Owen reached the door he stopped, looked back to where she stood alone watching him, and held her eyes for a moment longer. Then he was out the door and into the darkening night, leaving her to wonder about the tumultuous feelings that surged through her.

Chapter Four

Owen Williams worked the bristle brush across the tall mare's back, swept along the length of her side, and brought it down the horse's long flank. Carefully yet forcefully, he repeated his chore. Dipping the brush into a tall pail of water that had been warmed over the work stove, he brought the steaming liquid to the animal's back. Over and over he brushed, pulling out loose hair and flecks of dirt embedded from the day's work. The large brown and white horse occasionally snorted, flicking either her alert ears or wiry tail, but remained contentedly still, enjoying the attention.

Outside the open barn doors, the nearly full moon had risen above the eastern horizon in a sky filled with thousands of bright stars. Though the setting of the sun had brought with it a cooling of the day's heat, whatever breeze that managed to stir the air elsewhere was lost in the close confines of the horse's stall. Sweat ran in rivers down Owen's face, and the sleeve of his work shirt was damp from repeatedly wiping his brow.

Usually, working his way through the chores of caring for his own two horses calmed Owen's tumultuous thoughts after a busy day; the procuring of feed, the monotonous brushing, and even the shoveling of manure allowed him to relax, however long it took.

But this night was different...

Lately, the thought had begun to nag at Owen that the longer he remained at the Grant Ranch, the less he seemed able to soothe the raging emotions that had necessitated his coming in the first place.

When Owen had watched the doctor drive away into the whirling snowstorm six months earlier, he had known that the end of his mother's life was mere moments away. Watching her die, a shell of the vibrant woman she had once been, nearly broke him. At the instant she had finally given up the futile struggle to defeat her illness, there had been a part of him that had been relieved, and instantly ashamed for having had such a terrible thought. Never once had she opened her eyes. He had dug a deep hole in the frozen Colorado earth, listened while the priest had mumbled a few words into a stiff eastern wind, and then Owen and Hannah had set about formulating their plan for revenge.

The first thing he had done was rifle through his mother's belongings over Hannah's protests. No matter how many times he attempted to explain why it needed to be done, how it was the only way they would ever learn the truth, his sister still had fought him every step of the way, through every faded photograph, every scrap of paper containing a bit of their mother's handwriting, and even to the meager clothing she had afforded herself over the years.

But then his perseverance had paid off...

Folded into a small, worn book of poems wedged into a back corner of his mother's dresser, Owen had found a piece of paper on which Caroline had scribbled a few notes. Most of them were either illegible or nonsensical, but there was one pair of words that stood out:

SAWYER, OKLAHOMA

Neither Owen nor Hannah could ever remember hearing their mother speak about Oklahoma. They thought that Caroline Wallace had been born and raised in Colorado. So what was the reason for her writing? While Hannah insisted that whatever their mother had meant in making note of such a far-off place, it likely had absolutely nothing to do with the mysterious and absent man who had made her pregnant, then deserted her. Owen hadn't been so sure.

He had asked around the small town of Longbow, questioning anyone he thought might have some clue as to what his mother had meant in writing down the name of the town. Finally, after applying enough liquor to loosen the flapping tongue of Franklin Sullivan, who was what passed for the town's attorney, Owen learned that, in the years before he and Hannah had been born Caroline Wallace had left the town of her birth and headed to Oklahoma. The reason for doing so had been lost in the haze of years gone by, but the lawyer remembered the sliver of a conversation he'd had with Caroline upon her eventual return. In it had been a name.

"Grant, I believe, was the name," he'd muttered, his words slurred by alcohol. "Or was it Griffin? Hell if I can 'member!"

Whichever of the two names it was hardly mattered. Owen had packed whatever of their belongings fit into their dented trunk, sold their meager home for even less than the pitiful building was worth, and led them off in search of the unknown man who had helped give them life.

The mare's annoyed whinny brought him back from his memories; apparently he had been brushing too hard, lost in the rising of his temper. With a scratch behind the horse's ear, he apologized.

"Sorry, old girl," Owen soothed. "I'll try to be more careful."

Arriving in Sawyer at the onset of spring, they discovered that John Grant was a successful horse rancher, well respected, and an upstanding member of the community. No one would say a harsh word against him, not one offhanded slight. Owen had mentioned his mother's name to a couple of people, but no one seemed to recognize it.

He had not one thing to go on. He just knew he was right. He was certain John Grant was the man.

Owen's first impulse was to kick down the door to John Grant's ranch house, pull him out into the yard by his hair, and give him the beating he undoubtedly deserved. Hannah restrained him, arguing that they had no proof that the rancher was the man they were looking for, nothing but the drunken ramblings of Franklin Sullivan.

Over Owen's protests, Hannah explained that it was in their best interests to try to learn the truth before resorting to violence. Swallowing his pride, Owen had gone to John Grant's door, faced the man who just might be his father, and asked for a job. Fortunately, the ranch had just found itself a man short. John had looked him up and down, judging whether he was capable of backbreaking work, before finally nodding his head, taking Owen on right then and there. Within hours, he found himself working for the very man he had come to Sawyer to ruin.

"And here I still am," he muttered. "Still working..."

The worst part was that Owen had found he had little reason to resent John Grant. Unlike other men Owen had known who, in a position of authority, lorded it over those who worked for him, the rancher never shied away from any demanding, grueling tasks; he could often be found pounding away on a hot anvil, corralling a stubborn horse, or even performing the same menial task in which Owen himself was now engaged.

But Owen also knew that appearances could often be deceiving, as easily changed as a horse's shoe. It was possible that behind Grant's friendly exterior resided a conniving, manipulative son of a bitch fully capable of getting a young woman pregnant and then throwing her out on her ear. He believed that John Grant was such a man, and that if he looked long enough, watched him closely, his assumptions would be proven true.

"You should have been nicer when you came in the house."

Owen looked up from his chores to see Hannah entering the barn. She walked over to where he was working and leaned against the closed gate, resting her head upon her crossed arms.

"I didn't see much of a point in it," Owen argued, resuming his brushing. "Besides, you know I don't like to spend a lot of time around him."

"You say that like it's supposed to be some kind of secret."

"What's that mean?"

"It means that if it weren't for the fact that you're such a good worker on the ranch," she said, a bit exasperated with her brother, "and that I'm so completely likeable, I believe that John Grant would have asked you to leave his ranch a long time ago."

Owen snarled in answer. From the first moment they had set foot on the property, he had marveled at Hannah's ability to be so friendly, so *natural*, with the man who may have driven their mother to her grave. That she berated him for acting the way he did only made it worse.

It made him angry.

"Would it kill you to be nice to the man?"

"It just might!" Owen snapped.

"This whole thing was your idea!" Hannah persisted. "And it would be a lot easier if I wasn't the one who had to show a friendly face."

Once they had talked their way onto the ranch, Hannah had taken a secretarial position in Sawyer with Carlton Barnaby, the town's old lawyer. She put up with the man's come-ons and lecherous stares because the job afforded her the opportunity to look through whatever pertinent information she could get her hands on, in the hopes of finding clues that would link their mother with John Grant. It was a risky task, illegal in more ways than one, a crime for which she would undoubtedly be fired or even jailed if she was discovered, but Owen had convinced her that it was necessary.

"You know that the reason we were so late in getting back to the ranch was because I finally had some time alone with the files in Barnaby's office," she snapped.

"And that might have been worth a spit if you'd managed to find anything worthwhile!"

"It's like looking for a needle in a haystack, Owen!"

"Then look harder!"

"All of this...this scheming is starting to feel like it's too much to bear!" Hannah argued, throwing up her hands in exasperation. "Ever since we left Colorado, we've done nothing but lie every step of the way to each person we've met! You even changed our names!"

"What choice do we have?" Owen countered. "It's not as if we could have walked up to John Grant's front door and introduced ourselves as Owen and Hannah Wallace. Besides, as closely as you physically resemble our mother, I keep expecting him to see through our ruse."

"But 'Hannah Williams' sounds so ridiculous!"

"It's not forever. Just until we find the proof that Grant is guilty."

"If we find it, you mean."

Owen threw the horse's brush in such a fury into the closed pen door just beneath where Hannah leaned that she leaped back, shocked. Without pause, he lashed out, kicking at a pail near his feet, sending water soaring up into the heated air.

The horse who had until then been content under his caring touch became spooked, rearing up on her back legs and skittering nervously backward toward the rear of the stall. Quickly, Owen moved forward rather than shying away and gently laid his hand on the startled mare's front quarter, attempting to ease her agitation. With a soothing voice, he whispered to the animal, reassuring her that everything was as it was before his outburst. Finally, the horse's anxiety passed and she relaxed, save for a derisive snort and a furtive pawing of the ground with one hoof.

"It's all right, girl," he promised. "Everything's all right."

Owen turned toward his sister, ready to see her relieved that the horse's outburst was under control, but the look in her eyes stopped him cold; when she was pushed far enough, Hannah's reaction often resembled that of their mother. Though weakened by constant illness, Caroline's stare, made up of equal parts determination and pity, had always been able to quell his most intense angers. Now, Hannah's stare did the same.

"Have you ever stopped to ask yourself if you might be wrong, Owen?" Hannah argued, her voice as flat as a knife's blade. "And that John Grant might not be the man you're so desperately looking for?"

Owen wanted to argue, to defend himself against her, but found that he couldn't and remained silent.

"You carry around all of this...this anger," she continued. "No matter how much I try to reason with you and make you understand how completely wrong you *might* be, you never listen."

"Hannah, I—" he began, but she wasn't finished talking.

"You brought all of this with you from Colorado, just like the belongings you threw into our trunk, and if you don't learn to live with it, if you aren't able to walk away, it will destroy your life every bit as much as it destroyed our mother's."

Owen desperately wanted to step forward, to open the horse stall gate, wrap his sister into his arms, and explain that what he was doing was for both of them, for the honor of their mother, so that they could return to Longbow and erase the stigma from their mother's name. Instead, he could only stand mutely, his hand never straying from the mare's dark mane.

Hannah sighed, turned on her heel, and left him to his work.

Carter Herrick drew hard on his cigarette, savoring the burn of the tobacco deep within his lungs before blowing it out in a plume. The milky smoke pushed insistently against the closed window, swirling and dissipating upward. Soon the cigarette was little more than a nub beneath his gnarled fingers.

The room of his dead son was as dark as a tomb. Though two weeks had passed since Walter had slipped away, days from his fifteenth birthday, Carter couldn't bring himself to look upon the boy's belongings. No matter how many times his manservant lit the oil lamp on top of the dresser, Carter extinguished it. The blackness felt right, appropriate to match the melancholy that had settled upon his heart.

"And I can't imagine it will ever change," he muttered into the evening.

Oddly, his wife's death two years earlier, the result of a fall down the enormous staircase of their home, had been much easier to bear. In his own strange way, Carter supposed that he had loved Emma, his spouse of over thirty years, but her passing hadn't affected him any more than the changing of the seasons, something to be expected rather than marveled over. She had done what all good wives were expected to do: she had borne him a son.

But the loss of the boy was different...

When Walter had first fallen ill, Carter had regarded it as temporary. But the disease, something the old quack in town thought might come from the boy's brain, did not pass. What started as fatigue and dizziness became something far worse. For days on end, Walter was unable to get out of bed. No matter what was prepared for him, he was unable to keep down his food. And worst of all were the eye-splitting headaches ravaging him day and night.

Through it all, there was nothing for Carter to do but watch. His professional life had been spent amassing a substantial wealth, but no amount of money, no number of doctors brought in from Tulsa or Kansas City, nothing, could stop the fate that awaited Walter. When the boy died in the hours just before dawn, something of Carter went with him.

And that was why nothing mattered anymore...

Carter Herrick walked out of his dead son's room and down the long hallway of the second floor to his own office. Without turning on any lights, he opened a cupboard beside his oak desk, poured himself a stiff whiskey, and swallowed it hurriedly, before pouring another.

The hardest thing for him to accept about Walter's death was that it demonstrated how hollow his life had become. For days this bitterness gnawed at him. *My son isn't even cold in the ground and not one goddamn person has bothered to offer condolences!* At the boy's funeral, faces passed by one by one, but Carter was sure that everyone who was there came only because of the standing his ranch afforded him. It was then that he'd had a revelation.

He had discovered that he had power . . . and little else.

All his life, Carter felt as if he had been a step behind, not quite in a position for fortune to smile upon him. Certainly the deaths of both his wife and son were evidence of such hardship, but it was more than that. His ranch wasn't successful in the ways of others. His position in Sawyer was based on respect for his power rather than his person. And even when it came to love, he had failed to get what he had wanted.

And it was all because of one man . . .

"John Grant, you son of a bitch," Carter snarled.

Chapter Five

CHARLOTTE STEPPED OUT of the ranch house and into glorious morning sunlight streaming down from a cloudless sky. She'd always been an early riser, awakening shortly after dawn, but she was surprised to see how many others on the ranch shared her habit: cowboys scurried about working on chores; women were already hanging clothes on the wash line. There was activity everywhere despite the early hour.

Inside the house had been every bit as hectic; even as she washed herself from her basin and dressed, she heard the sounds of scraping chairs, clinking glasses and silverware, and male voices. Though she had been prepared to fix her own breakfast, she readily accepted the plate Amelia offered her, heaped high with fried potatoes, ham, and eggs. Even the coffee had been delicious!

This is the beginning of something wonderful, she thought.

Charlotte finished her meal, carried her dishes to the kitchen, and went out the back door.

She heard a burst of whistling, clapping, and hollering. It rose above the competing regular sounds. She followed the noise around to the front of the house. Hale stood next to the corral shouting encouragement to a couple of men as they herded a pair of horses into the enclosure. Once they had been brought safely inside the fence, he hurled the gate shut behind them, securing it with a sliding pole he used as a bolt. When he finished, he yanked off his hat and wiped his brow.

"There's no rest for the wicked, is there?" she teased him as she neared.

"I suppose not." He chuckled. "But then I suppose that explains why you're up and about so early."

Charlotte smiled at the easy way she and Hale kidded with each other. Though they had only met the night before, she felt as if she had known him for years; it was as if he were the brother she'd never had. She felt certain that the warmth and friendliness in his heart easily matched his bulk, maybe even exceeded it.

"Did you manage to sleep last night?" he asked, dropping his playful manner, if only for a moment, "what with it bein' your first night and all?"

"Yes, I slept very well; thank you."

"Most evenin's round here are very pleasant, once you get used to the sound of about a hundred horses roamin' ever' darn way," Hale explained. "As for myself, I'm usually so tired after a day's hard workin' that I don't know if I'd wake up even if a tornado pulled the roof off over my head!"

"Well, let's hope that it never comes to that."

"You can't ever tell about Oklahoma weather."

Before Charlotte could ask Hale what he was doing with the horses he had brought into the corral, she was interrupted by the loud, fevered sound of dogs barking. From around the corner of the nearest barn, dust rising in clouds from the striking of their paws against the ground, came a pair of mutts. One was much larger than the other, a fluffy white beast with slightly upraised ears. His companion was much smaller, black as the night sky, hurrying to keep up on legs a third shorter.

The white dog raced up to Charlotte and began to run awkward circles around her, playfully barking, his tongue lolling out, and his eyes never leaving her. Once the black dog managed to keep up, he stayed out of the way near Hale; Charlotte wasn't sure if it was because the mutt was wary of her or wise enough to avoid being trampled by his partner.

"Salt, you big dummy!" Hale shouted. "Don't you know that ain't no way to greet a lady?"

At the sound of Hale's booming voice, the white dog instantly broke away from his circling around Charlotte and leaped up on his hind legs, placing his paws squarely in the enormous ranch hand's midsection. With his tail wagging furiously, the dog clearly enjoyed the scratching he was receiving behind the ears.

"This here is Salt," Hale said in introduction, "on account of his color and that we figure he's got nothin' but rocks between his ears."

Salt gave a merry bark, as if he agreed with Hale's assessment.

"And this little fella down here is old Salt's constant companion," he explained, nodding to the little black dog who, upon being mentioned, inched back behind Hale's leg until he was nearly out of sight, giving a low growl for good measure. "He goes by—"

"Let me guess," Charlotte offered. "His name is Pepper."

Hale laughed heartily. "I suppose it were to be expected, weren't it!"

Charlotte bent down, straightening her skirt on the dusty ground, and carefully reached out her hand to Pepper. Skittish, the little dog leaped back, offering a hint of his teeth to go with his earlier warning. Patiently, Charlotte waited. Slowly, Pepper's fear and trepidation began to wane as his curiosity grew. His tiny black nose twitching this way and that, he eventually made his way to Charlotte's hand, allowing her to pet his small body and lifting his head as if in triumph.

"Looks like you're the sort who gets along well with dogs," Hale remarked.

"I had a special one when I was younger."

"Can't say that you've lost your touch, then."

"I suppose it's not something that ever really goes away." Charlotte smiled.

"I reckon not."

Now that Pepper was getting special attention, Salt became jealous and decided that he wasn't about to lose out, even to a friend. He jumped away from Hale and pushed his canine companion completely out of the way, before finally sitting down in front of Charlotte, waiting for the surely inevitable petting that was to come.

After a few moments of showering the two gluttons with affection, scratches and petting, Hale finally asked, "So what are you doin' out so early?"

Charlotte smiled playfully. "Hannah offered to have her brother take us both into town this morning. She thought I might benefit from being shown around a little before I was expected to start teaching."

"Ha...Hannah...asked you...to go?" he stammered.

Rising to her feet, Charlotte fixed Hale with a curious look. He stared at her for only a moment before turning away, color rising in his cheeks and his foot kicking nervously at the dirt.

"You're sweet on Hannah, aren't you?" she ventured.

"No...no...I—I don't know what you're talkin' 'bout," he answered.

"Tell me the truth, Hale," Charlotte insisted.

The man's mouth opened wide, as if he wanted to argue the point a bit further, but when his eyes met hers, it was clear that he could see the uselessness of lying. "I reckon that fact's 'bout as easy to see as that sun in the sky, ain't it?" he asked rhetorically. "It ain't too easy to bear knowin' that everyone on the ranch figured it out but her."

"I'm sure she knows." Charlotte smiled, despite her desire not to.

"Awww, now that's just great to know," Hale despaired, throwing his hat into the dust with a thud.

"But that doesn't mean that she doesn't think you're... nice," Charlotte offered as a salve to his wounded pride. "For all you know, she might have the same feelings for you."

"Then why hasn't she said somethin'?"

"Maybe it's because she's waiting for you to tell her exactly where you stand," Charlotte explained. "I'm sure it doesn't help that every time you are in the same room as her, you can't seem to say anything without mumbling like you've got your mouth full of mush."

"It's not that bad," Hale said defensively.

"I'd only just met you, but as soon as Hannah came through the door, I could hardly recognize you," Charlotte argued. "If I could notice it, then there is no doubting that she did."

"I just get so darn flummoxed!"

"Women want a man who's confident, someone who's not afraid to let them know how he feels."

"But I don't know how to do that!"

"You need to learn, then."

Hale's eyes suddenly lit up; it looked as if a light switch had been thrown. With his enormous hands, he reached out and grabbed her by the arms, momentarily startling her. "You can teach me!" he exclaimed.

"Wh-what are you talking about?"

"It makes total sense," Hale kept on, his enthusiasm so great that he lifted her up and off the ground as if she were a bag of feathers. "You can tell me everythin' that I've been doin' wrong, what with you bein' a woman and all! Hell, I ain't the least bit tongue-tied round you, which means that I must not feel the slightest 'ttraction to you!"

"Thanks a lot, Hale," she said sarcastically.

"Aw, you know what I mean." He chuckled, finally hopeful.

"Hale McCoy, what do you think you're doing with her!"

Both Charlotte and Hale turned to see Hannah striding toward them, consternation written across her face. As if what he was holding were ablaze with fire, Hale quickly set Charlotte down and stepped awkwardly back, looking for a moment as if he were considering running away.

"Why did he have you up in the air like that?" Hannah asked Charlotte once she had reached her side.

"He...he was..." Charlotte said, now the one to be tongue-tied.

"I was just showin' her how strong I am," Hale jumped in, the words tumbling from his mouth.

"Anyone with one working eye would know that,"

Hannah said with a chuckle. "You should practice with the horses instead."

Relief washed over Charlotte at Hale's quick thinking, although she was just as surprised that he'd been able to form a complete sentence while in Hannah's presence.

"Well...then I suppose...I should probably get goin'...what with all the chores to do...and all," Hale flailed, reverting to his bumbling ways.

"Bye, Hale." Hannah smiled.

"We'll talk when I get back," Charlotte added.

As he walked away, Salt and Pepper trailing happily at his heels, it was Hale who looked like a dog slinking off with his tail tucked between his legs.

Just as she had when she had first arrived, Charlotte took in all the strange sights and sounds of the ranch as the truck drove down the dusty drive and out onto the road to Sawyer.

Her bare arm rested on the open window, soaking up the warm sunlight; even with a gentle breeze rustling the tree leaves, the day was growing hot. Scissor-tailed fly-catchers dipped and dived beside the gurgling stream, the birds' beaks open as they tried to catch insects before retreating to what shade could be found in the summer afternoon. Only the wildflowers seemed unaffected by the heat, still standing tall under the glare of the sun.

Owen was driving, his left hand lazily steering the wheel; he didn't seem particularly concerned about his driving, making no attempt to avoid the depressions and deep holes that pocked the road. Hannah sat sourly between them, a hand raised above her head to ensure the truck's roof remained a safe distance away.

"You don't have to hit every hole in the road, you know," Hannah said, her voice broken as she tried to maintain her balance in the bouncing truck.

"Anytime you want to start drivin' yourself into town, you just let me know," Owen answered with indifference, as he purposefully steered the truck toward an enormous hole at the edge of the road. When the wheel struck, it was as if they had been caught in an earthquake; Charlotte clung tenaciously to the door frame, fearful she might be tossed outside. "If I were you, I'd keep my comments to myself. Otherwise, you can drive yourself."

"But you know that I've never learned to drive," Hannah argued. "Besides, the truck's needed on the ranch."

"Then put a cork in all the complainin'!" he barked. "You'd think you'd be grateful!"

Charlotte was both shocked and horrified by just how openly Owen disparaged his sister, especially while someone else was present. Though she had met him for only a moment the night before, it was hard to believe he was related to someone as outgoing and friendly as Hannah. Squirming in her bouncing seat, she found it impossible to sit quietly by as Owen belittled Hannah.

Clearing her throat, a touch of sarcasm in her voice, Charlotte said, "Thank you for taking us into town, Owen."

"See?" Owen said, turning to Hannah. "She knows what to say!"

"Maybe your sister would be more willing to give you a kind word here and there if you didn't throw everything back in her face," Charlotte interjected, resentment toward Owen twisting in her gut.

"Must not have much along the lines of manners up there in Minnesota," he retorted, his green eyes never wavering from the dusty road. "That is, unless something got lost on the trip."

"Don't pay him any mind." Hannah laughed, ignoring the rude and demeaning way in which he had spoken to her. "If there's one thing Owen has always been good at, it's arguing!"

Owen frowned. "I hope you remember how funny all this is when I've driven off and left you in Sawyer."

Biting her tongue to keep from adding fuel to the fire, Charlotte fumed while she stared out the window. Though the landscape tried to grab at her divided attention, full of long, open views the likes of which she had never before seen, she paid them little mind. If Hannah hadn't spoken up, joking about Owen's words, there was no telling what Charlotte would have replied.

He'd best not take that tone with me ever again!

"It's a lot different from Minnesota, isn't it?" Hannah asked, following Charlotte's gaze but not understanding its meaning.

"More than I would ever have imagined," Charlotte

answered truthfully. "I guess I'm used to a place with lots of trees."

"It's a far cry from where we come from in Colorado, too. There, just about everywhere you look is as pretty as a picture, full of snowcapped mountains, towering evergreens, and gurgling streams around every corner. And that's to say nothing about the flowers and animals!"

"It sure sounds beautiful," Charlotte said. "So then why did you come to Oklahoma?"

"Well...it's because..." Hannah struggled. "Because..."

"If Minnesota was so damn nice, then why in the hell did you leave?" Owen interjected.

For an instant, Charlotte thought about going into detail about the decision to leave Carlson, her family, and the only life she had ever known behind, but something stopped her. "I suppose it's because I wanted to see somewhere else," she answered simply.

"'Bout the same reason for us, Charlie."

"What did you call me?" she asked incredulously.

"Charlie." Owen smirked. "That's your name, ain't it?"

"I'll have you know that...isn't my name."

"Hey! Look here!" Hannah shouted. At first, Charlotte thought that she was trying to break up the building argument between Owen and herself, but instead Hannah leaned across Charlotte's lap and pointed excitedly out the open window. "What's that?"

Curious, Charlotte looked to where Hannah was pointing. There, just outside the limits of Sawyer, she saw a huge commotion. Men pushed and pulled on enormous poles, raising the bright blue and white fabric of a tent, occasionally hammering down a stake; the end closest to them was already straining toward the sky. Another man rhythmically turned a wrench, tightening the bolts on a barrier that looked as if it would run around the entirety of their working area. Other men were hefting large, rectangular sections of smooth wood from the back of a truck and carefully stacking them beside the tent. One man ran to and fro, shouting orders and encouragement.

"Must be the circus coming to town," Owen observed.

"That's not what it is," Charlotte contradicted him. "It looks like they're putting up a roller-skating rink."

"Really?" Hannah asked enthusiastically. "I've always wanted to try skating."

"How do you know what they're doing?" Owen frowned.

"One used to come to Carlson, every summer."

"She's right!" Hannah yelled, still craning her neck out the window. Nearing where the men worked, they saw that a sign had been put up announcing the coming of THE BLUE TENT ROLLER RINK!

"Huh." Owen shrugged.

"Did you ever go skating?" Hannah asked.

"Sure, there's nothing to it." Charlotte smiled. "Not if you don't mind falling a time or two."

"We'll have to go!" Hannah cried. "We'll just have to!"

Owen grumbled in his seat.

While Hannah pushed across her lap for a better view of Sawyer's new attraction, Charlotte decided to sneak a quick look at Owen, only to be completely surprised to find him already staring at her! Though her immediate instinct was to look away in embarrassment, something in his eyes refused to let her do it, holding on to her gaze. Because of the harsh things they had said to each other, she would have expected his eyes to be full of anger and annoyance, but what she read in them more closely resembled intrigue...maybe even interest. Charlotte couldn't help but recall how he had looked at her the night before, stopping just before he reached the door to turn back to her; though it had been too dark to see for certain, she imagined his expression had been much like how he looked at her now. Unbidden, her heart began to beat faster. Finally, he returned his gaze to the road and the moment between them was ended, leaving Charlotte to her confused thoughts.

Owen brought the truck to a sudden halt in front of the grocer's, stamping down on the brakes hard enough for the tires to skid. Charlotte got out with Hannah right behind her. The door hadn't even completely shut behind them when Owen hit the gas and was off again.

"See you later, Charlie!" he hollered out the window before heading back the way they had come, leaving a cloud of dust in his wake.

Chapter Six

CHARLOTTE STRUGGLED TO KEEP UP with Hannah as she led the way up and down Sawyer's Main Street, poking her head into every open doorway and introducing her new friend to each person they met. From Charles Cower, the heavyset butcher, to Anna Rodgers, the redhead sitting behind the cash register of the Five and Dime, everyone welcomed Charlotte warmly, happy that she had arrived safe and sound.

Good folks is good folks, no matter where they call home.

John Grant's words to her just after her arrival in Sawyer echoed in Charlotte's thoughts with every new face. Man or woman, young or old, well-to-do or struggling to make ends meet, all of them brightened up just a bit upon first meeting her, helping to ease what little of her nervousness remained.

It was nothing short of amazing.

But in the end, the most remarkable thing to her was the way Hannah carried herself; regardless of the fact that *she* too was a recent arrival in town, she acted as if she had lived in Sawyer all her life, giving a warm hug here and some good-natured sass there, all with a smile. Everyone they met seemed to love her.

Somehow, I doubt that Owen is thought of as highly as his sister...

Sawyer's school sat in the shadow of the town's water tower, only a stone's throw from Main Street. Farther out, heat shimmers rose up from where the road fronting the school disappeared down a hill before finally heading toward the surrounding countryside. Standing two stories tall, sturdily constructed of dark bricks, it looked brand-new, despite the BUILT IN 1912 chiseled into a stone near the roof. Even the flagpole looked as if it had recently received a fresh coat of paint.

It was all just as Charlotte had imagined it would be.

Standing in front of the same building in which she would soon teach children to read and write, to add and subtract, and even how to find faraway places on a map, Charlotte couldn't believe she was about to achieve her dream. She had often wondered what this moment would be like, gazing at *her* school, and she found that for all of her dreaming, the experience was more than she had anticipated. For all of the long years she had prepared, studying at her teaching college, planning and practicing for the opportunity she would find in Oklahoma...that time had arrived.

Stepping up to the front door, she gingerly ran her fingertips along the rough brick wall, savoring its touch and its radiating warmth. Though she would have enjoyed the chance to go inside and take a closer look, especially to get a glimpse at her new classroom, the door was locked.

"Maybe you'll be the one who can explain something to me," Hannah said.

"Explain what?"

"That." She pointed, calling Charlotte's attention away from the school.

"Oh my," Charlotte answered.

In the lot to the right of the school was a two-story home that initially appeared innocent of any special mention; painted a crisp white, it had a porch that ran the length of its front, lower floor, supported by thick wood columns painstakingly cut to resemble beveled marble. Tall, weather-withered evergreens stood silent watch, the ground beneath them littered with a mat of brown needles. From the street, a stone walkway split a row of trimmed hedges and led the way across the lawn, ushering a visitor to the steps and front door beyond. It looked just like many of the other well-maintained homes up and down the street. Beneath the overhang of the pitched porch roof was a sign reading: THE LOWELL FUNERAL HOME.

"Right...right next to the school?" she muttered.

"That's what I don't understand for the life of me!"

Hannah exclaimed, throwing her hands up in exasperation. "What do you suppose the reason could be? To
frighten the kids into behaving, I just bet!"

"That can't possibly be it," Charlotte disagreed.

Hannah just kept on, ignoring what had been said to
the contrary, her voice imitating a matronly old teacher
as she cackled, "You best sit down and behave, Elizabeth,
or else I'm going to march you right over to the funeral
home and you'll have to sit in the corner with all of the
caskets!"

"I wonder which one was here first," Charlotte said.
"The builder of whichever came second made a really
strange choice, don't you think?"

"Speaking of really strange," Hannah replied, her eyes
lighting up mischievously, "wait until you meet the woman
who runs the funeral home. I've met just about everyone
in Sawyer, and I can say without a shadow of a doubt that
she's as odd as a two-headed calf! Talk about eccentric!
When you finally encounter Constance Lowell, and you
most certainly will, I promise you'll never forget it!"

"You're making me nervous," Charlotte admitted.

"For good reason," Hannah smirked, "seeing as how
you're neighbors."

"What's she like?"

"I'm not telling. You're just going to have to find out for
yourself."

"I thought you said that everyone in Sawyer was
friendly."

"Oh, she's a friendly-enough person; it's just that...
well, she's...she's just cut from a different cloth, if you
know what I mean."

Charlotte wanted to learn more about this mysterious
woman, but to her, Constance Lowell sounded much more
interesting than frightening.

Having successfully sown the seeds of confusion in
Charlotte's thoughts, Hannah excused herself and headed,
a bit late, to her job at Carlton Barnaby's law office. Before
leaving, she suggested a place to eat and further explained
what passed for sightseeing in Sawyer.

"What time will you be finished with work?"

"At four o'clock," Hannah explained, "so don't forget to
be back in front of the grocer's. Owen will be picking us
up and he hates to have to wait. I know exactly how difficult he can be!"

"I'm beginning to know just what you mean," Charlotte
muttered.

Charlotte spent the afternoon getting further acquainted
with Sawyer; retracing her steps with Hannah, she took
her time to take it all in. When her feet began to hurt, she
decided to take a rest and have a bite to eat.

Milton's Diner sat between the hardware store and the
doctor's office. Facing the street, its green awning fluttered
gently in the listless breeze. Following Hannah's advice,
Charlotte took a seat at the lunch counter and ordered an
egg sandwich and a tall glass of iced tea. While she ate, the

waitress standing behind the counter, a snappy young girl named Emily who had an annoying habit of twirling her curly hair about one finger, regaled Charlotte with stories of the first settlers to arrive in Sawyer. It wasn't *that* interesting, but she managed to nod her head between bites.

I bet people don't come here for the conversation.

After dropping off a letter for her sister, Christina, at the post office, Charlotte glanced up at the clock above the bank and saw that it was nearly time for Owen to come for her and Hannah.

When Charlotte arrived at the designated spot, Hannah was nowhere to be seen up or down either side of the street. Concerned, Charlotte again checked the clock, but found that their ride was actually a few minutes late.

The smallest tremor of unease coursed down her spine at the thought of Hannah not arriving as intended. After the way he had spoken to her on the ride into town, Charlotte didn't care to spend time alone with Owen.

"Come on, Hannah," she muttered.

Her plea was not going to be answered. Charlotte saw the truck racing past the nearly completed roller-skating rink and heading toward her, a billowing cloud of dust rising behind it. Just as he had done when they first arrived in town, Owen slammed down on the brakes and brought the vehicle to a sudden, skidding halt.

At first glance, Owen appeared irritated, sweat beading on his brow and upper lip. Streaks of grime dirtied his muscular forearms and hands. A mess of stubble grew on his cheeks and chin, darker than the hair that stuck out from beneath his hat. Still, through the mess, Charlotte recognized he was handsome.

"Where's Hannah?" He frowned through the open passenger's window.

"I don't know. She said she'd be here at four."

"Don't make any difference, I guess," Owen huffed. "Get in."

Looking up and down both sides of the street, Charlotte still held out hope that Hannah would somehow appear. Instead, the only other person sweltering in the heat was an older man exiting the barber shop, tottering carefully by with the help of his cane.

"What are you waitin' for, an invitation or somethin'?" Owen growled impatiently.

For a long moment, Charlotte considered simply walking away and discovering a different way back to the ranch, even if that meant she had to cover the couple of miles by foot. *I'm tired of him being so rude to me!* But then something stopped her; as hotheaded as Owen had already been, there was no telling how he would react to her so openly defying him. Hannah laughed his tantrums away, but could she?

Reluctantly, angry both at herself for not standing up for herself more forcefully as well as at Owen's brash, bullying tone, Charlotte got in the truck, her exasperation instantly turning into surprise when he tromped down on the gas, whipped the truck about in an earsplitting, screeching turn in the middle of the street, and sent them hurtling back the way he had come.

"What do you think you're doing?" she shouted, holding on to the door frame. "Aren't you going to wait for Hannah?"

"If she ain't there when she said she would be, it means she's workin' late for that damn lawyer, and only the Lord knows how long that's gonna take," Owen explained, sliding a bare forearm across the length of his brow. "I don't know 'bout you, but sittin' in this truck when it's hotter than blazes don't sound like much of a good time to me."

"But what if she…"

"Look here, Charlie," he kept on, shooting her a sidelong glance and making the truck go even faster and more recklessly, "we've been doin' this for months, probably 'fore you even decided to come to this place. There ain't no doubt that I know what I'm doin', so just sit back, hold on tight, and don't do any more complainin', you hear?"

"Don't call me Charlie," Charlotte warned, instantly regretting her decision not to walk back to the ranch.

"Why in the hell not? It's your name, ain't it?"

With every harsh word that he spoke, Charlotte's dislike for Owen grew leaps and bounds until she could scarcely stand the sight of him. Never in her entire life had she met a man who was so obnoxious, so willing to say things just to irritate her. How utterly wrong she had been about him, especially after the way he had looked at her the night before.

He's nothing but a fool!

"What in the hell kind of name do you have, anyway?" he kept on, seemingly oblivious to how upset he was making her. "The only Charlotte I ever had the displeasure of knowin' was an old woman with a hunched back who spent all her damn time goin' back and forth to church, pointin' out everything the folks around her was doin' wrong." Owen chuckled. "But I suppose you have that in common with that old bird . . . what with your claimin' that leavin' Hannah behind was wrong and all!"

Without giving it any thought, Charlotte hit him.

It wasn't much of a blow, more of a glancing punch to the top of his muscular biceps than a solid hit, but Owen reacted as if he had just been kicked by a horse; the truth was that it almost certainly hurt her more than it did him. His green eyes grew wide as he held the steering wheel with one hand, rubbing his new wound with the other.

"What in the hell was that for?" he bellowed.

"Because you're the most disrespectful man I've ever met!"

" 'Cause I call you Charlie?"

"It's much more than that and you know it," she snapped, turning to face him with eyes full of anger.

"Whatever it was, it sure isn't enough for me to get hit!"

"Don't be such a baby!" Charlotte snapped, refusing to let him escape punishment for what he had done. "From the first moment I saw you this morning, you've done nothing but antagonize me! If it wasn't belittling that I came from Minnesota or making fun of my name, it was that I was new in Sawyer and absolutely had no idea what I was talking about!"

With every angry word, Charlotte expected to feel relief for finally expressing her frustration with Owen but instead found it growing. It didn't help that a sly smirk spread across his whiskered face; it was obvious that he wasn't chastised but amused.

"Didn't your mother teach you any manners?" he chuckled.

Owen's hurtful question easily shattered the walls of Charlotte's fury, breaking her will to fight. She turned away from him quickly, fearful that he might see the tears that welled in her eyes. Staring out the window of the truck, she somehow managed to answer him.

"My ... my mother died the day I was born ..."

Without any warning, Owen slammed down on the brakes of the truck, sending it fishtailing around the dusty dirt road. Panic-stricken, her hands fearfully braced against the dashboard, Charlotte worried that they were going to crash, hurtling end over end or into the ditch, but they somehow managed to hold to the road. When the truck finally came to a halt, she could barely hear the ticking of the engine over the thundering of her own heart.

"What ... what did you do that for?" she coughed through the clouds of dust raised by the truck's sudden stop.

For a long while, the only answer she received was silence. Her first expectation was that Owen's sudden stop meant he was going to tear into her about something, maybe even her mother's passing.

"I'm...I'm sorry for what I said," Owen replied softly.

He was staring forward at some distant spot, his jaw clenched tightly and his hands rigid around the steering wheel.

Following his gaze down the road, Charlotte saw that they were within sight of the ranch, just on the other side of the bridge. Faintly, she could hear the distinctive sounds of work, an errant whistle, the pounding of a hammer, and even the faint barking of a dog. If she wanted to, she could just open the truck's door and walk away...

"I shouldn't have said what I did," Owen continued, turning to face Charlotte with an intensity that forced her to look away. "Losing a mother is hard enough without some jackass makin' it worse. I know I was only foolin', but that don't mean you knew it."

"That's...that's all right," she answered. "It was a long time ago."

"Don't make it any easier to bear."

Charlotte had met other people stricken by the loss of a parent who carried their grief as if it were a physical thing. In the right moment, you could read their loss on their face as easily as words on a page.

Now, as he sat in the truck, Owen's grief was that apparent.

She struggled with the desire to say something, to ask him if her assumption was true, but she didn't want to pry. If Owen wanted to confide in her, he would when he was ready.

Regardless, his actions had demonstrated that there was much more to Owen Williams than she had been led to believe. Maybe, just maybe, he bore a passing resemblance to the man who had intrigued her the night before, stopping at the door to look back at her.

"Some days are worse than others," she admitted, finding the strength to look directly at him.

"I know just what you mean," he answered quietly.

Before Charlotte could say another word, Owen let up on the brake and gave the truck some gas. Even as the truck rolled over the planks of the bridge, her piercing eyes never left him.

When he caught her staring at him, he grinned. "What I just said don't mean I'm gonna stop callin' you Charlie, though."

"Then you should just get used to being punched in the arm."

Owen laughed. "I suppose I can live with that."

And so could Charlotte.

Chapter Seven

John Grant drove the old truck past the holding corrals where dozens of horses' necks were bent deep into their water troughs as a relief against the sweltering heat, headed past the open barn doors where soot-streaked men sweated over a blazing anvil, the heavy blows of their hammers sending off showers of sparks, and eventually past the last workman's cabin, heading away from the ranch house. Charlotte sat beside him, wondering where he was taking her and what mysterious job he had in mind for her to do. Why was it all so much of a secret?

While the truck bounced down the uneven road, Salt and Pepper ran alongside, furiously trying to keep up. Though Salt made much easier progress, an expression on his face that seemed to say he was just out enjoying the afternoon, Pepper yapped with every frenzied step of his small legs; Charlotte could not tell if his barking was out of some hostility toward the truck or frustration that he couldn't go any faster. Finally, he could do no more, stopping with a sharp flurry of barking before turning back the way he had come, Salt trotting along behind.

"Why won't you tell me where we're going?" she finally asked.

"You'll understand," John promised, "when we're there. "It's easier to see than it is to explain."

Too bad that patience was never a virtue I had very much of... Charlotte thought, and leaned against the door, resting her arm along the open window to catch a bit of breeze.

The rushing air cooled the sweaty heat that clung tenaciously to her skin. So far, every day since her arrival in Oklahoma had been about the same. Above, a blazing sun filled the mostly cloudless sky, relentlessly pounding down upon anyone or anything unfortunate enough to be under its glare. While Minnesota summers were both hot and humid, the nights were often filled with soft breezes and welcoming rain. Here, an open window offered no relief from a sweltering night.

"It doesn't rain much, does it?" Charlotte asked as she looked out at the meager scrub. "The ground seems awfully dry."

John chuckled loudly. "Some days it seems the ground gets more water comin' from my spittin' than it does from rain. If you listen just right, you can hear the tin roofs out on the shacks cryin' out like they was schoolchildren, rememberin' what it was like when raindrops was bouncin' off 'em!"

"It's just so unlike where I come from. Back home, we get so much water in the springtime that it can be quite dangerous, with all of the problems of flooding."

"Round these parts, things couldn't be more different." The older rancher nodded. "Most troublesome problem we got is when a wildfire gets a spreadin' out of control. The winds pert near whip 'em into a frenzy 'fore you know it. When one gets a head of steam, why, there really ain't no way of tellin' just where it'll all end."

"That sounds terrible."

"Sure is," John agreed. "One thing 'bout a wildfire is that it's a hell of a lot tougher to stop than it is to start."

"Then I suppose everyone around here is extra careful."

"If only that were the case. All it takes is a stray spark here or there, wherever it happens, and you got one goin'. Hell, if some fool tosses a match after he's done lightin' up his cigarette, 'fore you know it you're so deep in flames and chokin' smoke that it wouldn't be a surprise to see the devil lookin' over your shoulder!"

John kept on talking, switching from explaining the dangers of wildfire to describing the breadth and scope of his land, its history as his family's property, and even to carrying on about the wildlife that inhabited it, but Charlotte found it difficult to keep her mind on what he said no matter how hard she tried to pay attention. Instead, she couldn't keep her thoughts from traveling unbidden to Owen Williams and the strange way he had spoken to her the day before.

Still furious at Owen that he had decided to just leave Hannah behind in Sawyer, and had raced so recklessly down the dusty roads that led home to the ranch house, Charlotte had been shocked when he had slammed on the truck's brakes short of the rickety bridge. But that paled in comparison to her surprise at the words he had then spoken. Given the harsh, hurtful things he had said to her that day, she never would have expected him to have been so apologetic, so contrite and clearly emotional.

Owen had smiled at her when they'd finally resumed their journey to the ranch, and Charlotte thought they would continue their conversation, but he fell silent. Once they arrived, Owen hurried off toward the closest barn without a word or glance in her direction. Hannah appeared at dinner alone without a hint of her brother's whereabouts. Charlotte was so confused, so disheartened, that she'd even ignored Hale's attempts to get her attention.

Even as she lay in bed that night, listening to the strange sounds that emanated from the ranch grounds outside her window, Charlotte wrestled with the confusion Owen caused in her. On the one hand, he infuriated her; she couldn't remember if she had *ever* met a man more insufferable; never in her life had she been spoken to so rudely. But on the other hand, when she thought of how Owen had talked about the loss of his mother, the hurt look that had radiated in his eyes, and even the way he had smiled affectionately toward her, she decided that whatever impressions she had formed of him were wrong or at the very least...truly complicated.

Who was the real Owen Williams?

"We're here," John said, tearing her from her thoughts and bringing the truck to a stop.

Ahead of them, a small, dilapidated shack sat beside a shallow drainage ditch that had been baked bone-dry in the scorching heat. A tin roof had been tacked down over its shoddy, wooden frame, a hole cut into the roof where a dented stack belched up faint smoke. Its lone window was so small that it made the house look as if it were a child squinting up into the sun. The whole building sat off-kilter, its foundation sinking slightly and leaning to the left into the unsteady earth. A couple of scrawny chickens clucked while scratching in the dirt in a futile search for something to eat.

"I don't understand what—" Charlotte began, but before she could even finish her question, the answer presented itself.

The door to the cabin slowly opened and a small girl stepped outside, shielding her eyes from the early sun. Long blond hair hung limply past her shoulders and down onto her stained, blue blouse. The rest of her clothing, noticeably the dark skirt that hung so low that it brushed along the ground, appeared to have been cobbled together from other garments. From beneath her shaded brow, dark eyes regarded them intently. She was obviously quite young; Charlotte would have been surprised if she was as old as her sister, Christina, who was just fourteen. The girl looked unwashed; a smudge of grime colored her face just to the side of her chin; with growing horror Charlotte wondered if it could be a bruise. What most drew her attention was the girl's stomach, however. It was round and bulging with the unborn child she was carrying, pregnant nearly at the end of her term.

But before Charlotte could wonder aloud at what she was seeing, a man sauntered out from behind the small shack, and spat a thick stream of tobacco onto the scorched earth. Some of the dark juice dribbled down his whiskered chin. The sparse hair on his head was as white as snow, his face a wrinkled mess of canyons and deep valleys. He was thin as a scarecrow, his back bowed deeply, his shoulders and emaciated hips jutting awkwardly from his makeshift clothes. His beady eyes regarded them warily over a bulbous nose that looked to be red from too much drink. Charlotte couldn't even begin to guess his age, but was certain that he was old enough to be the girl's grandpa.

"Who are these people?" she asked.

"Come with me and it'll all be explained as best it can be," John answered as he opened the truck's door.

Before he could even start sliding from his seat, Charlotte reached out, snatching John by the wrist and holding fearfully tight. "Tell me why you brought me here," she demanded.

Even as she raised her voice in both unease and frustration, Charlotte couldn't help but let her eyes wander back to the dilapidated shack and its forlorn inhabitants. Neither the girl nor the man had taken a step toward them, each regarding their arrival with a blank expression. Apprehension spread across her and she wanted nothing more than for John to turn the truck around and drive them away.

For his part, John Grant remained calm. "I brought you here to this girl 'cause I believe that you can do for her what there ain't no chance I can," he explained carefully, reassuringly taking Charlotte's hand in his own. "I know I ain't been too forthcomin' with the details since you arrived, but that's not on account of me tryin' to deceive, instead it's 'cause I just want to help her . . . for reasons that I ain't exactly proud of. Trust me on this, Charlotte."

Finally, she nodded.

Unsteadily, Charlotte got out of the truck and slowly followed as John headed to where the girl stood, her meek face showing little reaction to her visitors. Out of the corner of her eye, Charlotte noticed the old man spit another dark stream of tobacco, while his gaze never left her.

With every step, she felt consumed by questions:

Who are these people?

What is their connection to John Grant?

Why are they staying all the way out here instead of back on the ranch with everyone else?

What reason does John have for bringing me here?

"Charlotte, I'd like you to meet Sarah Beck," John said in introduction. "Sarah, this is the woman I was tellin' you 'bout, the new schoolteacher here in town, Charlotte Tucker."

Up close, Charlotte was struck by the sudden realization that her initial observation of the girl might have been wrong; the girl was *very* young, younger than Christina. That this girl...this child standing before her was pregnant nearly nauseated her.

"Hello," she somehow managed, extending her hand. The girl took it limply, never bothering to make eye contact or utter a sound.

Sarah's only answer was to nod her head.

"Sarah and her father, Alan, came here a little more than four months ago, arrivin' from Arkansas," John continued to explain, his voice as free and friendly as if he were introducing acquaintances outside of church. "Had themselves a spot of trouble but were lucky enough to find themselves a place out of the storm, ain't that 'bout right, Alan?"

"Yep," the old man agreed with an ugly, coughing laugh. "Seems to be."

Charlotte smiled awkwardly, though she couldn't begin to see what could be so funny about their situation.

"Now, Sarah," John said, "why don't you just head on inside while Miss Tucker and me have a couple of words. When we're finished, she'll come on in and talk to you a mite 'bout what's to come."

"Yessir," the girl mumbled, and did as she was told. Though he hadn't been similarly instructed, Alan also ambled away.

Once she was sure they were alone, Charlotte again asked, "Why did you bring me here?"

"It's just like I told you," John replied. "I want you to help her."

"What can I possibly do?"

"You and I both know that if that girl don't get as much schoolin' as she can she ain't gonna have much of a future. Hell, even if she were to get a good education, odds are that it's gonna be a struggle every step of the way."

"And you expect me to be the one to teach her," Charlotte said, beginning to understand just a bit, "because she can't go into town..."

"I don't know what things are like up in Minnesota, but I reckon that they ain't gonna differ too much from the way things are here." John sighed deeply, his features taut and his voice growing a bit tired. "Around these parts a woman...a girl gettin' pregnant at Sarah's age, without a husband in sight, will set every tongue in town to waggin'. For much less offense than that, folks've been run out of town on a rail. To send her to your school, even havin' the intentions of a saint, wouldn't be right."

Charlotte knew that John was right. Back in her teaching college in Minnesota, one of her fellow students had become pregnant and the result had been scandalous. Even though the girl intended to marry the man and regardless of the fact that they had been together for more than a year, she had been shamed into leaving. The fate facing a girl of Sarah Beck's age would undoubtedly be worse.

"How old is she?" Charlotte asked.

"Thirteen is what I've been told."

"Do you know how much schooling she's had?"

"My assumption would be that it's a hell of a lot less than she should have," John answered in dismay. "But I ain't rightfully asked much. My hope is that spendin' a little time with her, talkin' to her a bit, will give you whatever answers you're lookin' for."

Still, Charlotte wavered. Though she eagerly looked forward to teaching her new pupils, the idea of instructing a pregnant teenage girl hidden far out of inquisitive eyes was not appealing. *What if I were to be seen with this girl and her father?* She felt certain that the answer to her unspoken question was a simple one: she would be ostracized like Sarah, and that was a risk she didn't feel comfortable taking.

"I'm sorry, John," she said apologetically, "but I don't think that I can teach her much. I'll not have much time to spend with her."

"Won't you try, Charlotte?" he answered before she could say any more, his calloused hands taking her by the shoulders, his eyes beseeching. "I know this ain't an easy thing for you to agree on, with you bein' new to these parts and all, but I feel like I ain't got any choice. I ain't gonna lie to your face by sayin' there ain't no risk, but whatever doubts you got, whatever reservations are makin' you want to walk away from here, I'm askin' you to put 'em down."

Until that moment, Charlotte felt certain that the reason John Grant was trying to help Sarah Beck was out of a sense of kindness, a neighborly way to offer a hand to someone down on her luck, but now she found the reason insufficient. There was more to all of this, something unspoken, but unfortunately, it was not enough for her to simply take him at his word. She needed more explanation.

"Who are these people to you?" she asked bluntly. "Why, John?" she insisted. "Why are you doing this?"

For a long moment, John simply stared at her, before breaking his gaze and looking off over her shoulder into the distance. From his expression, Charlotte clearly saw that he was struggling to find an answer. Finally, he said, his voice hard to hear, "I have my reasons."

Charlotte frowned, a bit put out that he wasn't being more forthcoming. "That's not good enough for me," she explained. "If I'm going to put my future in Sawyer in jeopardy, if I'm going to try to teach her..."

"Then how 'bout for now there ain't any such expectations," John suggested. "How 'bout you just go on in there and have yourself a little talk with Sarah, get to know her a bit, and then you can decide."

"But what if I choose not to teach her? Won't you be upset?"

"If that's the decision you come to after talkin' with her,

then that'll be fine by me. Even if I'm disappointed, leastways I'll have tried."

"I don't know if she can be taught."

"I ain't askin' for you to perform no miracles. All I'm askin' is she be given a chance."

Charlotte sighed and turned away from John, her arms folding over her chest as she absently kicked at a loose rock. While she still had a few strong reservations, it was hard for her to imagine what harm could come from just going inside and talking. From somewhere deep in her memory, a recollection from a much older time floated up; she had once stood outside another broken-down shack far out in the woods, and by taking a chance and going inside she had discovered her father, long thought dead. On that day, if she hadn't found the courage, Mason Tucker would surely have died. Maybe this was another such moment, another opportunity to save a life.

There's only one way to find out...

"All right," she said. "I'll go in and talk to her."

Chapter Eight

To CHARLOTTE'S CURIOUS EYE, the inside of the rickety, dreary cabin that Sarah Beck shared with her father at the far edge of the ranch property was nearly as uncomfortably cramped as the inside of the steamer trunk she had brought with her on the train ride to Oklahoma. The only difference was that her trunk carried a greater number of belongings.

Scarcely illuminated by the sliver of bright summer sunlight that slipped in through the front door and tiny, cracked window, the single room was barren. A pair of old mattresses lay toward the back, one on a frame and the other tossed haphazardly on the floor; Charlotte hoped that, given Sarah's current condition, her father was the one sleeping on the hard wooden floor. A wooden apple crate, its once-colorful label long since faded, lay beside the beds on its side, cluttered with a handful of items. Near the door, a beaten and worn table was pushed up against the wall; as it was missing one of its legs, this was the only way that it could be forced to remain standing upright. A pair of equally damaged chairs sat on opposite sides of the table, buckled and slightly bowed in the seat. A cast-iron stove threw off waves of stifling heat.

"Do you want some coffee?" Sarah asked meekly, still refusing to make eye contact as she reached for the pot on the stove.

"I'm afraid that I'm a bit too warm for that, but thank you all the same," Charlotte answered with a forced smile, wiping at the heavy beads of sweat that made her blouse cling to her skin. All the while, she did her best to avoid obviously looking at Sarah's very round, pregnant belly.

"Yes, ma'am." As quiet as a mouse, the young girl took a seat at the table.

For a moment, Charlotte could only stand and take stock of what an untenable situation she had allowed herself to enter into. Though she had heard her speak only a handful of words, she knew that Sarah Beck was facing an impossibly difficult future. *Even with some schooling, what chance does this girl have?* Even if Charlotte was to try her very best, to devote as much time and energy to teaching Sarah as she could, to instruct her in the most basic of things, it seemed unlikely that much change could be hoped for. To make matters worse, she would risk her reputation if she was seen with a pregnant teenager. That could destroy her own future.

On entering the Becks' cabin, Charlotte recalled another such shack and the day her father had returned to her life. With her beloved dog, Jasper, always by her side, she'd gone inside just such a place and discovered Mason Tucker, a man she then had not known was her father. But for Mason, so delirious from fever that he had mistaken Charlotte for his wife, her own mother, there'd been somewhere for her to take him, somewhere he could be nursed back to health and his ills made right. But where did Sarah Beck have to go? How could the hopeless future before her be avoided?

Glancing back out the door, Charlotte saw John Grant talking with Alan beside the truck; the rancher offered the down-on-his-luck older man a cigarette that was quickly, almost hungrily accepted. Though her instincts still told her to march back out and demand a return to the ranch house, to put meeting these people right out of her mind, Charlotte was unable to act upon them.

"All he asked was for you to talk to her..." she mumbled under her breath.

Sighing, she took the seat opposite Sarah.

"Mr. Grant said that you and your father came here from Arkansas," Charlotte began as a gentle way of starting to understand just how big a task lay before her. "Is that right?"

"Yes, ma'am."

"Did you have any schooling back where you came from?"

"Yes, ma'am." Just as Charlotte was starting to wonder if she would have to pry words from Sarah Beck as painfully as a dentist extracts rotten teeth, the girl added, "But it weren't much."

While Sarah spoke, Charlotte took a long look at the young girl. Strands of her limp blond hair hung down before her face. An outbreak of pimples stained her face near her thin lips and tiny nose. Thankfully, the darkened spot Charlotte had seen on Sarah's face appeared, on closer inspection, to indeed be dirt, not a bruise as feared, although the difference did little to staunch Charlotte's growing sense of apprehension and unease.

But what truly struck her as she stared at Sarah was the nearly overpowering fear that if she had ever found herself in a similar situation, if she'd become pregnant at such a young age, her life would have looked every bit as hopeless. *How could I possibly have gone forward with my life? What burdens would I have put upon all those around me?* Even with her parents' help, even with the best of intentions, the shame of what she had done would have consumed her. Though she had only the briefest encounter to assess how much help Alan Beck would be to his daughter, confidence in the man eluded her. Sarah obviously had nowhere else to turn.

Fighting down her apprehension and determined to, at the least, do as John had asked, Charlotte moved forward with her questioning. "Can you read or write?"

At the question, Sarah's eyes rose up and held to Charlotte's for scarcely an instant, faster than it would have taken her to even blink her long lashes, but in that fleeting moment a touch of shame revealed itself in her expression, a protected yet painful secret being pried loose. When she spoke, her gaze was again facing down.

"Just...just a bit, I reckon," she stammered, "but I ain't got much of a chance to do any practicin' or any such. My pa ain't the type to have no books just layin' 'bout. I seen a Bible or two when I weren't but waist-high, but since we weren't never much for churchgoin', I forget it all."

"But you do know how to read?"

Sarah nodded.

Determined to find out just how truthful Sarah was being with her, Charlotte began looking around the cabin for some means of testing her. Just as Sarah admitted, there wasn't a single book to be seen, but Charlotte's gaze settled upon a large sack of flour resting against the wall beside the stove. On it, stenciled in oversize red letters, were the words: MCGREGGOR FLOUR—THE VERY BEST FOR YOU AND YOUR FAMILY.

"Can you read what's written on that sack?" she asked, pointing.

Sarah followed Charlotte's request and her eyes squinted down at the advertising, her brow knit in furrows of concentration. With a nervous uncertainty, she nibbled on her thin, pursed lips. When she finally spoke, her voice lacked any trace of confidence or surety. "It's a flour sack...but them other words...are a mite hard," she stammered. "I don't know if I can..."

"Take your time," Charlotte encouraged her.

"It...it says...it says 'the ve-very...very...b-be-beast... very be-beast...'" The young girl struggled, each word coming out as unsteadily as a step on ice. Frustration was so apparent across Sarah's face that when she angrily folded her arms across her narrow chest there was no doubt that she wouldn't attempt to read another word.

"That's all right, Sarah." Being honest, Charlotte explained, "I just wanted to have some idea of where we might be starting from."

"Well, now you know," Sarah declared as the first tears began to well in her eyes.

Sarah's words, while the truth, were not what Charlotte wanted to hear; now she knew that Sarah lacked even the most basic understanding of reading. There could be no doubt that her skills in other subjects, writing and math quickly came to mind, would be equally poor. Teaching her anything would require a great deal of work as well as patience. They would have to start at the very beginning.

But just as Charlotte began to grasp just how enormous a task lay before her, she looked at the way Sarah sat in her chair, her face pointed down at the scarred old table-top, her shoulders slumped, and *knew* that she had never had the least bit of encouragement. Sarah Beck was beaten down, ashamed of her shortcomings, headed nowhere, and in that way looked to be even younger, even more of a child, than she really was.

"How long has it been since you've had any schooling?"

"A long time ago," Sarah admitted. "My pa took me out of school when I was younger 'cause he said it weren't doin' me no good, said learnin' never did him no good, neither, and he didn't want me wastin' my time. Besides, he needed me to help out farmin', and when I was away it just meant more work for him." She hesitated for a moment, before adding, "We was happy like that for a couple of years, makin' of that farm what we could...up till I wound up pregnant, and now I ain't nothin' but a burden to him."

"I'm sure that's not true," Charlotte tried to reassure her, but Sarah wasn't about to accept what she was offering.

"It was 'cause of what happened to me that we ended up losin' the farm," the girl disagreed. "My pa says it ain't, just like you did, but you can see it in his waterin' eyes."

"What's done is done. What matters is what you do now."

"Pa says that, too." Sarah smiled weakly. "But it don't make my burden any easier to bear."

"That's why you need to let it go," Charlotte explained, wanting to give whatever meager hope she could to Sarah, but the girl was already shaking her long hair in resignation.

"Some burdens are so heavy that you can't let 'em go. They just got a life of their own and there ain't no escapin'."

Charlotte found herself stunned by the severity of Sarah's words; the bluntness with which she spoke of her condition was unsettling. It didn't matter if it was becoming pregnant and causing her father to lose their farm that was her burden, or if it was her unborn child that she would be unable to get away from; either interpretation filled Charlotte with dread.

But it also filled her with resolve.

Charlotte had always been a fighter, both unable and unwilling to surrender to defeat without giving the task her all; her father had always claimed that she was stubborn to a fault.

Now, looking at Sarah's downturned eyes and hearing how resigned she was to her fate, Charlotte knew that if she failed to teach this girl anything, it would not be from a lack of trying, any consequences for her reputation around Sawyer be damned. She was to be the schoolteacher of Sawyer's children, so she would be so for *all* of them.

"So it's been a while since you've been to school," she voiced her thoughts aloud.

"Yes, ma'am."

"Do you remember anything at all?"

" 'Bout the only thing I recall as far as readin' goes is a story my mother used to tell me 'fore I went to sleep," Sarah answered, lifting her eyes only briefly before lowering them again. "It was 'bout a little girl in a bright red outfit who was bringin' her grandmother some food but found this mean old critter, a wolf with big teeth, had done beat her there. He'd dressed himself up in the grandmother's clothes and was waitin' in her bed, actin' and talkin' like a person, wantin' to eat the little girl, too."

"My grandmother used to tell me the same story when I was little."

Sarah brightened at Charlotte's words, smiling in a way that prettily lit up her face, a hint of a happier girl trapped by the harsher reality of her life, faint dimples showing on her cheeks. "My mother used to make different voices for each of the critters in the book," she said, "but I used to get a bit scared when she talked like the wolf, what with all the growlin' and snarlin' she did."

"Where is your mother now?" Charlotte asked, broaching the subject that had tugged at her from the moment they had been introduced.

Just as quickly as the smile had appeared on Sarah's face, it now vanished. Instead of answering, the girl got up from the table and walked over to the makeshift beds and picked up an item from atop the overturned apple crate. She paused for a moment, unsure if she wanted to reveal what it was, before returning to the table and putting it down before Charlotte.

"This is her," Sarah said simply.

The small, faded photograph was crooked inside the square wood frame, its enamel chipped and dusty.

Black-and-white, with a faint crease that ran all the way across its width, the picture showed a woman who appeared to have struggled with the weight of life every bit as much as her daughter.

Sarah's mother was neither ugly nor pretty, just plain, with mousy hair that, while long and straight, had been hastily piled on top of her long face in an obvious attempt to look more sophisticated. Her small mouth was bunched tightly, the woman uncomfortable at being the object of the photographer's attention at best, angry at worst. Still, Charlotte knew that the picture she held was Sarah's most prized possession.

"She died when I weren't waist-high," Sarah said simply.

"I'm sorry," Charlotte replied.

"It come on in the fall," the girl explained. "Pa said she'd been out in the rain too much...that a wet had done settled into her chest and it weren't comin' out till it killed her. Weeks went by and there weren't nothin' to do but listen to coughin' comin' from her bed.

"Last time the doctor come to look in on her, he was real quiet, like he was in a church or somethin'. He listened to her breathe, put his hand on her wrist, gathered up his things, and made for the door. Just 'fore he left, he turned to Pa and said he was sorry. Pa just nodded. She died that night.

"Since then, it's just been me and Pa and..." But her voice trailed off before she could say more.

In silent answer to Sarah's sad tale, Charlotte retrieved the locket she always wore around her neck, opened the tiny clasp, took a familiar look at what it contained, and held it out to the pregnant girl. Curiously, Sarah took it.

"This is my mother," Charlotte explained.

"She's pretty."

"Yes, she was," Charlotte agreed with a tiny smile. "But just like your mother, she was taken from me when I was very young, and just like you, about all I've got to remember her by is a photograph."

"You look an awful lot like her."

"My father has said that I'm the spitting image of her, especially the hair."

"What did she die from?" Sarah asked abruptly.

Charlotte's heart clenched tightly. She knew that there was no way she could tell Sarah the truth: that Alice Tucker had died in childbirth, leaving her newborn daughter behind to be raised without either of her parents. Thankfully, in Charlotte's case there had been her aunt and grandmother to lovingly take over and raise her, an essential task that she doubted Alan Beck would be capable of performing. In Sarah's fragile state, already feeling responsible for the predicament she and her father found themselves in, adding the fear of dying seemed unnecessarily cruel.

"My mother . . . had a weak heart," Charlotte managed.

For a long moment, neither of them spoke, content to sit silently, each staring at the other's photograph, the only sound a dog's distant bark. Charlotte was getting ready to speak, to again talk about furthering Sarah's education so that she could provide for her unborn child, when the girl spoke, her voice trembling: "I'm a bit scared to be a mother."

"I think that any woman, no matter her age, would be a bit frightened."

"Would you be scared if you were me?"

Charlotte nodded.

"Thing is, I ain't got no one around to tell me right from wrong with a baby. I ain't never had no time with one 'fore, 'cept for this one time on a train. What happens if I do somethin' wrong?"

"You have your father..."

"He ain't no woman."

"No, he's not," Charlotte agreed, her concerns about Alan's skills at child rearing already in question. "But..." She paused, the weight of what she was about to say heavy before plunging forward. "You have me."

"You'd...you'd help me?"

"I'll try, but only if you'll let me teach you proper schooling."

"I'll have to do learnin'...and you'll be my teacher..."

Charlotte began to smile a bit beside herself; that *was* what it meant. When she had first set foot in the Becks' small cabin, she'd already resigned herself to exiting as quickly as possible. But, after beginning to understand Sarah's predicament, she had been swayed. Now she would take on the task with everything she could muster. She would be a teacher. But before she could say as much, John Grant burst into the cabin and shouted, "Charlotte! We gotta go right now!"

"What...what's wrong?"

"The prairie's on fire!"

Chapter Nine

JOHN GRANT DROVE the truck recklessly down the dirt road, his eyes surveying the sky through the dusty windshield. Unlike the trip to the Becks' ramshackle cabin, a gentle drive that gave him and Charlotte plenty of time to look at the beautiful yet rugged landscape, they now hurtled sharply around corners, wheels sliding in the scrabbly, loose dirt, and bouncing over the many rocks and ruts that littered their path. Charlotte clung tightly to the truck's door frame, her feet pushed hard against the floorboards as she desperately tried to keep from bouncing off the seat. She wasn't brave enough to guess how fast they were going.

From somewhere close by, somewhere over the gentle rises of the hills before them, dark tendrils of smoke rose steadily upward to the cloudless sky, faintly billowing and spreading in the soft breeze. Charlotte couldn't be absolutely certain, but she thought that the plume came from near the ranch; still, to her eyes it didn't look particularly threatening, certainly not enough to have caused John to react in such a panicked way. Regardless, they continued to race onward.

"Is the fire near the ranch?" she asked worriedly as the truck roared around a tight corner.

"On or near," John answered grimly, his jaw clenched and his forehead deeply furrowed with concern.

"Could it be someone burning a brush pile?"

"It ain't. Too spread out."

"But I've seen plenty of little fires around the ranch," Charlotte kept on, gritting her teeth as they shot so quickly over a rise in the road that she would have sworn the truck's wheels had left the road. "It's probably nothing more than Hale getting ready to shoe a couple of horses or..." She paused momentarily, another sudden, treacherous turn silencing her tongue before continuing. "Or one of the cook fires is smokier than usual. I'd hate for us to get in an accident over something as simple as that."

John turned quickly to her, his eyes only leaving the road for a second, but Charlotte could clearly see how serious he was. "I've spent too many years ranchin' not to know when things ain't right. Lyin' to myself ain't gonna make it go away no matter how much I wish it were so."

Charlotte opened her mouth to speak but instead fell silent; she wished that there were words she could offer that would lessen his worry and stop their recklessness, but she knew there was nothing that would take John Grant's foot off the gas pedal. She remembered that they had been discussing wildfires on the way to the Becks' cabin; it seemed impossible that one could have just sprung to life. Scanning the growing smoke to which they drew ever closer, she could only hope that the rancher's worry really *was* for nothing.

No matter how preoccupied she was with her own safety, Charlotte's thoughts kept returning to her meeting with Sarah Beck. The thought of the young girl's burden weighed heavily as unbidden questions pressed for answers she did not have.

Why are the Becks staying on John Grant's property?

Who is the father of Sarah's unborn child?

Am I going to be able to teach Sarah enough before the baby comes?

Charlotte knew that the answers to these questions, as well as many others, would come only when she had the chance to have a long and very honest conversation with John, but now was not that time.

Crossing the narrow bridge that spanned the gurgling creek as it skirted to the south of the ranch, they raced around a gentle turn, drove down into a depression, and then shot up out of it as the ranch finally came into view. Charlotte couldn't suppress her gasp.

"Oh, my Lord!"

"Damn it all to hell," John swore beside her.

Before their eyes, at the edge of the corral pens south

of the livery stable and beside the first cluster of worker cabins, bedlam reigned. Within the nearly impenetrable smoke that pulsed and billowed into the blue sky, flickering tongues of red and yellow flame showed through, racing ever forward, with the fences caught in its advance already ablaze. Shapes ran around wildly in the gloom, releasing the stock. As she watched, horrified, Charlotte could hear the unmistakable sound of the fire's onslaught, a crackle and popping punctuated by an occasional human shout or a horse's terrified whinny, even over the ticking of the truck's engine and the pounding of her own heart. John had been right to worry.

"What...what do we do?" Charlotte asked.

John grimaced, his hands tight on the truck's steering wheel. "We damn well better stop it, that's what."

John brought the truck to a skidding halt just before the large barn that housed the ranch's horse tack. Though she was only a few feet from the open doors, Charlotte could hardly see the saddles, stirrups, bridles, reins, harnesses, and bits that lined the walls, so dense was the smoke. From the Becks' cottage where John first sensed something was wrong, it had looked as if the smoke was just gently rising up into the sky, but now, down on the ground where the fire raged, swirling, hot winds pushed the flames, choking out the light of the summer sun and gagging those unfortunate enough to inhale it. Charlotte coughed involuntarily, even as she held the sleeve of her blouse against her nose. Carefully, she moved around the truck as John shouted angrily.

"What in the hell happened?" he bellowed.

"We ain't rightfully sure, Mr. Grant," a man answered. Blinking in the stinging smoke, Charlotte thought that it might have been Dave Powell but couldn't be certain. "Come up outta nowhere, all sudden like, and 'fore we knew it, it was right on top of us! Been a struggle ever since."

"Any idea what started it?"

"None, sir."

"How broad is it? Is it all the way across the western flank of the ranch?"

"No, sir, it ain't. From what I can tell it's in a pretty narrow strip, just right here around the pens and barn. Thank the Lord that there ain't much of a wind or who knows how big a mess we'd have. If the wind was gustin', I'd be worried 'bout it reachin' all the way to Sawyer."

All around them, men darted about in the churning smoke, frantically shouting instructions. Charlotte felt terror rising within her. Just driving to the tack barn had been frightening, but barreling full speed into the teeth of a fire in dense, choking smoke was crazy! They might run headlong into something or someone they couldn't see. Frantically, she peered through the blaze for John. His reaction was remarkable; though he was clearly upset, he remained focused on getting control of the fire.

"Where's Del?"

"He was one of the first ones out to fight the blaze," the man replied. "Got one hell of a burn up his arm for his troubles."

John frowned. "Did anyone set about startin' a back-fire?"

"Hale's got a group of men over at the well haulin' buckets back to where the worst of it is," Dave answered; Charlotte was finally certain that it was he. "Blankets are bein' doused in the horse troughs and handed out and we talked 'bout that, 'bout startin' a backfire, but it ain't done that I know of."

"It's probably too damn late for that anyway," John said. "The fire's too close to us out here at the barn for it to do us any good, but keep it in mind if we think the ranch house is in danger."

"What's a backfire?" Charlotte asked.

"Backfirin's when you light a couple of small fires in the direction you think the big one is headed," Dave answered; John's attention was elsewhere, his determined gaze focused on the fire.

"But won't that just make things worse?"

Dave shook his head. "Nope, it don't. What a backfire does is take away the fuel that the fire's got to have in order to keep goin'. If it don't have nothin' else keepin' it burnin', it'll peter itself out, or at least make it easier for us to do it. Problem is that Mr. Grant's right . . . it's already too close to the barn and corrals for that. Startin' a backfire here *would* just make it worse."

"We're gonna need to get the shovels ready if it gets past the tack barn," John explained, formulating a plan of action. "There's a bit of a divide out behind here before it reaches the bunkhouse. We get that scrub brush dug up and we'll have the same advantage as if we burned it."

"I'll hand 'em out, but could I hook up a team of horses and try to get 'em to plow up the scrub? I'd be quicker."

"Won't happen," John replied surely. "Fire'll just spook 'em. You'll spend all your time keepin' 'em in line. Two or three men with shovels and hoes'll be enough to do the job."

"I'll get to it," Dave answered before disappearing out into the smoke.

Now that he had begun the process of trying to quell the raging fire and limit the damage to what had already been done, John turned his attention toward Charlotte, grabbing her insistently by the shoulders. "This ain't no place for you to be now, young lady," he firmly told her. "You need to head on out around this barn, follow the side wall till you reach the end, and just keep walkin' straight. Won't matter if you can see nothin' or not. 'Fore you even know it, you'll get out of this damn smoke and find yourself already headin' for the ranch house. Stay there till it's safe."

"But surely there's something I can do to help," she argued.

"You can help best by gettin' yourself out of here."

"Maybe I could get to the phone," Charlotte kept

on. "Maybe the fire department in Sawyer would be able to—"

"I'm sure that would have been helpful back in Minnesota," John silenced her, a worn worried frown creasing his already blackened features, "but here it won't do any good. The town's too far away, so we'll have to do our own rescuin'."

"But that doesn't mean that I can't—"

"Charlotte, listen to me," John said insistently, his earlier warmth now nowhere to be seen. "I'm tellin' you to get yourself up to the ranch house and stay there. If I had time to take you there myself I would, but I need to find Del and get on top of this, so I have to trust you to do as I ask."

"But why can't I—"

"Promise me you'll go, Charlotte," he demanded.

"Okay, I'm going. Just watch out for yourself. Be careful; be careful!" Charlotte answered, but John was gone, disappearing into the smoke and leaving her standing alone.

Charlotte stood within sight of the corner of the tack barn, the route that John had told her would take her safely back to the ranch house, unsure if she could go through with what she had promised. Chaos reigned in the midst of the growing fire, matching her own indecision. Reluctant as she was to openly disobey orders she knew were prompted by John's concern for safety, she couldn't go when maybe she could give help.

Around her, men worked frantically with blankets and

gunnysacks as they tried to put out the blaze; occasionally, bodies crashed into each other before righting themselves and getting back to whatever task they had set out to do. Even over the crackling and roar of the fire, she could hear snippets of voices.

"—over where we can do the most good!"

"If you ain't careful, it's gonna..."

"...the other bucket's in the..."

As if her feet had a mind of their own, Charlotte found herself drifting away from the tack barn out into the swirling mess of smoke and heat. In the end, she could not run away and do nothing.

Within her first few tentative steps, Charlotte was struck by the fire's frenzied rage; pressing waves of blistering heat washed over her as she ran to locate John, Hale, Del, or even Owen. The blaze's intensity was hard to bear. Even with the sleeve of her blouse pressed tightly over her nose and mouth, the heat burned the air from her lungs. She coughed, and coughed again, but she kept moving on.

Once she was far enough away from the tack barn, Charlotte lost all sense of direction; she wasn't even sure if she was walking toward the fire or away from it. As she struggled to maintain her balance, each of her senses was assaulted; the black smoke enveloping her, the never-ending sound of brush and wood burning, the acrid stench that it produced, the heat on her skin, even the sooty residue that lodged in her throat, all fought to upset her balance. As the men periodically wafted into her view, she had the illusion that she was dreaming, a nightmare from which she desperately wanted to wake up.

Suddenly, a shadowy form loomed up before her through the smoke and she collided with it hard, falling back stunned.

"Watch where you're goin'!" a voice thundered.

Even through the murky gloom of the fire, Charlotte had no trouble recognizing Hale's hearty voice. When he saw who it was who had run into him, his demeanor quickly changed.

"What the hell are you doin' out here?" Hale shouted. Streaks of soot ran black across his sweaty face. His clothes were soaking wet. He stood before the well pump, a pair of empty buckets on the saturated ground before it. Mud caked his boots and the cuffs of his pant legs.

"I want to help," she answered earnestly.

"This ain't no place for you," he growled, taking the same tack that John had when he had ordered her to leave. "Go on. Get on out of here. Now!"

"Don't go chasing me away, Hale!" Charlotte persisted, her back up and defensive, her voice rising in anger. "Just because I'm a woman doesn't mean I'm helpless!"

"You should be back at the ranch house with Hannah and—"

"I'm not Hannah! I'm here and I want to help."

"But if something happens to you, then—"

"Then what?" Charlotte demanded. "Why is it all right for you to take all of the risk, but I'm just supposed to run away and hide." When it looked as if Hale would argue, she quickly added, "And don't even think of telling me it's because you're a man!"

Hale stared at her for a moment, then seemed to realize that there wasn't any point in arguing.

"Once the buckets are full, they'll be too heavy for you to haul as quick as they're gonna be needed."

"Hale, I told you that—"

"But that doesn't mean that you can't haul wet blankets up to the men who're usin' 'em to beat down the flames."

Charlotte couldn't help but grin that Hale had relented and was going to let her help. "Just show me what to do."

Hale picked up a blanket from a pile that had been haphazardly tossed on the ground beside the well pump. With a few rapid pumps with one hand, he drew cascading water from the ground below. Hale held the blanket under the flow until it was well wetted, then handed it to Charlotte.

Pointing off behind him, Hale instructed, "Walk straight that way, but don't go bein' in any hurry, 'cause I ain't sure how far forward the fire's come. You could rush into it before you know it. Once you see the flames, find the men who're usin' the blankets, give 'em a wet one, and bring the other back to me. You understand?"

Charlotte nodded.

"Then go," Hale ordered, "but be careful!"

After she headed off in the direction Hale had pointed, it didn't take long for Charlotte to see the edges of where the fire blazed; through the thick, dark smoke, a crackling bright red and orange flame rose from the brush it consumed. The roar of bushes, grasses, and even fence posts burning was overwhelming, the heat nearly the same. While the area that was aflame wasn't very large, mammoth effort was needed to contain it. Three men waved blankets over their heads before bringing them crashing down to the ground. Another ranch hand poured water from a pair of buckets before quickly running back toward where Hale worked the pump.

Charlotte staggered; the soaking-wet blanket was so heavy! She wondered if hauling buckets wouldn't have been easier.

"I've got a new blanket!" she shouted, but no one appeared to hear her.

What am I supposed to do now?

Tentatively, she took a few steps closer; all of the men had their backs turned to her, so she couldn't tell who any of them were. Grime and sweat caked their shirts, their hats low on their heads. So intent were they on their tasks that Charlotte couldn't get their attention.

I'm not just going to stand here and do nothing...

To the right of the man closest to her, the fire had gotten to a small sagebrush bush, lighting up the full length of its small branches and the dry grass at its base. With the still-soaking-wet blanket clutched in her hands, Charlotte moved closer, intent to do her part.

Tentatively at first, she began mimicking the motions

of the ranch hands beside her; with her hands at the blanket's corners, she quickly brought it swinging over her head and crashing down on the hot, burning grass. Water flew in a widening arc, dousing Charlotte but also tamping down the bright flames. Over and over she swung, growing proud of herself as she saw her actions making a difference.

When one spot was taken care of, she moved to attack another. Soon her shoulders began to ache with the strain of moving the heavy blanket. But Charlotte didn't allow that to slow her down; she had actually begun to feel a sense of happiness course through her.

Suddenly, she bumped into something. Her first thought was that she had moved too closely to where the other men were working, but then a sharp pain flared in her elbow and forearm. Spinning, Charlotte was horrified to find that she had backed into the burning sagebrush bush. Yelping, she jumped away fast, dropping the blanket and swatting at her bare arm.

Quickly, the pain subsided, but it was then that Charlotte grew truly afraid; backing into the bush hadn't just singed her skin.

It had set her skirt on fire.

Chapter Ten

CHARLOTTE COULD NOT BELIEVE what she was seeing; the hem of her skirt burned brightly, flame hungrily devouring the fabric. Even as the sharp, pungent smell of her burning clothes rose to her nose, mingling with the dark clouds of smoke billowing all around her, she found herself in such shock, such complete denial of the pain she began to experience, that she was incapable of moving.

Put it out, you fool! You've got to put it out!

Breaking through the fear that paralyzed her, Charlotte began frantically slapping at the growing flames with her bare hands. Pain ran across her skin, a blistering heat, but still she kept on. Terrified, she saw the blaze grow despite her efforts, as if fighting the fire only spread it farther across her skirt.

Without warning, Charlotte was struck hard from the side and violently knocked to the ground, the air nearly driven from her lungs. A heavy weight fell on her legs, pinning her down. Hysterically, she began kicking her feet and flailing her arms in a desperate attempt to get free.

"Hold still, dammit!" a man's voice barked angrily. "If you don't quit moving, I can't help you!"

The gruff words stilled Charlotte's thrashing movements. Rough hands started slapping at her legs. It hurt!

What in heaven's name is happening to me?

Blinking rapidly through the thickening smoke, Charlotte tried to regain some semblance of control over what was happening to her. The man's weight and the way he was hitting her sent flares of anger rippling across her chest, so she began to fight, kicking and flailing her limbs.

"I told you to hold still!" the man shouted. "It's almost out, but—"

Lashing out wildly, she accidentally brought one of her knees up into the man's jaw. The sound was horrible, bone against bone. In an instant, he came crashing down on top of her, his chest landing squarely on her own, the brim of his hat bluntly striking against her forehead.

"What in the hell did...you do that for?" the man gasped.

Even with his face shadowed by his hat and the dark, swirling smoke, covered in streaks of soot and drenched in sweat, Charlotte recognized Owen, and her heart skipped a sudden beat. While he rubbed his aching jaw, his green eyes glared at her accusingly and with...something else... Though she had sat beside him in the truck, she'd never been *this* close to him before. Ridiculous as it was at this moment, she thought, *He is so handsome!*

"Ow-Owen?" she stumbled.

"Is that the way you thank a fella for saving you?"

When Owen spoke, his face was so near hers that Charlotte could feel his warm breath upon her skin. Even though he was a mess from fighting the fire, even though she had been burned and could have died in the fire, there was something about the situation they found themselves in that triggered a feeling in her heart that was different, nearly impossible to explain.

Owen's lips were so close to her own that Charlotte found herself in a struggle to resist leaning up and lightly, delicately touching them. In that instant, Owen looked at her and she knew, she *knew*, that he had had the same thought. His normally rough exterior, made worse by the fire, softened, she saw it in his eyes, but then like the flames all around them, it flickered before disappearing.

Before she could protest, Owen was up and off her, wiping his hands against his shirt as if to remove her imprint from his body.

"Charlie! What in the hell are you doing out here?" he shot out accusingly, swatting his dirty hat against his thigh.

Just as she had been unable to act when she had found herself on fire, Charlotte found herself incapable of replying to Owen's biting, angry words. Lying on the ground, she was only aware of the scene around her; for the first time since noticing her clothes were on fire, she saw the fire; the bush she had brushed against was now completely engulfed by flame and all of the dried grasses around it crackled and roared, the blaze reaching higher and higher toward the obscured summer sun somewhere above, the heat growing with every inch the fire consumed in its relentless march forward. She wondered which was angrier, the wildfire or Owen.

"You could've been killed!" he snapped.

"I was only trying to help..."

"Catching yourself on fire 'cause you're too damn foolish to stay away from a burning bush is a hell of a way to help out!"

"I didn't do it on purpose."

"What you intended doesn't matter a damn bit," Owen snapped, cutting her off. "All that matters is what you did, which was nearly get yourself burned alive, behaving like a stupid city girl who ain't got the sense to stay away from where she shouldn't be!" With every word, he grew more agitated, stabbing an accusing finger at her as if he were a lawyer and she on trial, charged with murder. "It's enough that I'm fighting to save this godforsaken ranch without having to look out for you, too!"

"Then maybe you should have just let me burn," Charlotte answered sarcastically.

Owen paused, only for an instant, before saying, "Maybe I should have."

Unable to control her wavering emotions, Charlotte

turned away quickly, not wanting Owen to see the tears that welled in her eyes. Owen's harsh words hurt as surely as if he had slapped her across the face. Shame colored her cheeks; it wasn't entirely sadness that wounded her, but anger that she'd allowed herself to think him a better person, someone capable of feelings she couldn't even fully describe.

But now that hope had been shattered.

The worst part was knowing that some of what Owen was saying was the truth; she had nearly gotten herself killed and, at the same time, she had taken him away from fighting the blaze. If only she hadn't been so stubborn, if she had listened to what John and Hale had tried to tell her, she wouldn't have found herself in such a predicament. All she had wanted was to help, to do her part to save whatever she could for the people who had been kind enough to take her in and make her feel welcome in Oklahoma. She'd made a mistake, that was all, but now it felt as if she couldn't have made a worse one if she'd tried. It would have been horrible enough to have had to be rescued by any of the other ranch hands, but for it to have been Owen made it much, much worse. That he had to be so callous, unforgiving, made it nearly unbearable.

"Why did it have to be you to come to my rescue?" she muttered under her breath.

Seemingly unaware of Charlotte's vulnerable state, Owen was relentless. "Get on back to the house before you cause more trouble."

Without another word, he turned and headed back to fight the blaze. Charlotte stood on wobbly legs, didn't even bother to brush her smoldering skirt, and did as he said, heading back to the ranch house.

Her eyes watered, but not just from the smoke.

Charlotte sat on the steps of the ranch house porch, watching as the sun lowered toward the western horizon. Because of the lingering smoke hanging in the evening sky, the colors were spectacular; the orange and reds were deep and vibrant, cascading into a purple where the rays struck the higher, darker sky as parts of the night mixed with what remained of the day.

Usually, the first stars would have begun to shine, but they were obscured tonight, leaving only the swollen moon, already at its zenith, to stand watch over her miserable mood.

For the most part, the fire had been put out. Enough of the black smoke had cleared for Charlotte to see the pair of small barns and the corral that had been destroyed by the fire; only charred husks still remained, smoldering but no longer aflame, save for the occasional flare-up that was quickly extinguished.

What little breeze there was carried with it the telltale signs of the wildfire's aftermath: the sharp, biting smell of wood that had been charred into ruin, the insistent shouts of tired men still pouring buckets of well water and dirt onto flames that still fought to stay alive, and even the occasional laugh or two, now that the worst had past.

But for Charlotte, the shame of her failure still stung as freshly as if it had just happened, maybe even worse. When she finally managed to return to the ranch house, she discovered that the women were doing all that they could: bringing food and drink to replenish the firefighters' strength, phoning Sawyer for all the assistance that could be mustered, and, particularly, tending to the wounded as they straggled up from the fire. The women rushed Charlotte to the parlor and pressed a damp, cool cloth to her burn. She briefly protested, claiming that she was capable of helping, but she was told to stay put and regain her strength. Exhausted and downhearted, Charlotte hadn't argued much, but just sat down. Eventually, she had made her way outside.

"Looks like it's almost under control."

Charlotte nodded in agreement as Hannah sat down beside her. She had been one of the first to arrive from Sawyer after receiving a call at the lawyer's office and had worked tirelessly ever since.

"Once, when I was a girl, there was a fire in Colorado that nearly burned the whole town to the ground. It got out of control so fast that there wasn't time to react. We were lucky today. If there'd been a stiff wind..."

Charlotte could only stare into the distance, watching the men work.

Although Charlotte knew that Hannah desperately wanted to ask her what had happened, she never asked directly.

Ever since she had left Owen and begun trudging back to the house, Charlotte had replayed his words over and over again in her mind, each time feeling a sting of shame and anger. How could he possibly speak to her in such a way? Confusion roiled her thoughts. He had spoken to her so differently in the truck, with an understanding and compassion she couldn't begin to explain or understand, but then, after he had put out her burning skirt, he had behaved like an angry husband when all she had been trying to do was help.

"I'm sure you were just trying to help," Hannah said, reading her thoughts.

"I was, but..." she trailed off.

"You didn't let anyone down because of what happened."

"Other than myself."

"That's just ridiculous! Whether we want them to or not, accidents *do* happen," Hannah argued, placing her hand on Charlotte's. "All you wanted was to do your part. You didn't plan to get burned. For heaven's sake. No one will hold that against you."

"Someone does..."

"If that someone is my brother, you just go right ahead and wallop him a good one or"—she smiled mischievously—"I could just do it for you."

"I don't think he deserves something that bad."

"Then you don't know Owen very well."

Charlotte was struck by just how honest Hannah's words were; she truthfully didn't know much about Owen Williams. Everything she had experienced so far was full of contradictions; he was rude and sarcastic one moment, then surprisingly kind and caring the next.

It suddenly occurred to Charlotte that if there was anyone who had a chance of explaining Owen to her, it would be Hannah. After all, they were twins, a fact that would undoubtedly give her special insight.

But just as Charlotte was about to ask a question, to begin trying to fathom whatever it was that was inside Owen, she saw Del Grissom and Dave Powell making their way up the dirt drive to the ranch house.

While both men looked to have suffered injuries from the fire, Dave appeared to be much the worse for wear. Gingerly he cradled one of his hands near his chest as he leaned on Del for support.

"Evenin', ladies," Dave called. "This where a fella gets fixed up?"

Hannah was up from the steps in an instant, hurrying to their side. She took Dave from Del's shoulder, careful not to bump against his arm, and asked, "What on earth happened to you?"

"You'd reckon I'd have learned that you pour the water out of the bucket, 'stead of lettin' it try to jump in 'longside." He chuckled, wincing at his own macabre sense of humor. "Just a dumb ole cowboy who don't know no better than to stick his hand in the fire, is all."

"Then we're all a bunch of dumb fools," Hannah replied. "Isn't that right, Charlotte?"

"I suppose it is," she added, holding up her own burnt arm.

Slowly, Hannah led Dave up the steps, onto the long porch, and into the front parlor where he would soon be swarmed with attention and his burns well taken care of, leaving Charlotte and Del alone in the approaching dusk.

"I'm sorry that you were hurt," Del said to her.

"It's only because I was headstrong enough to think that I could help."

"The fact that you tried shows your character."

Del's kind words soothed the unease in Charlotte's heart, but when she looked at him, eager to thank him, she noticed that he too had been hurt; the skin along his forearm and elbow had been so badly singed that it was practically black and the rolled-up sleeve of his shirt had been burned. Even in the gloom of near-evening she could see the first blisters on his skin.

Charlotte could not suppress a gasp. "You've been burned!"

"I suppose I have," Del answered simply.

"Let me take you inside," she said, rising from the steps. "You need to get that looked at right away."

"'Fraid I just don't have time for that 'bout now," he replied, looking back over his shoulder at the smoke rising from the still-smoldering buildings. "Regardless of how I feel, there's still too much work needs to be done and..." He paused, as if he was searching for the right words. "I owe at least that much to Mr. Grant."

"I'm sure he'd understand if you needed to get medical attention."

"I suppose he would, but I..."

Del fell silent just as the setting sun surrendered, falling over the horizon and beginning its nightly slumber. With what little light escaped the windows of the ranch house, she could see that his jaw was tight, his eyes narrowed.

Uncomfortable with the silence, Charlotte said, "When John and I first saw the fire it sure didn't seem like much to me, but he knew better. When he shouted for us to—" And then she caught her tongue, uncertain what, if anything, she should mention about the Becks. Even though Del was John's right-hand man, something stopped her from saying more. She was afraid that Del would notice her discomfort, but he seemed to be paying her little attention.

"Del?" she asked.

He looked at her, startled, then said, "I'm sorry, my head was elsewhere."

"Do you know what started the fire?" Charlotte asked, wanting to change the subject even if it seemed as if he hadn't known the last one.

Del paused, looking off into the distance for so long that Charlotte thought he had returned to ignoring her, but he said, "Don't know if we'll ever really know. Ain't nobody who'll admit to tossin' a cigarette butt or bein' careless; that's just how these men are. Only thing left for us to do is pick up the pieces as best we can and start back from the beginning. That's what you do when things get out of kilter this way."

While Del wandered back down the walk toward the remnants of the fire, Charlotte thought about what he had said.

Maybe...just maybe, Owen Williams, we can have a new start.

Chapter Eleven

OWEN SCRATCHED the wooden match to life and touched it to the oil lamp's wick. In the sputtering, uneven light, wild, deep shadows danced haphazardly across the barn's walls and ceiling. Even with the barn door thrown open and the moon now full in the sky, the darkness was not easily penetrated. Still, he could move about the barn freely, his eyes slowly adjusting to the remaining gloom.

The horse barn sat to the north of the main ranch house, far away from the smoldering fire, but the smell of burnt wood and brush clung to the air like a blanket. Faint echoes of shouts and shovels, axes and curses found him on the faint wind, like intermittent whispers on a radio. Even with the fire being all but extinguished and all of the men who had come from Sawyer helping, at this late hour there was still much work to be done.

And there doesn't seem to be any end in sight . . .

Past the workbench just inside the broad doors and hay dump on the opposite end, both sides of the barn were lined with stalls fitted with latched gates. Many of the stalls were empty; few of the horses that had been in their corrals had been brought in for the night. Still, some pairs of ears pricked up alertly, turning in his direction as he made his way down the wide aisle.

With every step, Owen felt an exhaustion and ache tug insistently at his ravaged and weary body. He had swung that drenched blanket so many times that he knew come morning he wouldn't be able to lift his arms above his shoulders. His stomach growled angrily. He hadn't had a bite since breakfast and he had no idea when that would change. Hell, when the time finally came, he'd probably be so tired that he'd fall asleep in his plate.

When Owen neared the first occupied stall, he hung his lantern on a rusty nail hammered into a beam, and checked closely to make sure there wasn't a chance of another fire being accidentally started.

A brown and white mare regarded him intently, her brown eyes never wavering from him, even as he leaned against the gate and tipped back his hat. The flickering lamplight had made the horse a bit skittish; one hoof pawed a bit uneasily at the ground, but she never tried to back away, allowing Owen to place his hand on her muzzle.

"Hey there now, Cinnamon, old girl," he soothed.

As his fingers scratched the side of the horse's face,

the mare leaned into his affections and gave a little snort. Owen had always been fond of horses, but Cinnamon was different, the bond between them stronger.

"Bet you've had a better day than I did." He chuckled. "Although both of us were forgotten at mealtime."

Reaching into the feed bag propped up just out of Cinnamon's reach, Owen gave her a handful of oats, which the mare devoured hungrily, her lips and tongue exploring every crevice of his hand.

"Don't worry now. There'll be more where that came from."

After slipping a full feed bag over Cinnamon's ears, Owen diligently set about doing his chores: scooping out manure from the mare's stall, hauling replacement hay back inside, and brushing down the horse's coat, while Cinnamon ate contentedly.

Usually when he brushed a horse, he allowed the bristles to travel the long distance across the neck, down to the shoulder, along the back, and finally to the hindquarters. While he was doing this, Owen was able to let his mind wander. He found it a peaceful, relaxing time in an otherwise hectic life. It was something he could do alone, without anyone else bothering him, and it had become a moment he treasured, just him and Cinnamon. But this night was different. Too much had happened for him to feel any sense of ease.

"Damn it all." He spat onto the stall floor.

Owen hated to admit it to himself, but there was a part

of him that regretted not letting John Grant's ranch burn to the ground; there was another part devastated by guilt for even *having* that thought. But when Owen had heard the first shout, seen the first plume of dark smoke rising to the sky, he had not even hesitated for an instant, rushing alongside the other ranch hands to frantically pump well water, hurriedly dig trenches, and wildly swing wool blankets. He'd done so willingly, even though he had known his actions benefited the man he accused of ruining his mother's life.

With annoyance, Owen brushed the sweat from his brow with the back of his hand. Helping John Grant had been the last thing he had intended when he and Hannah had come to Oklahoma.

The worst part was the way John had accounted for himself during the wildfire, doing every bit of the same backbreaking work he had asked of his men. Even now, he labored into the night, a leader who worked through deeds instead of empty words. He had never once shown fear in the face of losing everything he had worked so hard to build, never shown anger or frustration at a man not doing all he could, and never given Owen reason to confirm that he was the cad he believed him to be. It galled Owen, but it was all true.

But what had happened with Charlie was even worse.

Owen first noticed that she was feverishly battling the fire beside him at the very instant she backed into the burning bush. Terror grabbed at his heart like a vise. Not being aware of his feet moving, he was upon her, driving her to the ground trying to put out the flames. Even when accidentally kneed in the mouth, he hadn't felt anything but concern for her safety.

But then something in him had changed.

Falling on top of her would have been bad enough on its own, but when Owen had found his lips so achingly close to hers, where a kiss seemed as inevitable as breathing, when he had seen the emotion in Charlotte's eyes as plainly as speaking the words, he had become flustered, embarrassed, and had begun to say things he wished he could take back. He also wished he could have erased the hurt that appeared on her face, the tears he knew he must have caused, but try as he might, he had no idea how.

The strange, simple truth was that Charlotte Tucker had gotten under his skin. Twice now he'd looked like a jackass in front of her. Though he had somehow managed to douse her anger once by being honest, to do so now meant admitting feelings he couldn't possibly put into words. *What the heck am I supposed to do: walk up to her and tell her that I can't get her out of my mind? She'd laugh in my face!*

Consequently, he felt both hopeless and helpless, a new state he despised.

"Damn my stubborn hide, Charlie!" he swore.

Beneath his hand, Cinnamon twitched in annoyance, whinnying and throwing her dark mane; he must have been brushing her too hard, lost in his thoughts.

"Sorry, girl."

The sound of one of the doors being opened wider came from the front of the darkened barn. Stepping out of the stall, Owen was surprised to see Hale McCoy striding toward him, a scowl spreading across his face.

"What's the matter, Hale? Anything I can—"

Hale's fist slammed into Owen's jaw, sending him crashing to the floor and the horse brush flying into the darkness behind him, out of the range of the oil lamp. For a moment, everything went black. His head told him to get up and defend himself, but his legs wouldn't listen. All he could do was roll over.

"You had no right to be treatin' her that way!" Hale bellowed, his thunderous voice echoing around the interior of the barn. "What kind of man hollers at a woman like Miss Charlotte? Answer me, damn you!"

Even with his ears ringing and bright stars flaring before his eyes, Owen couldn't help but hear the man; it was replying that was the problem. He felt as if he had been kicked by a mule. Words fluttered into his mind but couldn't manage to make it to his mouth. He hadn't spent much time with Hale, they did different things on the ranch and besides, Owen had gone out of his way to not be friends with anyone, but it would have taken a blind man not to know better than to make an enemy of a man as large as Hale.

Gingerly, Owen rubbed his jaw, an ache sinking in all the way to the bone.

"I said, answer me, you no-good son of a bitch!"

"I would...if I had some idea...of what the hell you're talking about..." Owen finally managed.

"You know," Hale barked. "You know exactly what I'm talkin' about!"

And Owen did; it was the same thing he had been beating himself up over for the last half day; it was because of Charlotte.

"She was only tryin' to help! That don't give you no right to shout at her!"

"How do you...I thought...you were running the pump..."

"I was, but there weren't nobody there to take the last pair of buckets after they'd been filled," Hale explained, his voice a snarl, "so I took 'em myself. I managed to get there just as Charlotte was leavin'. She ran past me with a big mess of tears runnin' down her cheeks! I only hope that in all the smoke she didn't see me so she don't feel no shame other than what you gave her. I can promise you this: if weren't for the fire, I'd a give you a beatin' right then and there!"

Cautiously, Owen looked up. Hale was standing over him, looking as imposing as an enormous tree, his hands balled into angry fists, his face a mask of red even in the flickering light of the oil lamp. It looked as if he wanted nothing more than to be able to beat Owen into a bloody pulp.

In his need to disguise his feelings for Charlotte, he had

yelled at her. Owen found himself rejecting the smarter, safer course of action of telling Hale why he had yelled. That seeing her dress on fire had scared the living hell out of him.

Defiance flared in his gut. It was none of Hale's damn business.

If the man was to give him a beating, he was determined not to roll over and play dead. When it was over, Hale would know he'd been in a fight.

"Why the hell do you care?" Owen grinned through bloody lips. "Let me guess, you're sweet on Charlie, aren't you?"

For a long moment, Hale could only stare at the man at his feet, his eyes narrowed. Then, with the ease of an ox moving a plow, he lifted Owen from the ground by his shirt, his hat falling back to the ground, his feet nearly leaving it.

"You think this is somethin' to laugh at?" Hale asked incredulously.

"Got to admit it's a bit of a stretch."

Without warning, Hale dealt him another savage blow to the midriff, and the air exploded from Owen like a punctured tire. Crashing back to the unforgiving ground, he struggled for breath and couldn't find any; he could only manage to pull in air in deep gulps and empty gasps. He wanted to both vomit and inhale, to bounce up and black out, to scream in agony and laugh out loud. Through it all, he forced a grin to his face.

"Maybe I ain't hittin' you hard enough," Hale said, "if you're still smilin'."

"There's...there's better ways...of showing...Charlotte... how much you...care than...punching me..."

Owen expected to again be lifted off the ground, to once more be severely beaten for his stubbornness, but to his surprise, Hale laughed.

"Lots of folks think I ain't the brightest feller they ever met, but you've gotta be some special kind of fool not to understand what I'm sayin' to you," Hale said. He squatted on his haunches so that he could look Owen in the eye. "I ain't gonna hit you no more, Owen, but you listen up and listen good. I ever see you talkin' to Charlotte the way you did today, what just happened is gonna seem like fallin' out of bed compared to the state I'll put you in. That's a damn promise, understand?"

And Owen did.

Without another word, Hale walked over and took down the oil lamp, using it to light his way to the barn doors and out into the night, leaving Owen to be swallowed by the darkness.

Alone, Owen found himself laughing. Everyone on the ranch knew that Hale was in love with Hannah. To insinuate that he was attracted to Charlotte was ridiculous, a charge Owen knew was not true.

As for his own feelings for her, that was another matter.

*   *   *

Carter Herrick stood on the small landing that jutted out from his second story office, the cigar in his hand slowly sending smoke drifting up into the sky. Before him was the land that had been passed to him by his father, had given him his immense wealth, and had caused his to be a name feared. Besides the opulent house, buildings of all shapes and sizes dotted the gently rolling hillsides, standing watch over pens of cattle. Men worked hard at their tasks, employees all, every one of them mindful enough not to be caught looking in his direction.

None of this matters... not a damn bit now that I cannot pass it on to my son...

Ever since he had decided to destroy John Grant, to make him pay for what he had denied him, what he had stolen and taken away, Carter had still not managed to find relief for the ache that filled him. It burned his gut day and night, a constant gnawing.

But it was not for lack of trying.

There had been hopes for the fire; imagining the Grant Ranch utterly engulfed in flames, becoming a towering funeral pyre for that rotten son of a bitch, was a comforting possibility. Carter had wanted to be able to watch from his landing, whiskey in hand, as everything John Grant had amassed was taken from him, burned to the ground, nothing left but ash. It had seemed the most pleasant of dreams, but had proven as difficult to grasp.

But it could have been, if not for my man's failure...

Months ago, it had come to Herrick's attention that one

of Grant's men had acquired a gambling debt he could not hope to pay. A string of bad luck had created an unshakeable belief that the next hand of cards would surely offer salvation for his troubles, but believing in that lie had only sunken him deeper. One night, when the man had been leaving Sawyer's lone tavern, he'd been jumped by a couple of rowdies and been beaten up a bit, a warning to pay up.

And that was when Carter Herrick had stepped in...

The offer he had made to Grant's man, to cancel all of his debts outright, had proven far too tempting to turn down. Accepting had put the man in Herrick's pocket, a tool to be used however he saw fit. In the beginning, he'd asked the man to do little, a petty theft here, a harmless lie there, just enough to get him used to doing as he had been told. Setting the fire had been his first real test, and the results had been significantly less than Herrick had hoped.

Herrick had believed the man to be capable of executing such a simple task, but his incompetence had proven too much to overcome. He'd lit the fire, but somehow his conscience had gotten the better of him. Another of Herrick's spies on the ranch had reported that the man had even gone so far as to battle feverishly against the blaze *he* had created. The damn fool was only making matters worse for himself.

Another gamble like that would cost the man his life.

Since the fire had failed, another act against Grant would need to be planned, something that would sow seeds of distrust among the bastard's ranch hands. Whatever was settled upon, Herrick was sure his new hireling would argue against it, fearful that it would draw attention to his own involvement, but the man's protests would be ignored. *Why should I give a damn about his reputation? He should have thought of what the consequences might have been before running up such a gambling debt! He will do as I tell him!*

All that mattered was ruining Grant.

Carter Herrick had been a much younger man when his dream had been stolen from him, but the pain lingered through the years, as fresh as if it had only happened yesterday. When Caroline Wallace had left Sawyer, rejected him, a piece of his heart had gone with her. Though he had spent a small fortune desperately trying to find her, it had been to no avail. When he had finally, reluctantly agreed to take a wife, as his overbearing father had demanded, little pleasure had come from it. Not until the arrival of Carter's son had the ice in his chest thawed, but with the boy's death, winter had returned, a blizzard from the midst of which he had no hopes that spring would ever come again.

Behind him in his office, a pistol lay on the ink blotter of his oak desk. Carter didn't need to look at it to know it was there. He had received it years ago as a gift and had come to enjoy keeping it well cleaned and polished enough to see his reflection in its ivory grip. Now he saw it for what it was: an instrument to be used for his deliverance, its iron as hard and cold as his son in the Oklahoma earth. Most nights, whiskey in hand, Carter contemplated using it, thought about ending all of his misery and heartache.

What a relief to be rid of this world...

Where once he had been a broad, robust man who thrived on his conviction and personal strength, he had been transformed against his will; heavy, dark circles hung beneath his green eyes, his once-broad shoulders slumped under a weight he could not possibly carry, and even his clothing was shabbier than he would once have ever considered wearing. He was a shell of the man he had been. He was nearing the end. There was no use in denying that he'd soon join his wife and son in death, though his would be because of his own choice and at his own hand. Carter Herrick vowed but one thing.

Before I go, I'm going to make sure I'm not alone...

Chapter Twelve

CHARLOTTE STOOD IN HER CLASSROOM on the school's second floor and looked out the window as the sun cleared the trees on the eastern horizon. It was a beautiful day, a majestic August morning without a cloud in the sky but with a breeze that she hoped would keep the heat at bay. Throwing open the windows, she breathed deeply of the fresh prairie air and tried in vain to settle her nerves.

To say that Charlotte was anxious would have been a tremendous understatement. She should have been tired, could not have had more than an hour of sleep the night before because she couldn't stop wondering what this day would be like, but she was so full of nervous energy that she swore she could have *run* from the ranch to Sawyer.

Everything that she had done in her life had been in preparation for this moment: all of the time spent at her teaching college in Minnesota, all of the encouragement she had gotten from Rachel and her father, Christina and her grandmother, and also all of her hopes and dreams. Today was why she had come to Oklahoma. Today was the day in which it would all come together, when she would begin her life as a teacher.

So why can't I stop thinking about Owen?

It had been almost a week since the fire and in that time she had only ever seen him from a distance, walking from the corrals to a horse barn or slowly sauntering back to his cabin. Not once had he come to dinner at the main house, and Charlotte suspected that Mrs. Grant was fixing him a plate to take to the cabin. He had also stopped driving Charlotte into town. Hannah took her brother's eccentricities in stride, saying that Owen was just being Owen, but there was no doubt in Charlotte's mind that he was avoiding her. She wasn't, however, about to swallow her pride and seek him out.

The truth was that she was still mad at him. There was no excuse for his treating her as he had during the fire. Whenever Charlotte thought of the words he had spoken in anger, it made her heart race in an unsettling way. Still, she couldn't completely suppress her excitement, particularly when she remembered his lips so close to her own, but all that did was thoroughly confuse her more.

Tenaciously, she clung to what Del had told her on the steps: that when things didn't go your way, you had to pick up the pieces and start at the beginning. She wasn't sure exactly what it was she had with Owen, only that they needed a fresh start.

But how do I do that? Should I just confront him or will that only embarrass us both?

Behind her, Charlotte heard the sound of a throat clearing. She turned quickly, a bright smile on her face as a welcome greeting to her first arriving student, but was surprised to find an older woman standing in her doorway, her arms folded across her chest and her face stern.

"I suppose that you are Miss Tucker," the woman declared.

"I am," Charlotte replied. "And...you are...?"

"My name is Paige Spratt, but you will call me Mrs. Spratt," she answered, apparently offended that Charlotte had presumed to ask.

"I'm the new teacher." She smiled uneasily.

That smile was not returned.

The first thought Charlotte had when looking at Paige Spratt was an unpleasant one: she resembled a buzzard. Thin to the point of looking sickly, even emaciated, she seemed to be all sharp angles and bones, swimming in a black, unfashionable dress. Her brownish hair, pulled back into the tightest bun Charlotte had ever seen, was touched by grey at the temples. A long neck, bulbous nose, protruding lips, and too prominent teeth completed the picture. Other than a slight hunching of her shoulders, she stood ramrod straight, prim and proper in her carriage as well as dress. Even her black shoes were matronly, one of them tapping a cadence out on the floor just outside the door, as if the threshold of Charlotte's classroom were a line Mrs. Spratt wasn't particularly interested in crossing.

"I would have thought that you would have sought me out by now," Mrs. Spratt continued, her face as sour as if she had bit into a lemon. "After all, I've been teaching here for over twenty years and might have been able to give you a bit of advice about what you should expect. I would have thought you eager for knowledge from my years of experience."

"I'm sorry if I've offended you in any way," Charlotte explained, "but when I was hired, I wasn't given much information about whom I should contact once I arrived in town. I was told that someone would contact me."

"Well, we all know what happens when assumptions are made," Mrs. Spratt cut her off dismissively.

Charlotte couldn't stop her temper from boiling at the audacity of the woman's words. The truth was that, ever since Charlotte could remember, she'd had a short fuse, eager to jump into a confrontation and defend herself. At that particular moment, she wanted nothing more than to correct Paige Spratt's misconceptions, to give every bit as good as she got, but decorum or politeness held her back. After all, letting her oversize temper run wild was what had landed her in trouble with Owen, and maybe she should try a different tack.

"Again, I'm sorry if I've offended you," she offered neutrally.

"Oh, I wouldn't worry about offending me, my dear," Mrs. Spratt replied in obvious insincerity. "I've seen many a young girl like yourself come and go through these parts in my time. Little Miss Know-It-Alls thinking that they have all the answers when the truth is they have a brain the size of an egg. Few of them make it more than a school year or two, rushing back to wherever it was they came from or scurrying off to marry the first foolish man who gave them any attention. Truthfully, I usually don't even bother to remember their names."

"It's my intention to be here for a considerable time," Charlotte answered defensively, giving voice to feelings she was not even sure she'd had before she spoke of them.

"I'm sure that right now, standing here talking to me, you honestly believe that to be true, which is wonderful, my dear, just wonderful," Mrs. Spratt said with a sweetness that was as false as it was sickening. "But if you really want it to be true, you have an awful lot of things to learn about . . . your clothes, for instance."

"What about them?" she asked, suddenly self-conscious.

"Just look at you!"

Charlotte did just that, looking down at the outfit she had carefully picked out for such a very special day. Rachel had bought it for her as a graduation gift in St. Paul, at a marvelous little shop whose owner was an older man with a handlebar mustache. One of her most prized possessions, it was delicately wrapped and put in the bottom of her steamer trunk, only worn when needed. The blouse was white, embroidered at the cuff with a delicate blue frill that ran an inch up the wrist. Pleated along the front, it had ivory buttons that shone in the sunlight. A dark blue skirt fell to mid-calf. She couldn't imagine what could be wrong about her clothes.

"I... I don't understand..."

"No proper young woman goes about with the top button of her collar undone unless she's advertising what's to be found beneath the fabric!"

"How dare you say that..." Charlotte began, her hand involuntarily flying up to her open collar, a fashion trend that all of the girls she knew followed.

"And the color doesn't do a thing but distract the children from the important lessons," Mrs. Spratt continued, her list of complaints not in the least bit out of steam. "That sort of meandering pattern is too noticeable, too vulgar. You truthfully should be no more noticeable than the blackboard! Their time here with us should be as fundamentally sound as their days in church. A proper school instruction shouldn't be about having fun, being entertained, laughing and whatnot, but filling their empty little heads with knowledge. Anything else is simply a waste of time."

The sudden realization dawned on Charlotte that had Paige Spratt been her teacher when she was in school, they wouldn't have gotten along at all. *What happened to make her this way?* If Mrs. Spratt wanted to be as plain and boring as the blackboard, she'd certainly succeeded, but that wasn't the path Charlotte had chosen.

"A waste of time?" Charlotte echoed.

"That's exactly right!" Mrs. Spratt answered enthusiastically, mistaking the parroting for agreement. "Besides, you'll have enough other things to worry about around town without being a bad teacher besides."

"Worry about? Like what?"

"Like being a single lady and all of the problems that causes!"

Now it was Charlotte's turn to fold her arms over her chest. She didn't say a word, knowing that Mrs. Spratt couldn't wait to continue.

"Everyone knows that a single woman your age, without morals, is usually completely desperate to find a man," Mrs. Spratt obliged, speaking in a tone much like she were telling a secret. "Tongues around town are already wagging about what kind of standards you must have. Imagine, a strange, single woman who chooses to live out on a horse ranch! My word!"

Charlotte barely repressed the sudden desire to slap Mrs. Spratt; it came at the exact instant she understood why all of the teachers before her had given up their jobs so quickly.

"What you need is to find a stable man, a good Christian man with upstanding credentials in the community." Mrs. Spratt talked on, oblivious to Charlotte's angry expression. "Lord only knows what kind of sordid men can be found out on a horse ranch! Filthy degenerates, more often than not! A compassionate man is what you need to find, and until you've done so, people will whisper and think far less of you." And here her voice dropped to a low, conspiratorial whisper. "They might even get the idea that you're nothing but a whore..."

It was that one word, *whore,* that broke Charlotte's control over her temper and loosened her tongue.

"Now you listen, Mrs. Spratt, and you listen to me closely!" she barked, feeling a faint tremor of thrill for maintaining enough decorum to use the woman's proper name. "If you think that I'm going to stand here and nod my head while you insult me, well then, you've got rocks in yours and should've retired years ago!"

"Why, I've never been so insulted in all my life."

"And another thing," Charlotte snapped, taking her turn at cutting her fellow teacher off. "Your way of teaching might work fine for you, it might allow you to bore your poor students to sleep, but my way of teaching will work just fine without any input from you! If I want your advice, I'll ask for it! Until then, keep away from my classroom and I'll stay away from yours!"

And with that, Charlotte stepped back and, since Mrs. Spratt had never even bothered to step over the threshold of her classroom, shut the door in her face with a satisfying click. For a moment, Charlotte was proud of herself, but then regret began creeping into her chest.

On my first day of school, before my first student had arrived, I've made my first enemy...

*   *   *

The rest of the day had been relatively uneventful. After the initial excitement of her students' arrival, fifteen boys and girls who looked at her curiously and expectantly, a few gossipy whispers shared among them, Charlotte had settled into her first day as a teacher.

Some of it had been strange; hearing herself referred to as "Miss Tucker" was something she doubted she would ever get used to. Writing on the blackboard, occasionally squeaking the chalk, which resulted in a serenade of giggles, was going to need practice. But the nerves that had plagued her when she had first arrived slowly dissipated, and her confidence grew with each passing moment. She was stern when she needed to be, encouraging whenever a child faltered, and capable when asked a question.

Today, I am a teacher...

The one moment that stood out in her day, besides her confrontation with Mrs. Spratt, was when she caught Emily Hagemann absently staring out the window instead of concentrating on the lesson being taught. When Charlotte had to ask her to pay attention, Emily had exclaimed, "Oh, fiddle! It's such a wonderful day, too!" and the whole class had burst into sniggers, and Charlotte had had to suppress her own laughter.

That would have been me, many years ago...

When the last student had left and the room had been tidied up for the night, Charlotte shut off the lights and left the school, heading for downtown Sawyer; Hannah would be waiting for her so that they could drive back to the ranch. Suddenly, just before she could even begin to wonder if Owen would be behind the wheel of the truck, a voice called out to her.

"Well, I reckon you must be the new teacher in town."

Charlotte stopped at the sound and looked around, but couldn't see who had spoken. She was in front of the funeral home beside the school, but there was nobody in sight. Then she noticed a woman standing beside the evergreens that framed the walk in front of the funeral home.

The woman was tiny, short enough to be dwarfed by the evergreens to either side of her. Dressed all in black from pillbox hat to sturdy oxfords, she pulled close the shawl draped across her shoulders, even in the waning heat of the summer day. Using a cane, she tottered toward Charlotte.

"You are the new teacher, aren't you?" the woman asked again.

"I am ... my name is Charlotte Tucker..."

"My, what a pretty name, a name that fits a young woman in the prime of her life," she remarked. "So much better than 'Constance Lowell,' don't you think so? I swear, my father gave me the name of an old lady at birth, some woman with one foot already in the grave."

"Well ... I ... I don't think ..." Charlotte sputtered as the realization dawned on her as to whom she was speaking. This was the woman Hannah had been warning her about when they had first visited the school.

What was it that Hannah had said...that Constance was a bit of a loon?

"Have you ever wondered what type of music you would like to have played at your funeral?" Constance asked bluntly.

"I...I really can't say that I ever have."

"It's truly such a difficult choice, one that most people don't ever stop to consider!" the woman explained as if it were the most important thing in life. "You could choose a hymn, a stirring piece of music that practically launches people out of the pews; you could have a choir, a simple piano, or even a ragtime band! The choices never seem to end and regardless of how much thought I've given the matter, I can never manage to make up my mind. And don't get me started on the flowers..."

Which seemed like good-enough advice for Charlotte to hold her tongue, but Constance wasn't willing to wait.

"There're roses and irises and big bouquets of this and that and—"

"It does sound complicated," Charlotte interrupted, glancing at her watch.

"Oh, it is, my dear! It really is!"

Charlotte was about to excuse herself, to say that it was nice to have made Constance's acquaintance, but she had left the conversation for a moment too long, an insufferable silence that Miss Lowell couldn't avoid filling.

"Have you ever wondered why people don't send invitations to their own funerals?" she asked. "After all, invitations are sent for weddings and for anniversaries, two moments in life that are quite personal, so why shouldn't you be able to invite who you want to your own funeral. I can't stand the idea of Anne Rider gawking over my casket, but I just bet you she'd come!"

"I really need to get going, Miss Lowell," Charlotte explained. "Hannah will be waiting for me."

"There are so many preparations when giving a loved one a decent send-off!"

"—meet someone and get—"

"I have to hurry so that it's all in place before the fateful day arrives!"

"I need to catch my ride back to the ranch."

"You never know when your time will be up, nosiree!"

"We'll talk again soon, okay?"

Even as Charlotte walked away, Constance kept right on talking.

Chapter Thirteen

SARAH BECK TOSSED down her pencil in frustrated anger, bouncing it off the old scarred table and down onto the floor with a clatter. It rolled until it was underneath the stove, and she sent the wadded-up paper she had been using to work out a math problem following it to the floor. Tears filled her eyes and her lip quivered, a sob barely held in.

"I ain't never gonna understand any of this! I ain't never!"

Charlotte sighed, forcing herself to take a deep breath for both their sakes. They'd been working together for days, doing the same kinds of problems over repeatedly in the futile hope that Sarah would begin to understand.

"Perhaps it's my fault," Charlotte offered in encouragement. "I may not have explained it clearly enough."

"It ain't yore fault!" Sarah said stubbornly. "I ain't never gonna learn it!"

"Getting angry isn't going to do either of us any good."

"I'm too stupid!"

"You're not stupid, Sarah," Charlotte corrected her. "Don't say that."

"I am so! I'm just a dumb old prairie gal. I'll never amount to anythin'."

Unfortunately, this was the pattern that had presented itself in the days since Charlotte had agreed to John Grant's request to teach Sarah. Every night after school, in the hours before dinner, John drove Charlotte down the long and bumpy road, to the shack. Regardless of the subject, arithmetic, or reading, or even basic spelling, Charlotte was shocked at how little schooling the pregnant girl had had. Most nights, she went home deeply frustrated, unsure of what avenue remained to her, unable to determine what she should try next. But every day she came back; true to her word, she would not quit trying.

What frustrated Charlotte the most wasn't necessarily that Sarah was a poor pupil, but rather that she lacked the incentive to get better. Every night seemed to end in protests that she wasn't smart enough to learn anything. No matter how Charlotte insisted that wasn't true, no matter what encouragement she offered, Sarah was convinced she couldn't learn.

Still, Charlotte didn't feel that she could push Sarah too hard. Because of her pregnancy, she tired quickly. Besides, Charlotte knew that she was still doing all of the chores around the ramshackle cabin: washing dirty clothes, doing the cooking, and tidying up. Most nights, Alan was nowhere to be seen; other evenings, he lounged around with a wad of tobacco wedged in his cheek. His apathy concerning Sarah's condition made Charlotte furious.

"Did you try to read the book I left for you?" she asked, hoping to move to a more acceptable subject.

"I tried, but I didn't get too far...some of them words were harder than I thought they'd be..."

"Well then, let's go over what you didn't understand."

The book had been one of Charlotte's favorites when she had been a little girl back home in Minnesota: L. Frank Baum's *Wizard of Oz*. Rich with bright illustrations that she hoped would tell the story without the need to understand every word of text, the copy she had borrowed from the Sawyer library had definitely seen better days. Worn to near-baldness on the spine, dented on each and every corner, and even missing its title page, the book still pleased Sarah. When Charlotte had presented it to her, the girl's eyes had widened in wonder.

For the next twenty minutes, Charlotte followed along as Sarah read, offering encouragement and assistance in equal doses. Occasionally there would be a word, like *contrary* or *supposedly*, that Charlotte expected Sarah to struggle with or stumble over, but the girl surprised her by pronouncing perfectly. Other times, she would crash up against *clatter* or *vision* and be incapable of making her way past them without help.

"You're doing better tonight." Charlotte smiled. "You really are."

"It does seem a bit easier," Sarah said, uncomfortable with giving herself any credit.

They had just read past the part where the Scarecrow joins with Dorothy and Toto on their long journey to the Emerald City when Sarah gave out a surprised yelp, dropped the book, and scooted back her chair.

"What is it?" Charlotte asked in confusion. "What's the matter?"

For an instant, she thought that Sarah must be in pain, so drastic her reaction, so wide her eyes, her hands flying to her large belly. But then a smile of wonderment blossomed across the girl's face, spreading from ear to ear, and brightening the whole room.

"It…it was the baby…" She beamed. "I felt him movin'!"

"Oh, Sarah!" Charlotte exclaimed. "That's amazing!"

"Give me yer hand!"

Before Charlotte could either agree or decline, Sarah reached out and snatched her by the wrist, lifted her shirt, and brought her teacher's unsteady hand to the bare skin of her stomach.

"I don't know if I should…" Charlotte tried to argue.

"Wait for it," Sarah hushed her.

Seconds passed with neither of them moving; Charlotte had to remind herself to breathe. The skin on the girl's belly was taut, as smooth as marble, and warm to the touch. Suddenly, there was an insistent push just beneath the skin, punching or kicking that jabbed against Charlotte's palm near the thumb, an unmistakable sign of life not yet born, but living all the same.

"Did you feel that?" Charlotte asked, followed by the recognition of how silly such a question was.

Of course she did...

Sarah nodded enthusiastically in honest answer.

"Is it often like this?"

"This ain't the first time I've felt him," Sarah explained earnestly. "But usually it happens just when I wake from sleepin', but it don't often amount to a whole lot more than a tap here or there, nothin' like the wallop he just gave me!"

"He?" Charlotte asked. "Are you sure it's a boy?"

"There ain't no way that it's a girl givin' me that much grief, don't you think?"

"I wouldn't be so sure. When I was a little girl I was a hellion and a half. I can only imagine how much of a tussle I had inside my mother."

With those words, Charlotte couldn't help but imagine what this moment must have been like for Alice Tucker; she had said good-bye to her handsome new husband, sending him off to war, without even knowing that she was carrying his child. By the time she knew, by the time Charlotte would have been kicking her the way Sarah was being kicked, Alice would have thought Mason to be dead, leaving her a widow. So what had her reaction been the first moment that her child had made her presence known?

Had Alice been as happy as Sarah was, humbled at the miracle of life? Or had she been repulsed, just one more reminder of her lost husband and that she would have to raise a child alone? The fact that she had died while giving birth gave credence to the later. It nearly broke Charlotte's heart at the thought of imagining her mother crying not tears of joy, but of heartbreak. But just as she felt her own tears begin to well, it was Sarah who pulled her away from such morbid thoughts.

"I wish his, I mean, the baby's father…was here to feel this," she said, whispering so softly that her voice could barely be heard.

Sarah's words were like a blow to Charlotte's chest. From the moment she had met the Becks, the question of who was the father of Sarah's child had reverberated around her thoughts, but she had not ventured to ask. Now the matter sat like a firecracker, its fuse lit, filling the room with expectation, an explosion that seemed destined to occur.

But some firecrackers' fuses fizzle…

Not this one…

Charlotte knew that she could no longer hold her curiosity at bay, particularly after what Sarah had said. Though Charlotte knew that it really wasn't any of her business, she pushed forward, prying a bit in search of the truth.

"Where is he, Sarah?" she asked. "Where is your child's father?"

Sarah eyed her closely, clearly weighing whether she was willing to divulge anything further; Charlotte didn't know what she would do if Sarah chose to remain quiet, but thankfully she didn't have to.

"Can you keep a little secret?" Sarah asked.

"Of course I can."

"His name was Andrew...Andrew Watkins..." she said as tears drifted steadily down her flushed cheeks, "and he was the...only man I ever loved...and he ain't alive no more..."

Watching the painful emotions wash over Sarah nearly broke Charlotte's heart in two. When she was younger, she'd loved to read about a love unrequited or lovers who weren't allowed to be together, but to witness such sadness firsthand was heartbreaking. It was hard enough for her to even *understand* love, since she couldn't honestly say she had ever found it, but that didn't mean she failed to appreciate its value. Charlotte wondered if she would ever meet a man whose absence would make her cry...and she suddenly found herself thinking about Owen; bringing her to tears was something he seemed good at.

"Do you want to talk about him?" Charlotte asked.

"You wanna listen?"

When Charlotte nodded, Sarah brightened for an instant. "The first time I ever seen him was outside the mercantile back in Colton; that's our home in Arkansas," she explained. "'Bout made my heart bounce just lookin' at his blue eyes, feelin's I ain't never had 'fore. When he come up to talk to me, I didn't have no idea what to say, so I just nodded my head a bit till he started laughin', and whatever was in that laugh broke the hold on my tongue. 'Fore long, we was meetin' up whenever we could."

"And you fell in love with Andrew?"

"It was the strangest sensation, fallin' in love. 'Bout the only thing I compare it to would be jumpin' off a big cliff. Once you're past the edge, there ain't no particular reason to be graspin' for a line a safety. You just keep on fallin' anyhow, so you might as well enjoy it the whole way down."

Charlotte couldn't help but laugh; it was a better way of explaining love than any she'd read in a book.

But then Sarah's face darkened, and Charlotte knew that she had come to what had taken Andrew away from her.

"My pa said Andrew come from better than us," she said softly. "See, Watkins was a name back home, 'portant people, folks with money, so that must of meant Andrew was just amusin' himself with us poor people and 'bout the time he got what he wanted outta me he'd be up and gone faster than a runaway train. But Andrew weren't like that; he really weren't! What with the sort of words he talked to me, the way he looked at me or held me in his arms, there weren't no doubt that he woulda stood by me if he coulda, if he'd gotten the chance, no doubt at all!"

To hear the heartache in Sarah's voice was nearly enough to make Charlotte wish she hadn't asked about the baby's father, but now it was too late for any regrets. Patiently, she waited, unable to ask further.

"He died not ever knowin' he was gonna have a son."

A hesitation, then a correction: "A baby. He was struck by some drunk drivin' a milk truck, right in the middle of the afternoon." By now, the tears were falling as steadily as the rain beginning to tap against the cabin's windows, as if it too shared in Sarah's sorrows. "I found out the next day I was pregnant, just 'bout the same time I learned he was gone. Love is just like fallin' off that cliff," Sarah said, "'cept sometimes you hit the ground."

Charlotte stood under the leaky edge of the Becks' roof, trying in vain to stay dry in the face of the growing rainstorm. It had come on suddenly, a squall with mean intentions, peals of thunder still distant but coming. Wind swirled her skirt against her feet, the dry earth slowly turning to mud. Though it should still have been light, dark clouds had rolled in, blotting out what had remained of the day and hastening night's arrival.

After talking about the death of her unborn child's father, Sarah had become exhausted and Charlotte had put her to bed. There'd been no protest and she'd drifted off to sleep the instant her head had touched her pillow. Not wanting to do anything that might disturb the girl's much-needed sleep, Charlotte had stepped outside, content to wait in the rain for John to come and pick her up.

Perfect weather to match my mood...

Sarah's story still affected her deeply, a keening in her heart. She'd imagined something different, something simpler, easier to understand, not such a heartbreaking story of loss. But there was something else, not a jealousy, but similar, for Sarah had at least known love, even if she had lost it, while for Charlotte, she had never loved at all, a void that now seemed much greater. Involuntarily, she laughed at her stupidity.

"I don't think what you're doin' is the least bit funny."

Charlotte was so surprised by the voice that spoke beside her that she practically jumped out into the rain.

Alan Beck leaned out of the deep shadows that draped over the house, unsteady on his feet, the unmistakable smell of alcohol on his breath. He was unshaven and unkempt, and the snarl on his lips parted long enough for him to spit a disgusting stream of tobacco out into the storm. His mouth hung slack, his breath ragged, a huge wad of chaw visible through his brown teeth.

"Excuse me?" she answered. "What do you mean? Funny?"

"Teachin' that girl book learnin' ain't gonna do her no good," he groused, punctuating his words with a jab of one gnarled finger. "Fillin' a woman's head up with such shit ain't in the least bit funny, if'n you ask me."

"I'm sorry you feel that way, Mr. Beck, but I have to disagree with you," Charlotte fired back, her dander rising.

"You just mark my words!" he barked, taking an aggressive step toward her. "Ain't nothin' good is ever gonna come outta a gal disobeyin' her papa! I told her that snobby prick she got tangled up with wouldn't do nothin' but screw her and leave her and that's exactly what he did! I reckon she done told you all 'bout it! Leavin' her without a husband or father for that kid, how in the hell's she ever gonna amount to anythin'?"

"Yes, she will! By getting an education, that's how! You should be supporting her however she needs it instead of tearing her down and drinking!"

Charlotte's words struck Alan as clearly as if he had been struck by lightning. "I'll show you for back talkin' me like that, girlie!" With a lurch, he reached awkwardly for her, one arm raised to slap her.

Balling her fists, Charlotte waited for the violence to arrive, intent upon defending herself as best she could. But as suddenly as it had begun, it came to such a quick halt that it frightened her, as Alan dissolved into a fit of coughing and hacking up phlegm that incapacitated him.

At the same moment, the headlights of the truck suddenly swung up over the low hill before them, cutting the gloomy rain like a knife. Without hesitation, Charlotte ran toward it, pulling at the door before John could even bring the truck to a halt. As she climbed in and sat down, she pondered the question: what was the reason John Grant took such an interest in the Becks? He had been so secretive that, for a moment, she had the crazy notion that he might be the father of Sarah's child, but no sooner than she had had the thought before she dismissed it. A blue-eyed boy had taught Sarah to love and now he was gone, never to know the child who had been born of it.

Chapter Fourteen

OWEN ROSE WHILE the first of the morning sun still ducked under the distant horizon. The ranch house, set up a bit higher than the other buildings on the property, was beginning to outline itself against the sky. Very little was stirring at such an early hour; a few horses whinnied and neighed inside their corrals, and he could hear the first birds of the day chirping in a tree somewhere close. A light in the kitchen window told him that someone else on the ranch had awakened before him but was nowhere to be seen.

He was alone, just the way he liked it.

Inside the cabin, his sister still slept soundly on the cot beside his own. Quietly, he'd slipped a worn shirt over his work pants and boots before going out. He ran a hand over his stubby chin that was in desperate need of a shave. Sleep still cottoning his head, he stretched a sore kink out of his back, snatched up a wooden bucket from beside the front door, and headed off into the morning for his water.

Nearby, the work of rebuilding from the fire had already begun. The wrecked barns and charred fences had been demolished and cleared away; the only obvious signs of the fire that still remained were blackened earth and dead shrubbery. In the end, the damage had been minimal, even if the fear of worse had not been. Hale had been placed in charge of the reconstruction and, with loads of enthusiasm and a penchant for backbreaking labor, had been intent on finishing the work quickly.

All the better to keep him out of my hair, Owen thought.

In the days since his confrontation with Hale in the horse barn, Owen steadfastly stayed out of the man's way, save for an occasional run-in around the supper table up at the ranch house; he avoided the cramped dining room at breakfast and dinner for another reason. Avoiding Hale wasn't something he did out of fear, but rather caution. Ever since Owen had arrived at the Grant Ranch, he had done his best not to draw any attention to himself. In order to learn if John Grant really was the man responsible for ruining his mother's life, if he was his and Hannah's absent father, the last thing Owen needed was an extra pair of eyes on him. *Work hard... keep your head down and your eyes open.* If there were bad blood between him and Hale, it would be a setback; Owen regretted mouthing off in the horse barn; it made things much worse than they needed to be.

Even though he had done his utmost to avoid Charlotte, by steadfastly skipping any meal she might attend, skirting the main ranch house, and even excusing himself from driving her and Hannah into town, sometimes he wondered if he wasn't making his situation worse. By not seeing Charlotte or talking with her, he found himself *thinking* of her all the time: while he did his chores, while Hannah rambled on about her day at the law office, and especially when he lay in his cot at night, trying unsuccessfully to sleep. Even when he should have been out gathering evidence pointing to John Grant's guilt, he was wondering if Charlotte hated him for all he had said and done. While his head was pulling him one way, his heart pulled another. Reluctant as he was to admit it, he was falling in love.

Rounding the back of a cabin, Owen neared the well that served the bunkhouse, where the workingmen employed by the Grant Ranch lived. Constructed of mortared stones and odd pieces of brick, with a simple winch and bucket, the well provided water for cooking, drinking, or whatever other personal use might be needed, including, in his case, letting a groggy man have a much-needed shave.

Owen loosed the rope line from the winch and tossed the bucket down into the darkness of the hole, hearing it land with a gentle splash. When he pulled it back up, straining easily at the winch, he whistled a tuneless tune, echoing the chorus of morning birds.

Before the bucket reached him, he knew that something wasn't right; a nauseating stench rushed up to meet him, a smell, a *particular* smell that he couldn't quite place, assaulted his senses. Despite his strong desire to let the bucket drop, he managed to draw it up.

Once the bucket was in view and he had pulled it over to the well's ledge, the pungent odor grew stronger. Owen expected to find something in the water, a dead animal or horse manure, but the bucket's surface just rippled as usual. Pouring out the water on the ground yielded no further answers and, after he had smelled the bucket, he began to wonder if it was the pail itself; someone could have untied it, used it for something else, and put it back not realizing what damage had been done.

After untying the bucket from the rope, Owen attached his own wooden pail and repeated the process. His bucket came back full of water as foul smelling as before.

"What in the hell is going on around here?" he muttered.

"It's kerosene," John Grant announced.

He stood beside the tainted well in the bright early morning sunlight, his face filled with concern. His jaw was set tight and his flat, contemplative eyes traveled back and forth from the well to Owen's bucket where it sat on the ledge. John touched its edge and rubbed his fingers together. When his tongue touched his thumb, he spat on the ground. "Kerosene, all right."

All around him were the men who had been summoned after Owen's discovery. Hale stood closest to John, his thick, muscular arms folded across his broad chest, while Del and Clyde Drake, another ranch hand whom Owen didn't know particularly well, were opposite, closer to himself. Every face was pensive, worried.

Owen hadn't known whom he should talk with first, but had settled on speaking with Del, who had always treated him right and seemed particularly levelheaded. Surprisingly, the Grant Ranch's best man hadn't immediately sought to inform John of the matter, joking that he hadn't wanted to interrupt his boss's breakfast, but Hale, who had overheard their initial conversation, thought otherwise, and told them in no uncertain terms that if they wouldn't disrupt Mr. Grant's meal, he most certainly would. On this particular matter, Owen couldn't help but see things Hale's way. Clyde had just been finishing his eggs and bacon and was swept up on their way to the well.

"You sure about that, boss?" Del asked.

"I am," John answered gravely. "Ain't no doubt 'bout it."

"How'd kerosene get in our well?" Hale asked the obvious.

"Ain't rightly certain how it got there, but I aim to find out," John replied.

"Maybe when they was diggin' this here well, they struck

oil and didn't even know it." Clyde laughed, his speech drawling. He was a short and thickening man, his potbelly threatening to spill over his belt line, his blond hair going dirty and grey at his temples. When he smiled at his own inappropriate joke, his stained, crooked teeth retained a smile that kept on even when no one else laughed.

"This ain't likely to be an accident, I reckon," John observed.

"Why not?" Del asked.

"It must be intentional tamperin'. There ain't no other explanation."

"Maybe it's that a lantern fell down the well," Hale offered. "Maybe someone came out here in the night, thirsty or whatnot, maybe they'd been doin' a bit of drinkin' and weren't right on their feet or were overly tired and just stumblin' round. Either way, they put it on the ledge and bumped into it, causin' it to fall, plain and simple. The lantern sinks and the oil floats round on top. Seems like it could've happened, just that way."

"Could be," Clyde echoed. "Could be that right there."

"We could ask around, see if anyone will admit to it," Del offered. "This ain't like droppin' a match that set the ranch on fire. Somethin' like this here ain't so hard to fess up to."

"Even if no one comes clean," Clyde said, "and I ain't sayin' they wouldn't, don't mean that that ain't the answer."

John remained silent for a while, his mind struggling

with all of the possibilities that might explain what had happened, although it looked to Owen as if he wasn't giving Hale's suggestion much of a chance.

"Owen," John finally began, turning to face him, "there wasn't anyone else around when you come out here this mornin'?"

"I didn't see anyone."

"Did you look around?"

"No. Not until I pulled up the bucket."

"Were you the first person to use the well today?"

"Probably."

"Your place is just over yonder?" John nodded over Owen's shoulder.

He followed the older man's gaze. The sight of the cabin, indistinguishable from most of the others on the ranch's grounds, set off a fluttering in his chest, completely unexpected, as if there was something about his living inside of it that was about to change. Owen's nerves went drum tight. He could see in what direction John Grant was headed. Cautiously, Owen nodded.

"Livin' right there and you didn't hear nothin' last night," John kept on, "no sounds of commotion or somebody rootin' round, up to no good?"

"No, I didn't."

"Nothin' at all?"

"If someone was out here, they must have been taking pains to keep quiet."

"Anyone else hear anythin' last night?" John asked, his eyes examining each of their faces.

In turn, every man replied that he hadn't.

An unsettling silence settled around the well as each man's thoughts remained his own. Owen felt no closer to understanding what had actually happened than when he had discovered the stricken well. Whatever the final explanation, he knew that John Grant was slowly and surely arriving at his own conclusion, one that, deservedly or not, made Owen quite unsettled.

I don't like where this is headed...not one bit...

"I ain't followin' all this here thinkin'," Del said, breaking the quiet. "If you don't think this is an accident, how did kerosene get down the well?"

"I think it was put there."

"What?" Hale exclaimed, his hands flying from his chest and his mouth hanging open. "You mean someone tried to ruin it on purpose?"

"I do," John replied simply.

"But what about the idea of it bein' a lantern?" Hale kept on.

"One of the lanterns don't hold enough oil to explain the amount that's down the well. Oil settles on top of water, so if it was what fits into a lantern, it would take only a couple of pails full and you'd have most of it out. What's comin' up here is a lot more than that. One sniff of a bucket would tell you that clear enough."

"Why in the hell would someone do that?"

"The bigger question would be who would do such a thing," Clyde offered.

John's tone darkened. "Right now, I don't know, but rest assured we're gonna find out, come hell or high water."

"You reckon it's someone here?" Hale asked. "Someone on the ranch?"

"Can't be," Del answered.

"Don't see how it could be any other way," John contradicted. "Be a hell of a walk for a fella to come up from the edge of the ranch property, 'specially when takin' into account the oil he'd be haulin'. Drivin' close enough, comin' 'cross the road over the creek, would be a sure way to get noticed."

"Then it's someone here," Owen said. And *he* would be one of the first to be suspected. On the surface, it made a lot of sense. He and Hannah were two of the latest arrivals to the ranch, and while his sister was outgoing and well liked, he had gone well out of his way to be aloof and even unfriendly with the other men; and he was, as John had already established, living close enough to the well to have been able to pull off the crime without being noticed. Somehow, the fact that he had been the one to *report* the tainting of the well would be conveniently overlooked, people assuming that he had alerted them to throw them off his trail.

When he looked at the faces of the men gathered around

the well, he saw that they were thinking similar things. Even Del, whom Owen had trusted enough to inform of what had happened, even he was stealing glances in his direction, suspicion in his eyes.

Everything Owen had done since he had arrived in Oklahoma, all of the time devoted to discovering if John Grant was his real father, hung in the balance. If the suspicion of his involvement grew too great, he could be asked to leave the ranch, regardless of what excuse he offered. After the death of his mother back in Colorado, he had sworn over her freshly dug grave that he wouldn't rest until he made the man responsible for her suffering pay. If he were to falter now, if he were to fail to fulfill his vow...

He couldn't allow that to happen; *he just could not...*

When the gathering around the well broke up, Owen couldn't help but notice the way Hale kept looking back at him as he walked away.

"I couldn't give a damn whether he likes the plan or not!" Carter Herrick thundered, his fist clenching so tightly that the lit cigar clutched between his fingers snapped in two. "Who does he think he is to question what I have ordered? Ruining that well was what I asked him to do and by God, he'll do it, any consequences to his own person be damned!"

Clyde Drake shifted uncomfortably from one foot to the other and then back again. He'd been on his feet all day and was utterly exhausted, but no matter how much he wanted to sit down in the chair opposite Herrick's oak desk, he understood that he couldn't do so without first being invited; it hadn't taken him long to learn that a man in Herrick's employ never dared do anything without his boss's approval.

"I don't think he likes havin' me lookin' over his shoulder," Clyde ventured. "He feels like you don't trust him."

"And why in the hell should I?" Herrick shouted, tossing his broken cigar at his employee, the lit piece bouncing off Clyde's chest and sending a shower of smoldering tobacco cascading to the floor. "Maybe if he hadn't been so damned concerned about stopping the blaze that he had set, he wouldn't find himself in such a delicate position!"

"You're right, Mr. Herrick." Clyde nodded. "I don't understand what he was thinkin' 'bout..."

"If only he'd let the blaze grow, Grant would be destroyed and his debt would be repaid," Herrick said as he got up to pour himself another whiskey; to Clyde's displeasure, no offer was made for a glass of his own.

"His heart just ain't all the way in it, boss."

"Thank you, Drake." Herrick sneered sarcastically. "I'm so happy that I have a smart man such as you to tell me these things."

"It ain't all bad," Clyde explained. "He done what he should've when Grant was talkin' round the well. He kept his head and didn't say nothin' suspicious. Ain't no one gonna be lookin' at him. Ain't no way that he'll be suspected of dumpin' the kerosene."

"Who does Grant suspect?"

"Can't say for certain just yet, but it looks as if the attention's turned to the fella that done first reported it. Man by the name of Williams."

Herrick nodded. "All the worse for him."

"Course…" Clyde began tentatively, struggling to choose his words carefully, "that don't mean our man still don't think you done made a mistake by actin' the way you did."

"And I told you I didn't give a damn what he thought!" Herrick roared.

"Now, boss…it's…it's just that…well, he might have a bit…of a point is all I'm sayin'," Clyde continued, beads of sweat dotting his brow. "If it had only been the fire, then it could be seen as nothin' more than an accident, a cigarette butt or somethin', but now we gone and ruined that there well, it makes things pretty clear that someone is out to do the ranch harm. From this point on, Grant's gonna be watchin' close."

"Let him, for all the good it will do."

"It's just that—" Clyde began, but Herrick's scowl silenced him.

What Clyde left unsaid was that the other man's concerns were also his own. In fact, his own position was even more precarious; he hadn't been at the ranch long and his boisterous nature always drew attention. Even if he were to be scrutinized by accident, he would have to be a fool to think that Grant wouldn't take a long look at him as a possible suspect, so it was still possible that his connection to Carter Herrick could be found out. But there was no way for Clyde to give voice to his concerns; the man who gave him orders was not the kind who would stomach weakness.

"What happens if we get found out?" Clyde asked.

"Then that would mean you weren't doing your jobs as you should," Herrick spat angrily. "What your task requires is both a low profile and an attention to detail. You are to follow my instructions to the letter, nothing more. When you deviate from the plan, *that* is when you will fail. You're both being paid a substantial amount of money, so the last thing I want to hear about are excuses and failures! Success is the only outcome that will be tolerated, so if Grant learns about what I am planning, if he finds out about my involvement, it will be your lives! Am I making myself clear?"

"Ye-yes, sir, you are," Clyde stammered.

"You tell your fellow saboteur every word that I'm telling you tonight. If he has a problem with what he's being asked to do, remind him of how solid his standing at that godforsaken ranch would be if word got out about his gambling problem. That should serve to silence his tongue."

"What are you gonna want us to do next?" Clyde asked.

For a long moment, Carter Herrick was silent as he

stared out the window into the night sky. When he finally turned, a malicious smile curled the corners of his mouth in a way that unnerved his lackey.

"Now is the time for us to be bold," Herrick answered. "Now is the time for drastic measures..."

Chapter Fifteen

WITH THE DINNER PLATES cleared from the table and the men headed back to the remaining chores of the day, Charlotte joined Amelia Grant and the other women in the kitchen to wash dishes. Positioned at the end of the working line, she dried each plate, glass, and piece of silverware that came her way, joining in the easy talk and ready laughter. It felt comfortable, different, yet still similar to the life she had left behind in Minnesota, a part of her new life, a future she felt glad to be pursuing.

Charlotte had no more than put the last plate in the cupboard when she heard a light rapping on the door frame beside her. When she looked, she was surprised to see Hale, although the look on his face didn't appear as warm as usual.

"Can I talk to you?" he asked softly.

"Sure," she answered. "Just give me a minute to finish up."

Outside, the night air was cooler than usual, but still pleasant. Charlotte rubbed her arms for a bit of warmth, marveling at the thousands of stars in the clear sky as night swallows dived and dipped, illuminated for an instant passing against the bright moon.

Hale stood out on the walk that led from the drive to the main house, uneasily shifting his considerable weight from one foot to the other, looking around him as if he was either expecting someone else to join them or worried that someone would; as far as Charlotte could tell, no one else was about.

"I hope I wasn't interruptin' anything important," Hale said.

"Not at all." Charlotte smiled, the look of seriousness on his face causing a ripple of worry in her chest, so she could not help adding, "Is something the matter?"

It had been a while since Hale had said anything about his romantic attraction to Hannah, but Charlotte had noticed that he hadn't been quite as shy as he normally was around her; over lunch the day before, he had even managed to make eye contact with Hannah without blushing a crimson red. Charlotte had begun wondering if he would even need any more of her advice, but she suddenly worried that Hale had somehow managed to voice his feelings, only to receive the sharp sting of rejection in reply.

"How well do you know Owen?" he asked.

Hale's words momentarily stunned Charlotte. "What . . . what do you mean?" she stammered. "I . . . don't understand . . ."

"I'm askin' only 'cause I know you've spent some time with him," he explained, his brow intently knit, "what with your drivin' back and forth from town and talkin' with him round the ranch. I need to know what kind of fella he is . . . whether he's a good sort or . . ." He left the last unsaid.

"Why are you asking me this, Hale?"

"Look now, just tell me if you know what he's . . . up to."

"And I'm not telling you a thing until you tell me why you're asking," she shot back, cutting him off.

For a long moment of silence, they simply stared at each other, two stubborn people who were each reluctant to give an inch, willing to fight hard for information. Though his physical size was imposing, it was Hale who finally relented.

"All right then." He sighed. "You got a right to know."

Reluctantly, Hale described to Charlotte what had happened that morning at the communal well, about how someone had fouled it with kerosene and that John Grant had concluded that the perpetrator must be staying on the ranch. Though Hale did not speak of his suspicions, it was clear who he held responsible.

"And . . . and you think it was Owen . . . ?" she asked incredulously. ". . . You suspect that he did it . . . that he put the kerosene in the well . . . ?"

Hale slowly nodded.

"No, Hale, he couldn't have done it!" Charlotte argued, grabbing him by the arm. "I just know that you're mistaken; you have to be! There has to be an explanation. You're talking about Hannah's brother!"

"Just 'cause they're blood don't mean he's as good a person as she is. I got a brother who's a hell of a piece of work, always drinkin' and gamblin' and even whorin'," he explained, suddenly realizing the words he had chosen, hastily adding, "if you'll pardon my language."

But Charlotte's mind was already elsewhere, paying Hale's cursing scant attention as her thoughts raced over the implications of his accusations.

While there was little doubt that Owen Williams had a rough exterior, needling and antagonizing her with his sharp tongue and wit, he had also revealed something more to her...something that confused her feelings for him. She thought of him so often that it kept her up at night.

In the days since Owen had shouted at her during the wildfire, Charlotte had begun to view his actions differently; it struck her that maybe the reason he'd shouted at her, had insisted that she go to the main house, was really because he was scared of what could happen to her if she stayed. After all, he had helped her when her skirt caught fire. She could still remember his lips so close to her own and the look on his face. This was not a man whose heart was unfeeling.

"Owen may be many things that you can take offense at," she said defiantly, "but he's not the sort of man who would do what you're accusing him of. Absolutely not!"

"This ain't somethin' that's been come to lightly," Hale insisted. "But rather than argue it with me, try to see it my way."

"Which is?" she shot back, her hands on her hips.

"Between me and Del, we know each man and woman livin' here on the ranch and can vouch for 'bout all of 'em," he explained calmly, his eyes desperate to get her to understand. "Those that we don't know ain't more than a couple, a handful, but ain't none of us know Owen, not really."

"Only because you haven't tried."

"He hasn't let us."

"That still doesn't mean that he's the one who did it!"

"He lives just next to the well," Hale argued, sticking to his conclusions. "When he told it, he said there weren't no sounds out by the well, but if there were someone out there, he'd of had to have heard it!"

"But he was the one who reported what happened at the well! If he had been the one who did it, why draw attention?"

"He must've . . . must've wanted to . . . to look innocent," Hale stumbled, forgetting the strength of his convictions, if only for a moment. "Besides, him and me had . . ." he continued before his voice faded.

"You and he, what?" Charlotte demanded.

"It's nothin' . . ."

"Hale McCoy, if you don't tell me what's going on between you and Owen," she snapped, determined to learn all that he was hiding, "I swear to you that not only won't I help you with Hannah, I *might* just put a bug in her ear about how horrible a man I think you are!"

"You...you wouldn't..."

"Oh, I most certainly would!"

From the look in Hale's eyes, he knew instantly that Charlotte meant what she said. With a heavy sigh, his broad shoulders sagging, he said, "Owen and I...well, I...I punched him..."

Charlotte's eyes grew as wide as saucers. "Why...why did you hit him?"

"Because of the way he treated you during the fire."

"You saw that?"

"I was takin' a couple of buckets from the pump when I saw him knock you to the ground."

"He was trying to help me!"

"At first," Hale agreed. "But then I heard how he yelled at you and saw the tears in your eyes when you walked away."

Charlotte imagined what must have passed through Hale's thoughts, watching as he had been, as she emotionally broke down. Shame of embarrassment colored her cheeks.

"When I confronted him, he made me so damn mad that my temper got the better of me and I hit him."

Though there was a part of Charlotte that couldn't help but feel thankful for how Hale had stood up for her, she knew that it was no excuse for the bad conclusions he had made. "Just because he spoke to me that way doesn't mean that he was responsible for fouling the well."

"I understand that you don't wanna believe it, I do, but no amount of wantin' it to not be so is gonna change the fact that it looks an awful lot like Owen is guilty. I came to you 'cause I figured you'd be honest . . ."

"And I have been."

Hale nodded. "Then I guess I just gotta do my job and find who's to blame."

"He didn't do it, Hale!" Charlotte said emphatically.

"We'll see."

With that, Hale turned and walked back toward the barns, leaving her alone on the walk.

Charlotte's heart ached as anger, bewilderment, and so many other emotions that she couldn't even describe descended on her, vying for her thoughts. There was only one way in which she could hope to settle them.

Determinedly, she headed toward the horse barn.

Charlotte found Owen at the back of the horse barn on the far eastern edge of the ranch grounds. In the light of a flickering oil lamp that hung beside a stall, his bare arms glistened with sweat. He didn't notice her until she stood before the stall where he was tending to a brown and white horse. He tossed a bristle brush into an empty pail with a clang and leaned against the closed gate, a mischievous smile on his face.

"What brought you here, Charlie?" he asked.

"Who are you, really?" she replied, her voice tighter than she'd intended.

"Beg your pardon?"

"I want to know who Owen Williams is," Charlotte answered, her hands knotted into tight fists, the nails of her fingers digging into the flesh of her palms. It was reassuring to her that there was no one else around. "I want to know what kind of man you really are."

"Did you get a crack on the head?" Owen chuckled, tipping his hat back and wiping his brow.

"Answer me," she insisted, stepping so close to him that only the wood of the gate separated them. "Are you the man who shouted such horrible things at me during the fire, who takes pleasure in teasing me about my name?" She paused. "Or are you the man who apologized and said he understood what it was like to lose a mother?"

Charlotte could see that her words had struck a nerve when he sucked in his breath. Then he quickly covered his reaction, choosing to laugh it away, but she wasn't willing to play along. Quickly, she reached up, seizing his face and turning it back so that their eyes met. "For once, I want you to be honest with me."

Slowly, Owen nodded. "What kind of man am I?" he repeated.

"That's something everyone wants to know." Charlotte looked him straight in the eye.

"Everyone?" he asked.

"For now, let's just start with me."

"I'm a good guy." Owen grinned.

"Then why did you shout at me when my skirt caught fire?"

"I suppose this is where I should just lie to you," Owen answered, a sly, confident smile again crossing his handsome features, "just say I didn't want to be a nursemaid while I was trying to do my job, but it looks to me like you aren't going to take that as an answer."

"I'm not," she agreed.

"Then I suppose it won't hurt to tell you the truth. I shouted at you, because I wanted you to get the hell out of there. I was afraid that something terrible would happen to you. Like you catching on fire when I was not near enough to help you."

"Why couldn't you have just told me that? Why did you have to yell?"

"Because." He shrugged.

Charlotte gave him a look that said, *I don't believe you...*

Owen sighed. "Because if I had told you the truth about why I didn't want you to be there, I was afraid that you might guess the reason *why*."

"Is this also why you've been avoiding me?"

"I reckon so."

From the first moment she laid eyes on him in the

ranch dining room, they seemed to be playing a game; and, as with most games, they were destined to play until there was a winner.

"So instead of being honest, you chose to be mean to me."

"I did."

"And then Hale came and punched you for it."

Charlotte's words appeared to take all of the wind out of Owen's sails. Slowly, his pride deflated; he was like a poker player who had believed his cards to be unbeatable, right up until the instant his opponent laid down a better hand. "So that's what this is all about," he finally answered.

Now it was Charlotte's turn to shrug.

"He came in here all in a snit, talking about how badly I had treated you, and then I made things worse by suggesting that he was only mad because he was in love with you."

Charlotte laughed. "That's ridiculous! Even a blind man could see that he's in love with your sister!"

"And I'm sure not blind."

"Then why did you say something so stupid?"

"Sometimes taking a beating is easier than admitting the truth."

"Which is?"

Owen wasn't willing to answer that question, instead choosing to steer the conversation to a different subject. "So Hale's the reason you're here talking to me."

"He didn't ask me to talk to you."

"But you're here because of something he said to you. Let me guess. He told you about the well."

She could see that Owen had become defensive; he leaned away from her, folding his arms across his chest, his eyes never leaving her. There was no point in talking about the particulars, what he had discovered, whom he had told, even why Hale suspected him; there was only the fact that he was being accused.

"He thinks that you did it, that you were the one who ruined the water."

"I didn't do it," he declared adamantly.

"I know."

"If that's the case, then why are you here?"

Owen's words wobbled Charlotte's resolve. She had been unsettled by Hale's brash accusation, but there was much more to her rushing to Owen's defense than the belief he was not guilty; in fact, she didn't know exactly why she defended him.

Maybe it was the way he looks at me...

"I came because Hale doesn't believe you."

"We both know that."

No easy reply presented itself to Charlotte, so she remained silent.

"I think I know why you came out here."

"Why's that?"

Slowly, with the calm, assured intensity of a predator stalking smaller prey, Owen stepped back and pushed open the horse gate. Behind him, the horse whinnied but made no move to leave. When Owen stepped toward her, the look in his eyes made Charlotte move back involuntarily.

"Because you have feelings for me," he ventured.

"I came because I would hate to see anyone falsely blamed for something they didn't do," she lied, uncomfortable with how close to the truth he had come.

"That's not it," Owen answered.

"Besides," Charlotte kept on, unheeding, "Hannah has been such a good friend to me ever since I came here that I owe her enough to look out for her brother."

"That's not it, either."

"Well, I'm sorry, but you're mistaken."

More quickly than the hungry flames that had leaped from the burning bush to set her afire, Owen closed the space between them, leaning down to tenderly place his lips against hers. His hand found the delicate small of her back and drew her closer, pressing her body against his. Shocked at first, she found herself giving in to her impulses. The taste of his lips, the feel of his whiskered cheek as her hand rose to touch it, the musky smell of his sweat, and even the sound that rumbled deep in his throat, all combined to overwhelm her. She strained to meet his advances, her mouth just as hungry as his; her eyes closed as she enjoyed a feeling that was as intoxicating as it was new. When Owen finally broke from her, she had no idea how much time had passed since their kiss began, but somewhere deep inside her, she knew that she would be counting the hours, days, weeks until she was in his arms again.

"That's why you came here tonight," Owen said softly, his hand still on her back.

"Owen," Charlotte answered, "Hale still thinks that you did it."

"Shhh," he quieted her with a finger against her lips. "Not tonight. There'll be time to deal with that later."

Chapter Sixteen

TIRED FROM A LONG DAY at school, Charlotte trudged up the walk to the main house, the sun still high enough for its rays to warm her skin. The whole day had flummoxed her, with her thoughts swimming back to the kiss she had shared with Owen the night before, and she'd had a hard time focusing on her students. Minutes felt as if they were hours, Paige Spratt was even more annoying than usual, and Charlotte wondered if Owen would be the one to come drive her and Hannah home; she was greatly disappointed when he was not.

Charlotte had just entered the front door when Amelia Grant approached her, absently wiping one hand on her worn apron, an envelope clutched in the other.

"John picked this up at the post office when he went into town." She smiled warmly, placing the letter into

Charlotte's hands. "I was certain that you'd want to have it as soon as you got home."

Even if she hadn't seen the postmark, Charlotte would have known who had sent it by the slant of the handwriting; Christina had written to her.

"It's from my sister." She beamed.

"Go on up and enjoy your letter."

"Thank you, Amelia!" Charlotte shouted over her shoulder as she dashed up the staircase to her room two steps at a time, her earlier fatigue and confusion utterly forgotten.

She opened the door to her bedroom, banged it behind her harder than intended, and dropped down onto the foot of the bed. Tearing open the envelope and unfolding the letter, several pages in length, she smiled at the sight of Christina's familiar script.

My dearest Charlotte,

Since you've been in Oklahoma for a little while, I thought that you might like to get a letter from your sister! We were all so happy to hear that you had arrived safely, but if I'm being honest, I'm pretty lonely here without you... don't tell Mom!

Life in Carlson hasn't changed much since you've gone, but then it never changed much when you were here, did it? I've spent a lot of time walking in the woods around Lake

Washington, like we used to do when I wasn't waist-high to you. While I'm having a good time, I doubt it's as exciting as the adventures you're having!

Everyone here is the same... Mom was pretty sad after you left, I even found her crying in her room one afternoon, but she's better now... Dad kept telling her that every Tucker left home at one time or another, just like he did, but that might have made it worse. Grandmother had a bit of a trouble with dizziness, but now she's better and having her friends over for cards like nothing ever happened... you know how she is!

Enough about us, how are you? I can't tell you how proud I am that you're a teacher and that you've set out to have a life of your own! Every day, you'll be meeting new people and doing things that you've never done before. That sounds like the greatest thing in the world, but I don't know if I'll ever be able to do that... I've never been as outgoing as you. It's easier for me to stay where I know things than try something new. But now that I watch you succeed, it makes me want to strike out on my own! Who knows... someday I might be the one who gets to take the train out of town... maybe I'll get to have a career, a new life out of Carlson. I'll keep hoping and studying, all right?

I love you so much, Charlotte! Don't forget how proud I am of you!

Your sister,
Christina

P.S. Have you met any nice men? I'm your sister and have a right to know!

Happiness blossomed brightly in Charlotte's heart as she finished her sister's letter, putting it carefully back in its envelope. She hadn't known it when she'd returned to the ranch, but something from home had been just what she'd needed. Although Christina's own self-confidence had often been lacking, she had never wavered with her unflagging support of her older sister.

Christina's postscript made Charlotte laugh; she had no idea whether it was right to call Owen a "nice man," but he had certainly had an impact on her. Whenever she thought of the man who had shouted at her, who had made light of her name, who had shared his feelings about his mother, or who had kissed her so passionately, she found her heart beating faster, filled with emotions she had never imagined.

I've definitely met someone...

But there was another matter that needed her attention, something that involved a man who was most certainly not nice. If her stay in Oklahoma was to remain pleasant, she couldn't wait any longer to do something about him.

"Git after it! Git after it! Git after it!"

John Grant whistled and shouted, encouraging a pair of cowboys who were desperately trying to coerce an unbroken colt to follow their commands. His tan ears were pricked high, spittle flew from his mouth, and he held his head up and alert. Whatever movement the men made as they worked in tandem, the horse attempted the opposite, his hooves rising up before slamming down into the earth as geysers of dirt shot up at every step. To Charlotte, it looked like an awkward dance with only two willing participants.

Suddenly, the horse bolted hard to his right, directly toward one of the ranch hands who now was trapped between the obviously upset animal on one side and the fence on the other. The hand grimaced, preparing to be struck, but at the last second the horse veered slightly, just clipping the man with his front quarter. The blow was still tremendous; the man fell hard on his rump, his hat flying off in a cloud of dust.

"Dang it all!" he shouted.

"All right there!" John bellowed. "That's enough of that for now! Why don't we let that horse run around some and work some of that gol-damn steam out of what bothers him, then we'll give it another go!" When he turned and noticed that Charlotte had come up behind him, watching a few steps away, he added, "Sorry 'bout the language, young lady."

"Nothing I haven't heard before, I'm afraid." She smiled. As the cowboys made their way from the corral, she said, "That looks dangerous."

"It is," he agreed. "Horses don't know their own

strength. This one's wild and don't take to tamin'. Course you gotta convince him otherwise, and that's when a fella's most likely to get hurt."

"How long does it usually take to . . . convince them?"

"A bit longer than I'd like!"

Watching John Grant smile as he talked about his horses, about his livelihood, Charlotte could see why he inspired such loyalty in Hale, Del, and all the other men. John was equally quick with a smile, a shouted order, or even the quiet surety of purpose she saw during the fire. He was friendly and a charmer. Charlotte wondered if she too hadn't been taken in when she had agreed to teach Sarah Beck.

"How about for this horse?"

"Give him a few more of these sessions and he'll start comin' round."

"That's how I feel about some of my new students," Charlotte said with a chuckle. "Whether it's reading or writing, arithmetic or geography, I have them do it over and over again in the hopes that they'll finally learn a little of what I'm trying to teach them."

"None of your students could possibly be as hopeless as some of the mustangs we got comin' through here."

"Other than Sarah, you mean."

John's eyes narrowed and there was a beat of tension that passed between them, if only for an instant. "I didn't quite mean it like that," he answered. "How're things goin' with her schoolin'?"

"Better than I'd expected, to tell you the truth. We've been working on building her reading skills, and while she can get frustrated quite easily, she tries as hard as she can to sound out the words," Charlotte explained, pausing before dropping her reason for coming to speak with him. "But there is a problem, a big one, although it's not with her."

"What's that?"

Charlotte proceeded to tell John about her frightening encounter with a drunken Alan Beck outside the shack; she recounted his horrible rant about how his daughter couldn't learn a thing, his inappropriate advance toward her in the pouring rain, and the fact that she had feared him. When John asked why she hadn't told him when he had come to pick her up, she explained that she'd been too shaken to think clearly, and that now, after she'd time to give the matter thought, she'd decided to talk to him about it.

And I've been awfully preoccupied with Owen...

"I hate to say it, but I was afraid this might happen, though I sure hoped otherwise." John frowned. "He looks the sort, like a man who's been beaten down a bit and finds a drop of courage in a bottle 'cause he ain't got none of his own to spare. Ever since him and Sarah arrived, he's been hangin' over the lip of that bottle, and from what you're sayin', looks to me like he finally fell in."

"I don't know if I can go back there until I'm sure it isn't going to happen again," Charlotte admitted.

"I guarantee you that it won't, even if I have to stay out there with you the whole time. This is too darn important to me to have anythin' gummin' it up."

"Why?" she asked, the question already out of her mouth before she could contain it.

"Why what?"

"Why is my helping Sarah so important to you?" Charlotte plunged recklessly forward, deciding that knowing was worth any potential risk. "When you took me out to the shack the first time, you asked me to give your offer a chance, to trust you, and to try to teach her something. I've done that. Now it's *you* who should trust in *me*. Why would you want to risk our standing around town for someone you scarcely know?"

John was quiet for a long time, moving only to wipe his brow with a handkerchief. With every passing second, Charlotte felt certain that he would not tell her anything, but finally he nodded.

"Life is full of a lot of things, some of 'em funny, some sad, even some angry, but the hardest thing I've ever tried livin' with is regret," he began, his eyes wistfully staring off into the distance. "When you're young, you'll do all sorts of things, foolish and whatnot, things you wouldn't if only you'd had a few more years on your bones to know better."

John paused, falling so silent that Charlotte could hear the rebellious colt's tail swishing away persistent flies.

"Even a young lady such as yourself," John continued, "even though you comin' to Sawyer, leavin' your home in

Minnesota, is the first step in what's sure to be a long life, I reckon even you've got a handful of regrets."

"One or two," she agreed, her thoughts again racing to her erratic relationship with Owen.

"Well, I've got one that weighs down on my soul." John's tone darkened. "Somethin' I can't rightfully make up for, and let's just say that when I first took a gander at Sarah Beck and her situation, it was the sort of reminder a God-fearin' man ain't likely to ignore.

"In an instant, a man can make the sort of mistake he spends the rest of his life tryin' to make up for. Me askin' you to teach that girl, to try to help her make somethin' better outta the mess of her life, it ain't much, but it's 'bout all I got these days."

When John finished, he turned to look at her, allowing Charlotte to be witness to the competing emotions written on his face: anger, disgust, and shame colored his cheeks. There was much that she could assume from listening to his words, much that reflected poorly on him, but she resisted the urge to leap to any improper conclusions. She knew that she had been allowed to share a part of John Grant's secret, an honor that was both flattering and troublesome.

"I know it ain't the whole truth, least not spelled out as simple as a story you might read to your students," he said, "but is it enough?"

"It's more than I knew before."

"It is at that."

Given the modest success she had gained in trying to understand John's interest in Sarah Beck, Charlotte felt optimistic. Ever since Hale had told her that Owen was suspected of fouling the well, she had considered how she might come to his defense. Since John was the owner of the ranch that was being threatened, he would be directly involved with any finger-pointing. If she wanted to clear Owen's name, there was no one better with whom to talk.

The only way I'll ever know is to ask...

But before she could say a word, Charlotte was surprised to see a commotion start on the opposite side of the corral, cross within spitting distance of the startled horse, and head directly toward where she and John stood; fast as lightning, she understood that it was Salt and Pepper, one after the other, racing just as quick as their legs would carry them. Though they were definitely interrupting, she couldn't help smiling. She hadn't seen them underfoot since the day of the fire when they had been frantically racing back and forth from the ranch house to the nearest barn, as if they couldn't decide whether they wanted to be brave and fight the fire or fearful and hide in the house.

"And what are you two little rascals up to today?" John asked in false consternation.

As if he were providing an answer, Pepper began to yap furiously; Salt only occasionally barked one deep woof, filling in what his partner left out.

"Sounds important," Charlotte commented.

"More than likely it ain't nothin' more than one of 'em tipped over the water bucket we keep out for 'em and they're too lazy to head down to the creek." He smiled. "I suppose I should go and see."

"You wouldn't want to make them angry," she said, wondering if they usually got their water from the well that had been tampered with.

"No, I would not," he answered, giving no hint that anything was wrong. Turning to leave, he only made it a step before stopping. "I promise you that I will take care of Alan, so are we settled?"

Charlotte nodded, her moment to stand up for Owen lost in a furious riot of barking dogs.

It was coming on dawn when Clyde Drake stepped out of his cabin, leaned against the railing of the porch, and lit himself a cigarette. His bleary red eyes were underlined by dark circles, testament to his almost sleepless night. Taking a deep drag, he waited for the tobacco to settle him, to calm his nerves. Absently, he rubbed at his throbbing temple.

It's a hell of a mess I've gotten myself into . . .

The orders Clyde had been given by Carter Herrick weighed heavily upon him. It was a dangerous, bold plan. While the chance for the destruction of Grant's property and injury to its hands was great, so too was the chance of Clyde's own discovery. To make matters even worse, his fellow conspirator was again dragging his feet, complaining about the risk they were taking. They had been up half the night arguing about it. In the end, Clyde knew that he would have to be the one to realize Herrick's demands.

Clyde Drake had never been the brains of an outfit, instead always content to be the muscle who did what he was told. At the orders of others, he'd beaten defenseless old men, burned houses down to the ground, slapped around women regardless of their age, and even robbed a bank in Kansas. He'd never regretted what he had done, content to fill his pockets with the money he was paid, even if that cash soon disappeared on whiskey and whores. But even a man such as he could clearly see that Carter Herrick was growing unbalanced and that his desire for revenge on John Grant was consuming him. He was becoming reckless, willing to risk it all as he became more and more desperate. But the real problem was that he wasn't risking his own neck, but those of his men.

"And that means me," Clyde mumbled to the dawn.

Carter Herrick wanted John Grant ruined, not dead. But there was going to come a time when Clyde was going to have had enough of dancing around the matter. Ruthlessness was a trait he had in spades. He had no problems with killing the man, even if that contradicted his boss. The man whom Herrick held in his pocket would undoubtedly try to stop Clyde, but he'd only get dead alongside Grant.

But first Clyde would do what Herrick asked. He'd do it carefully, cautiously, but he *would* do it.

Stamping out his cigarette butt, Clyde went back into his cabin in search of an elusive couple hours of sleep.

Chapter Seventeen

I swear, one of the things that I've never been able to decide on, no matter how hard I try, is in what season would it be the best to die," Constance Lowell declared, her withered hand rising to her chin in a pose of reflection. "Of course I know that we get no choice in the matter, but that doesn't stop me from wondering, all the same."

Try as he might, Owen could not think of a way to escape the old woman short of simply running away.

Owen cringed; he had been planning this moment for a couple of days, thinking that it would be nice to come and surprise Charlotte as she finished her day of teaching. After their passionate kiss, he'd resumed his job of picking Hannah up outside of the law office where she worked, but on this day he had made arrangements for his sister to get home by other means, leaving him free to pick up Charlotte after school.

He'd come early, parking on the street opposite the school. The wide, treeless road hadn't offered any shade from the relentless beating of the summer sun, the truck's cab roasting like an oven, so he had taken refuge under the paltry shade offered by a young maple tree in front of the funeral parlor; still, it had afforded *some* protection.

Owen hadn't even noticed her approach.

"They all have their ups and downs, pros and cons, as my father was fond of saying at great length," Miss Lowell kept on, either oblivious or uncaring about his indifference. "Spring can be beautiful with all of the flowers, but even in these parts it's likely to rain. Summer is so very pleasant, but what if the day is just as unbearably hot as this one? Fall is my favorite time of year, but once again it's a question of weather. Even winter, with an invigorating chill in the air, there's a problem in trying to dig a hole in the hard ground! I just don't know!"

... how I'm going to get out of this!

"Which one would be your favorite, young man?"

"Umm," he stumbled, unprepared for her question, "I suppose I'd say fall."

"But have you considered the problems of—" she started, but Owen had already managed to tune her out.

Of course, Owen knew all about Constance Lowell; if you spent enough time in Sawyer, she was sure to be mentioned. The stories were many, each more unbelievable than the one before. He'd heard about the time she had stood up and applauded a particularly strong sermon for the burial of the town's longtime grocer, about how she often showed up at weddings clothed only in black from head to toe, and about how even at her own father's funeral it seemed to everyone in the congregation that she was having the time of her life. Somehow, Owen had always managed to avoid her...until now.

"Do you ever wonder how people will find out how you died?"

"Excuse me?" he asked, her question jarring him.

"Because I wonder about it all the time," Constance chirped cheerily. "For most people you meet, word of their demise is circulated in print, written up in the obituary column in the newspaper, but for someone of my stature, maybe it would be broadcast over the radio," she kept on as her eyes twinkled at the possibility.

Suddenly, the school bell rang, as pleasant a sound as Owen had ever heard in his life, and a sigh escaped his lips.

Children rushed out of the school's front doors, boys and girls of all ages running past them down the walk like foxes intent on returning to their den, talking all the way. Constance paid the children no attention, prattling on as if they were not even there.

"Word of mouth would almost certainly carry news of my passing to most in town, going from ear to ear, especially over the telephone, but among the important people in town, I suppose—"

Finally, Charlotte came out of the school just behind

another woman, an odd-looking lady who went off down the walk in a huff without a word.

Looking at Charlotte made Owen's heart do funny things. There was no point denying he thought she was beautiful; the way that the streaming sun shone through her blond curls as they lay on her white blouse sent a tremor through his chest. When she finally noticed him, her lips curled into a curious smile, and he left Constance in midsentence.

"Is something the matter?" she asked when he had reached her side.

"Why would there be?" He smiled slyly.

"It's just that I wouldn't have expected to see you here," Charlotte explained. "You usually make me walk home."

"Today's special."

"Really?"

"I thought...I thought that maybe you might like to come somewhere with me," he managed. "There's a place that I found when I first arrived from Colorado, a bit outside of town and near the river, that I wanted to show you. I was hoping that we could talk...talk about the other night..."

"About our kiss?"

"Among other things, I reckon."

"Won't Hannah be angry that we've left her in Sawyer?"

"It's already taken care of."

Owen could see that Charlotte was pretending to think

his offer over, teasing him a little, but he already knew she was going to accept.

"All right." She nodded. "I'll go."

"Right this way." He smiled, taking off his hat and waving it toward the truck, heat shimmering off its metal body.

As they drove off, Charlotte waved at Constance Lowell, who was still rambling to herself in front of the funeral parlor.

Charlotte felt a tremor of nervous excitement as Owen drove the truck past the school and headed out of town. She had never been in that direction; her route from the ranch led through town and stopped at the school, never farther. Today would be different. With a cool breeze rushing in through her open window, they passed the last house on the outskirts and kept on going.

For a little while they drove parallel to the railroad tracks, traveling in reverse of the route Charlotte had taken when she had first come to Sawyer. She remembered a fenced-in herd of cattle here, a formation of rock there. But then the road turned away and Owen drove them down into a depression where the sparse wild grasses stood still unmoved by the wind.

"It's not far," Owen assured her, his tone casual, his hand lolling out the window.

"You're not going to tell me what it is you're taking me to see?"

"It's a secret."

Even though she didn't know where they were going, Charlotte felt glad to be traveling there all the same. Her day at school had been difficult; another uncomfortable exchange with Paige Spratt about the benefits of wholesome, married life had been followed by an afternoon spent with rambunctious kids who were sick of being cooped up in the heat. Well, so was she.

She was glad to be with Owen...

"I hate to admit it, especially to you," he said, breaking their shared silence, "but I'm impressed, Charlie."

"With what?"

"With you being a teacher," Owen explained, taking a quick glance at her as he guided the truck along a curve in the road. "It takes an awful lot of guts, something special, to get up there in front of a classroom and try to teach a bunch of kids. Heck, I don't think I have it in me." He laughed. "About the first time someone gave me any guff, I'd light into them in such a way that I'd be certain to get fired."

"It's not that hard. I'm more impressed with what you do."

"Driving you back and forth to the ranch?"

"No, not that." She laughed. "With how you work with the horses."

"There's nothing to it. All you need to do is learn their language."

"It's not any different with children."

Owen shook his head. "I've seen the way they act up. They're more stubborn than any horse I've ever met."

"Remind yourself about that the next time one of your favorites doesn't want to get into its stall for the night."

"You might have a point there," he replied, and they both laughed.

The road gently dipped and rose before them until turning to the right beside a lonely stand of trees that stood silently watching, one of them leaning so far to the right that it looked to be giving them directions.

"Here it is," Owen said.

Charlotte's eyes widened in wonder. The road had come to a sudden end, vanishing into a broad watering hole. Brilliant rays of sunlight, a kaleidoscope of color, reflected off the surface as if it were made of glass. Along the shoreline, thin reeds broke through the water, reaching for the crystal blue sky above. A swallow drifted a few inches above the surface before it suddenly darted down to snatch an unwary bug for its meal. Charlotte was surprised and delighted by what Owen had introduced to her. She got out of the truck, leaving the door open behind her.

"It's beautiful," she said when Owen joined her. "How did you find it?"

"Whenever I arrive somewhere new," Owen explained, "I like to look around to get the lay of the land, so when I dropped Hannah at the lawyer's office, I'd go exploring to see what there was to see. I've taken every road out of town for miles, hoping all the while that no one will notice how much gas I've been using." He laughed. "I found this place by accident."

"Maybe it was meant to be."

"I don't know if I believe in that sort of thing." Owen shrugged. "But I'm glad to have found it nonetheless."

Owen led Charlotte around the edge of the water, a startled frog jumping in as they approached. He held out his hand to steady her when they climbed a difficult rise. Farther ahead, under the shade of a lone tree, an outcropping hung out over the water. The view was magnificent. Wiping her brow in the heat, Charlotte had an urge to jump in and cool down, which made her laugh. Owen spread out a horse blanket he had brought along. From somewhere, he produced a couple of apples.

"It isn't much, but it was all I could scrounge."

"It's more than enough."

For a while, they were both content to just look, enjoying each other's silent company. A clump of daisies grew nearby; Charlotte plucked at their delicate white petals, letting the faint breeze pick them up and whirl them down to the water below. Owen absently skipped small stones across the water, counting the loud kerplunks of their journey on the pond.

"This makes me a bit homesick," Charlotte said wistfully.

"I didn't bring you here to make you sad."

"And here I thought that was exactly why you brought me." She looked at him with a teasing frown. "But I grew up on a lake in Minnesota and I guess I just didn't know how much I missed it until now."

"There were plenty of lakes in Colorado, too, but I don't miss any of them."

"What was it like?" she asked, turning to face him.

"What was what like?"

"Growing up in Colorado. Aren't there things you miss about it, about your childhood?"

Owen's mood darkened; the change was so marked and sudden that it took Charlotte aback, but she wanted to know all about him, to understand him.

"There isn't much of my childhood that I miss," he finally answered, his voice as sad as the limp breeze.

"Because of your mother's death?" Charlotte prodded.

Charlotte felt Owen begin to close up, to erect the walls he relied upon to block out all that was unpleasant. She could only imagine how often he had resorted to that tactic, but it was obvious that he'd had a lot of practice. But then his eyes found hers and held, softening as a low sigh of resignation escaped his lips. She knew then that their kiss had changed him, at least toward her, allowing him to open himself, if only a crack.

"My mother was a wonderful woman," he began, his eyes somewhere distant, "kind and caring, always ready with an encouraging word. She liked to sing, to struggle at the stove, and insisted that I get a proper schooling. I thought she was beautiful, in the way that most sons regard their mothers, but others also thought her pretty. I never knew her to speak ill of anyone, even when they deserved it. Through all of that, she was resigned to keep burdens to herself. I've no doubt that was what killed her."

"It was the same with my mother." Charlotte nodded. "Her crosses became too great for her to bear."

"I am sorry, Charlotte."

She couldn't suppress a smile at his using her real name. "I wish I could talk to her, if only for a minute."

"I'm sure you would have plenty to say."

"Much more than a minute, I suppose," she agreed.

"Even though I had years to talk to my mother, I don't know if I ever said all I wanted," Owen admitted.

"Was it an illness that took her?"

Owen nodded. "It was hell for us to watch her get sick. Being so damn helpless made me furious. My mother became ill gradually, not all of a sudden, like she'd broken a leg. It started with a weakening of her body; she'd get a bit breathless from time to time, need to go lie down after being on her feet for only a couple of hours. Then her appetite vanished, no matter what Hannah made for her, and she started to lose weight so fast I thought she'd just dry up and blow away. It wasn't long before she was in bed all the time. In the days before she died, she cried in her sleep. The worst part was accepting that the doctor couldn't do anything for her. I always thought that was what doctors were supposed to do, make bad things better, but sometimes it's just too late.

"Hannah and I were with her the morning she died and

it was the first time I had seen her at peace in years. I'm thankful that I was able to share her life, without question, and that I could care for her when she needed me the most, but the ache of missing her never seems to go away."

"It gets a little easier over time."

"I hope so."

"Had your father passed before your mother?"

Owen looked away quickly, his face a mask of distaste. "I never knew him," he spat. "I never knew who he was."

"I'm sorry," Charlotte murmured, regretting her thoughtlessness. "I shouldn't have asked."

Her apology lifted the gloom from his eyes. "It's all right. I think this is all a feeling I've held in for too long." He laughed weakly. "I guess I never really realized it until now, but I'm carrying the same burden that my mother bore, in some way. Maybe if I continued to hold it in, I'd end up just like she did, my secret eating away at my insides."

Charlotte couldn't help but think of the secrets that she kept, as well as those that had been kept from her. Her father had kept her whole family from knowing that he was still alive after the war. She herself honored Sarah's vow of silence as to the identity of the man who had fathered her unborn child. Even Hale's secret, his love for Hannah, obvious as it was, was never Charlotte's to tell. From the moment she had seen Owen in the dining room, she had known that there was *something* about him that wouldn't be easily told, something he kept hidden. Now, she found herself hoping he would reveal it to her.

"I came to Oklahoma because..." he began, before his voice trailed off.

"Owen," she interrupted, "you don't have to tell me right now if you don't want to," letting him off the hook although she desperately wanted to know the reason. "Whenever you choose, it's up to you."

But Owen had decided that this was the time.

"Hannah and I came here because I think that John Grant is our father."

Charlotte was shocked. She felt as if she had been struck by lightning, a freight train, or a massive boulder crashing down a hillside. It was almost impossible for her to believe what Owen had said. Over and over she searched for the words that would convey her surprise, but she continued to struggle, her eyes wide and her jaw slack. Finally, it was Owen who filled in some of the blanks, though they presented issues of their own.

"My last name isn't Williams," he explained. "It's Wallace, the same as my mother. Hannah and I changed it when we left Colorado. If my suspicions about John Grant proved correct, it would have been pretty stupid to walk onto his property with a name he would easily recognize."

"Owen...Wallace..." Charlotte struggled.

"It wasn't my intention to deceive you, but we couldn't take any chances. John Grant is my father. I truly believe it to be so."

Now everything seemed even crazier in Charlotte's head; Owen and his sister had traveled to Oklahoma for a reason, changing their names to avoid suspicion, scheming to get close to the man he believed had to be their father. But to think so poorly of John Grant, to carry so much dislike for the man who had invited her into his home, had shown her nothing but kindness, seemed ridiculous. It couldn't possibly be true. How could Owen believe such a thing?

"But you don't know for certain? You have reason to doubt it?"

"A few," he admitted, "but when I'm absolutely sure of the fact... I'm going to ruin him."

Chapter Eighteen

OWEN KNEW IN A HEARTBEAT that he had said too much. There was no denying that it had been liberating to let go of his burden, to talk about his mother and the horrible way in which she had died, and that comfort had loosened his tongue. He hadn't seen the harm in revealing what he believed about John Grant because regardless of how difficult it was to hear and know, *it was true*. But now that it had been let free, now that he saw the wide-eyed, open-mouthed disbelief in Charlotte's face, there could be no going back... only forward.

"What are you saying, Owen?" she asked, her voice rising, shrill and confused with every word. "Why would you want to ruin John if you know him to be your father? Why?"

"Because of what he did to my mother," he explained. "Because he abandoned her."

"He didn't make her sick!"

"It was because of him that she was forced to leave here and go to Colorado, living alone as she struggled to raise two children, twins born out of wedlock!" Owen heard himself shouting. "I'm sure that it was because he chased her away, denied her when he found out she was pregnant! He was ashamed of her, embarrassed. She would have had a better life, a different life, if it weren't for him!"

"What proof do you have that John is your father? You said yourself that your mother kept her secrets. If she didn't tell you, who did?"

Struggling to keep his temper in check, not at Charlotte but at the remembrance of his grievances against John Grant, Owen explained his conclusions: how he and Hannah had discovered that their mother had once, in the time before their birth, lived in Sawyer, how he had found what remained of a letter, dating back to Caroline Wallace's time in Oklahoma, that mentioned John Grant by name, and spoke of him being the man she could never stop loving, even if he had chosen to reject her; and how when he had first laid eyes on John *he had known*; deep in his gut he was certain of John's guilt.

"But that doesn't prove anything," Charlotte protested.

"It proves that he broke my mother's heart."

"Possibly, yet it doesn't give you any concrete evidence that John is your father, either. Who knows what the real story is, or whether there even is one worth talking about? Maybe she loved him from afar, but instead he loved

Amelia. Maybe he couldn't break off his engagement, or his feelings, and your mother couldn't accept that. The truth is that you don't *really* know, Owen. You don't know enough to go off half-cocked, wanting to ruin a man!"

Owen rose to his feet in frustration, kicking distractedly at a clump of flowers. When Charlotte doubted his conclusion and offered other scenarios, he was nonplussed.

What in the hell did you expect her to say?

If he was honest with himself, he hadn't known what he expected, but Charlotte's disagreement unsettled him; it even caused his confidence in his cause to waver, made him question how sure he was of what he was doing. Because he was beginning to care for her, her opinions carried weight with him. For six excruciatingly long months, he had persuaded himself that John Grant was the man who was responsible. He had uprooted their lives in Colorado and come to Oklahoma under an assumed name because John Grant *had* to pay for what he had done to Caroline Wallace. But what if he accidentally destroyed an innocent man? What then? What would his mother think of that?

More important, what would Charlotte think of that...?

Desperately, Charlotte struggled to show Owen how flimsy a basis he had for his accusation. His relentless pursuit of the truth was understandable, but he was letting his need cloud his better judgment. He was leaping to conclusions and grasping at straws. If he were to follow through with his plans for revenge, the consequences for him and Hannah would be too great to bear. She had to convince him that there was another possibility. But how?

"He rejected her because he got her pregnant," Owen murmured as he paced back and forth in front of Charlotte, the certainty slowly vanishing from his voice. "He didn't want to take responsibility for what he had done."

"John Grant doesn't seem the sort of man who would turn his back on a woman with child," she countered.

Charlotte thought of the way John spoke about Sarah Beck, of the great lengths to which he had gone, at certain risk to his reputation, to ensure that the girl got an education. He had taken in Sarah and her father, complete strangers from Arkansas, and put them up on his land. When Charlotte had pressed him about them, John had told her of his own regrets, a moment in his life when he had been unable to do right by someone. Had he meant Owen's mother? She'd never asked, but there seemed little doubt that all the Becks had, their bedding, food, and firewood, had to have been provided by John. How could the same man who had taken them in have completely rejected Owen's mother?

It just wasn't possible.

No matter how she felt about *why* John had become involved with the Becks, Charlotte did not feel free to tell Owen about Sarah. She knew that he would leap to whatever conclusion painted John Grant in the worst light; he might even go so far as to wonder if the girl's unborn

child belonged to the rancher. Charlotte didn't like keeping silent, but there appeared to be no other choice. While
Sarah had asked her to keep her secret, the identity of the
man responsible for her pregnancy, it was the secret of her
very existence that Charlotte felt needed to be kept.

"Have you thought about talking to John about it?"
Charlotte asked hopefully. "Because of the letter you found,
it's obvious he once knew your mother. If you told John
you believe him to be your father, if you were honest with
him, you would finally learn the truth."

"He'd lie."

"Why do you think that?"

"Because he's a coward," Owen said. "Once a coward,
always a coward."

"Maybe he doesn't even know."

"How could he not?" Owen snapped, turning to her,
the color rising in his face.

"Have you considered that your mother might have
left Oklahoma without telling him? Sometimes, when a
woman finds herself with child, especially when she isn't
married, she doesn't think as clearly as she should." Charlotte need look no further than her own mother's experience; Alice Tucker had been erroneously told that she
had lost her husband while he was at war, long after she'd
found out she was pregnant. It had all proven too much for
her to bear. On the day she had given birth to her daughter, Alice had chosen that she no longer wanted to live. "An
unmarried woman is scared and vulnerable. It's possible

that the shame of what had happened caused her to run away."

"Then he should have gone after her and brought her back."

"Maybe he tried," she soothed. "After all, look how hard it was for you to find him."

"It's too late for that."

"It's never too late for you to find your family, believe me." Charlotte couldn't help thinking of the man she had found out in the woods when she was just a child; he had been Mason Tucker, her father, and he had been a part of her life ever since that fateful day.

Charlotte regarded Owen with tenderness. It was as obvious as the beauty of the day that this whole affair, the uncertainty of it, was tearing him apart. Sympathy filled her heart, making her want to hold him in her arms as she had only days earlier; at that moment, nothing else seemed to matter, erasing all of the things that weighed on them both. But she knew he was too worked up. Instead, she would have to find another solution.

"What about Hannah? What does she think?"

"She came here with the same determination I had," Owen explained, "to learn the truth and make sure that the man responsible for abandoning our mother was punished. That was why she got the job at the lawyer's office."

"With Carlton Barnaby?"

Owen nodded. "With Barnaby's trips to the courthouse,

it gives Hannah plenty of time to go through his files to find some mention of what happened to our mother."

"Isn't that illegal?"

"All that matters is learning the truth. If that means breaking the law, then so be it."

"What has she learned? Has she discovered anything?"

"Not explicitly." Owen frowned. "But Hannah did discover mention of a claim of rape that occurred in the year before our birth. Barnaby had been contacted regarding it, but it mysteriously stopped without much mention with all of the principal names involved blacked out. It doesn't mention him by name, but I think that it's possible this was a claim filled against Grant for assaulting my mother."

"Owen, no! He couldn't have done it!"

"I know you don't want to believe me, but it truly *is* possible."

"Does Hannah believe it? Does she think that this speculation incriminates John?"

Owen frowned. "She's not as convinced as I am...nor is she as vengeful."

"Shouldn't that tell you something?"

"Only that I'll have to discredit that bastard on my own."

"What about *my* doubts?"

"They're all 'maybes' and 'what-ifs.' I know in my bones I'm right."

Suddenly, the events of the last couple of days reassembled themselves in Charlotte's mind. She had been too overwhelmed, dreaming about their passionate kiss and the romantic way he had come to surprise her with a getaway to the pond, to wonder what else was at stake, but Owen's mention of discrediting someone jarred it loose; he wasn't the only person compiling evidence toward proving a man's guilt.

"The well!" she exclaimed.

"What about it?"

"You've *got* to go to John and tell him the truth," Charlotte explained, suddenly energized by her revelation. "If you're right about him being your father, if he knew that you were his son, there's no way he would believe that you were responsible for pouring the kerosene into the well!"

"That wouldn't make any difference at all."

"He thinks that you did it. Maybe he thinks you also started the fire."

"So what?"

"But if he—"

"Think about what you're saying," Owen swiftly cut her off, and resumed his nervous pacing. "John Grant may be a bastard, but he's no man's fool. If I were to tell him that Hannah and I were his children with Caroline Wallace, wouldn't he wonder just why I had come here and what I wanted from him?"

Charlotte felt her chest tightening with his every word.

"If my suspicions are true," Owen continued, "then we've been living under our father's roof all this time, taking his pay, and sharing his dinner table right alongside his other family, all the while keeping our mouths shut. We've been here for months, Charlie. I suspect the next question he might ask us is why we waited so long to tell him what we knew. And how would I answer him...that I wanted to be certain before I ruined him?"

"Which is true..."

"Exactly! And then he either wouldn't let me out of his sight, or would have Hale throw us from the ranch faster than a gunshot."

Charlotte hated to admit it, but much of what Owen said made sense. Telling him about the possibility of his being John's son wouldn't do him any good; instead it might end up doing him harm. It all sounded so preposterous, so outrageous, that she couldn't imagine anyone believing it, let alone John. If only Owen had come clean when he and Hannah had first arrived, things could have been different. But he was right; it was far too late now.

And that was what truly scared her. If the investigation into the fouling of the well continued to focus on Owen, and from what Hale had told her, Owen appeared to be the only suspect, he would eventually be accused. Even if charges were never filed against him, he would still be banished from the ranch, an act that would tear them apart. She wasn't certain of exactly what they had together; she doubted that Owen knew, either; but whatever it was, she desperately wanted to hold on to it. They were only at the beginning of what they could become together; if she could help it, she would do anything that she could to keep it from ending.

"So what do you do instead?" she asked. "Hale is loyal to John and won't give you a moment's peace until he knows the truth."

"Then maybe we should help him find it."

"What are you talking about?"

It was clear that Owen had been giving a great deal of thought to the matter; he knelt down before her, a determined look on his face, hands punctuating his words as he spoke. "There's much more to this than you can see if you only think about me," he explained. "Even that morning after I'd gone to Del, wondering what had happened, I couldn't see it. There is a question, the important one, which you still haven't asked."

"And what is that?"

"Since we both know that I am not the one responsible for polluting the well or starting the fire," he said, gently taking her hand in his, "who is?"

Owen was right; until that moment, Charlotte hadn't imagined asking herself that question. She had been so intent on proving his innocence that she had never wondered *who* actually was guilty. Suddenly, hope sprang up through the depths of dark worry that had surrounded her.

"You're right," she answered.

"When we all stood around the well that morning, there was one thing John was sure about," Owen said, "that kerosene didn't get down that well without someone's help."

"But whose?"

"That is the question we need an answer to, but there's definitely someone besides me who wishes John Grant harm."

"So how do we go about learning the truth?" Charlotte asked. "Where could we possibly start? Neither of us has been there long enough to really know each person who works on the ranch," she said, thinking aloud. "Besides, everyone worked so hard fighting the fire, would someone who deliberately set the blaze *really* do that? I just can't imagine there is someone out there who is duplicitous enough to do such a thing, as well as dirty a well."

"I can't... I just can't believe I never wondered about it before now... I can't," Owen said, the words spilling out.

"Wondered about what?"

"The fire," Owen answered, the edges of his lips curling up in a rueful smile. "Until now, I've never questioned what happened... I'd just assumed it was an accident."

Charlotte recalled her talk with Del on the steps of the ranch house just after the fire had been contained; he'd believed that it had been an accident, a thoughtless toss of a match that no one would ever fess up to.

"What are you saying?" she asked.

"What if the fire wasn't an accident," he suggested, "and the well polluting wasn't a prank? Who hated Grant enough and what else is he planning to do?"

*   *   *

Owen couldn't believe that he hadn't realized the connections before now; while it was obvious that the well had been intentionally ruined, he had never contemplated that the same could be said for the fire. Pouring kerosene down a well was malicious, mean intentioned, but not likely to do permanent damage. But setting a fire...If he and everyone else at the ranch hadn't risked their lives to put it out, there was no telling how big a catastrophe would've occurred, who might have been killed. How bloodthirsty a person was out there?

"This is crazy." Charlotte shook her head.

"Is it really?" Owen asked in answer. "Think of all the things that I've said to you about John Grant, about the hatred that I have for him. We would have to be spectacular fools to think that there's no one else out there that feels the same. He's not a good man."

Charlotte rose to her feet and walked over to where Owen stood. Gently, she took his hands in her own. "I told you, Owen." She looked deep into his eyes, holding him firmly in place, unable to look away. "I think you're wrong about him; I know that you are. If you hold this in your heart, you're making a huge mistake."

Owen thought of all Charlotte had said to him. She had tried to be persuasive, and in many ways she had been, making him look twice at facts he had previously taken for granted. Hatred had been his food for so long that he couldn't imagine backing away from its table, but he wavered now, unsure of where he stood. He thought back to how competently John Grant had acted during the fire, the sure way he had commanded men, Owen included, and wondered if it was possible for the man to be such a spectacular liar, a wolf in sheep's clothing.

If it were anyone other than Charlotte reminding him of Grant's qualities, he would have dismissed her without a moment's thought, but since it was Charlotte telling him these things, he had no choice but to consider what she said. Every moment he spent with her, he found himself more respectful of her logic. Her voice, her smile, her touch were what had drawn him to her, but there was more to her than beauty. She had compassion and understanding. That she had so much faith in him made him stronger, made him more eager to think matters through.

"Maybe," he admitted.

"It's possible that we're wrong about all of this," Charlotte continued. "It could have been an accident that started the fire and I can't really blame anyone for being unwilling to step forward and admit to it. Maybe the same thing is true about the well."

"That was no accident, Charlie."

"I'm sure you're right, but maybe the reason for its happening isn't as malicious as we think. It could be that someone's angry that he isn't making more money or that he had to muck out the horse stalls one too many times in a row and is trying to get back for it. I'm sure worse acts have been committed for even more childish reasons."

A part of Owen desperately wanted to accept what Charlotte was suggesting. Maybe he was jumping to conclusions, grasping at the wildest of straws, when the answer was much simpler. He could see that she wanted to believe another explanation. It would be so easy to just nod his head and tell her that she might well be right.

A silence settled between them, stretching on as each was deep in thought. Owen was fine with the stillness, patiently allowing it to linger, happy to be with her, even if the subject of their conversation was difficult. Gradually, he became aware that Charlotte was still holding on to his wrists; when she saw him notice, she became self-conscious and pulled away.

"I hope I didn't ruin your day by worrying you."

"It's my fault," she protested. "I shouldn't have pressed you about your mother."

Owen tenderly touched Charlotte on the chin, turning her face up until she was again looking him in the eyes. "I'm glad that you did," he reassured her. "I've never told anyone about what happened to my mother before. No one else seemed worth telling until you came along."

Charlotte beamed, his words clearly making her happy.

"Do you remember the first time that I drove you and Hannah into town?" he asked.

"When you were so mean to me?"

"Why do you have to say it like that, Charlie?"

"Because you *were* mean, terribly mean."

"Let's forget about that for a moment. I remember that you said that you wanted to go to the roller-skating rink," Owen said.

"And you thought that it would be a terrible idea..."

"How would you like to go and show me that I didn't know what I was talking about?"

Ever since the day he, Charlotte, and Hannah had driven by as the roller-skating rink tent was being erected, Owen had thought about it. In the weeks after, every drive gave him more food for thought, but mostly it gave him pause. Families and courting young lovers flocked to the rink, laughing and falling as they tried to manage the trick of staying upright on their skates. He'd wanted to broach the subject to Charlotte for a while, but it had never felt right until now.

"Are you asking me on a date?" she asked, unwilling to let him off easily.

"Aren't we on a date now?"

"You didn't give me any forewarning about today..."

"Then I suppose that's what I'm asking."

"Would it be all right with you if I asked Hale and Hannah to join us?" she asked, and when Owen gave her a sour look she added, "The more that you're around Hale, the more it's going to look like you're not capable of being a criminal. Besides, he'll be so interested in your sister, you'll be lucky if he even looks your way."

"You're probably right about that." He chuckled.

"Then it's a date."

"It is at that." He tilted his head toward hers.

When their lips touched, Owen was again filled with a strange sensation, a feeling that had been missing from him for so long he'd forgotten how it felt; he was filled with the conviction that his life was much, much better than it had been the day before...

Chapter Nineteen

W E'VE GONE OVER THIS I don't know how many times, Sarah. You should be able to figure out the answer by now."

"I know...I just don't...I just can't figure it out..."

Charlotte and Sarah again sat at the worn table in her cabin. Although the evening sun had begun its slow descent to the western horizon, its light still streamed in through the small, broken window, splashing color on the wall behind them. Since Charlotte arrived they had been working on arithmetic, a subject that Sarah had found exceptionally difficult. The problems she had been given weren't particularly hard, addition and subtraction of sums greater than one hundred, but they confused her.

"Remember to work your way from the right to the left."

"Where?" She looked at Charlotte pleadingly.

"The bigger number, the number on top," she answered patiently. "You may have to make changes to it in order to be able to subtract the smaller number, the one below it."

"What kind of changes?"

Charlotte sighed. It seemed to her as if they had already had this conversation, every day since she had first come to the cabin. It was frustrating, slow going. No matter how much she tried, Sarah kept running into the same problems again and again. To the girl's credit, the more they went over it, the more likely she would be to be able to remember the lesson being taught. The task required a tremendous amount of patience, but it wasn't all that different from working with her students in town. Still, Charlotte was worried about Sarah.

The change in Sarah's appearance since the last time Charlotte had seen her was dramatic: her hair was dirty and unkempt, snarled around her shoulders; her face was drawn and tired; dark circles underlined her eyes; fatigue rode her as if she were a plow horse. She sat now with her shoulders slumped, her head on her hand, propped up by her elbow. She seemed thinner than she should have been, as if she hadn't been eating properly. Charlotte supposed that her condition was due to her pregnancy, but she wondered if she should say something.

"All right," she encouraged. "I'll get you started and then you can do the rest."

While Sarah returned to her problems, her tongue lightly clenched between her teeth in deep concentration,

Charlotte thought about how happy she was that Alan Beck wasn't around. Ever since she had spoken to John about Alan's inappropriate advances toward her the last time she had been to the cabin, she'd wondered how he intended to keep the man away.

In the end, it hadn't been very hard.

She and John had driven to the cabin just after Owen brought her back to the ranch after school. At first, the ride had been uncomfortable for her. While they drove, she stole careful glances at Grant, hoping to see some resemblance between him and Owen and Hannah, but there weren't any obvious characteristics they shared; she knew this wasn't enough to rule out his parentage. She herself was said to be the image of her mother and looked nothing like her father. Still, after what Owen had told her about John, she couldn't help but wonder if she were mistaken and he *was* the villain Owen thought him to be. But then John had started telling her about a stubborn horse, his laughter rolling out his open window into the countryside, and she had forgotten all of her apprehension. Within minutes, she was convinced her defense of John Grant had been correct.

When they had finally arrived at the cabin, John honked the horn. Sarah had come to the door, but there had been no sign of Alan. Just as Charlotte was about to ask where he might be, Sarah's father had stumbled out from the rear of the cabin, a disheveled mess. He wore the same clothes she'd last seen him in with the addition of a dark stain that ran down the full front of his shirt. One of his boots was missing, though he didn't seem to mind. A green bottle hung limply from his fingers, and when he saw them he brought it to his lips. The sight of him made Charlotte's stomach turn.

"He's as drunk as a skunk," she observed in disgust.

"I wonder where he gets it," John said. "I tell you there ain't no bottle of booze in the supplies I brought out here."

"Maybe I shouldn't be here today."

"I told you that I'd make sure you weren't bothered by him. Take me at my word and trust in it."

John got out of the car and ambled over to the Becks, grabbed Alan firmly by the elbow, steered him away from the cabin and down the slope of a nearby hill. Alan didn't seem to like John's grip one bit, but wasn't capable of breaking loose, so he had no choice but to go along.

"Back to the lessons, ladies," John called over his shoulder. "He won't bother you."

Sitting with Sarah at the table, Charlotte knew that John would keep Alan away for as long as was needed, allowing for her to teach the man's daughter whether he wanted her to learn or not.

Charlotte was lost in thought, pondering the ranch troubles, when Sarah suddenly collapsed against the tabletop. Her scream split the silence that had descended upon them. She tipped out of her chair and landed hard on the wooden floor, as sobs began to rack her small body, and her shoulders shook. It happened so quickly, so surprisingly, that for an instant Charlotte could do nothing more than watch openmouthed.

"Sarah!" she finally shouted. "Sarah, what's the matter?"

But the girl was inconsolable, unreachable, fat tears rushing down her cheeks in a flood of emotion that showed no sign of letting up. Her body slid slowly from the table to the floor, to lie on her side. Her hands reached under her heavy belly, cradling its weight, as if the baby were in her arms, as her knees drew up and spittle ran from her mouth.

"Is it the baby?" Charlotte pleaded in panic. "Sarah, is it your baby? Is it coming? I can't do anything for you if you don't tell me what's the matter!"

Sarah's crying went on and on, rising in strength and timbre, echoing around the tiny room in an unending wail. The pencil the girl had been using on her numbers was still clutched tightly in her hand; Charlotte had to pry her fingers apart to work it free, fearful that Sarah might hurt herself with it.

"Sarah! Sarah!"

Unable to get any response, Charlotte rose to her feet and looked around for something, anything that might be able to help her. For all that she knew, Sarah's baby was coming early, about to be born on the floor of a filthy cabin far from any doctor.

If it were to happen, Charlotte had *some* knowledge of what to do; her grandmother and Rachel had been midwives back in Minnesota, and though she had never actually assisted in a birth, she'd listened to them talk about births enough that she knew the basics. She'd need blankets and boiling water and...

I need help and I need it now...

Charlotte quickly ran from the cabin and out into the Oklahoma evening. She felt helpless and alone, as if the cabin were an island surrounded by countless miles of sea. She shouted for John, again and again, her voice sounding small and weak. There was no response; she had no idea where he and Alan had gone or if there was any chance they could hear her.

She ran for the truck, but found that John had taken the keys with him; even had they been in the ignition, Charlotte knew she couldn't leave Sarah in order to get help, and she doubted she would have been able to raise the pregnant girl into the cab.

Rushing back into the cabin, Charlotte again knelt down beside the weeping girl, pushing stray strands of hair from her face and wiping the spittle from the corners of her mouth. Sarah continued to sob, her tears and gasps for breath audible in the quiet room.

"Sarah, listen to me," Charlotte said softly, doing all that she could to take the fear out of her voice. "Look at me, Sarah. I know that you're upset, but you need to put it out of your head and look at me." Though Sarah's crying never lessened, Charlotte kept trying. "You can do it; I know you can. Think about your baby, Sarah. Think about the child you've carried all this time."

Charlotte had no way of knowing how to reach Sarah, but she finally managed to get to her by talking about the baby. Sarah's sobs subsided. Her eyes, open and wet, searched Charlotte's face.

"There you go! That's the way!" Charlotte rejoiced. "Is it the baby? Can you tell me if it's because of your baby that you're so upset?"

"I'm . . . I'm so tired . . . I'm so tired all the time . . ." Sarah sobbed.

"It's not your baby?" Charlotte pressed.

"I . . . I don't think so . . ." She shook her head, her chin wrinkled, holding back another flood of tears.

"Oh, Sarah," Charlotte gasped, tears rising unbidden to her own eyes, tears of relief at the realization that the girl's baby wasn't about to be born after all.

They sat that way for a while, the two of them on the floor, Sarah's head in Charlotte's lap as she slowly stroked the girl's hair, trying to calm her. Eventually, Sarah's outburst subsided and they were blanketed in silence, the only sound an occasional crow's caw from outside. The sun's rays slid down the wall beside them, as if it were going into hiding, a child playing a game of hide-and-seek. While the sun set, Charlotte's anger rose.

That worthless, drunken old fool!

It was clear to Charlotte that Sarah was, as pregnant as she was, still shouldering the entire burden of her and her father's household. No matter how much John provided for them, he was limited in the things that he could do. Cooking, washing, and chopping firewood for the stove were all chores left to the Becks. Charlotte wondered just how many of these fell upon Sarah while Alan crawled into a bottle. It was as if the girl were his wife; no, it was worse, as if she were his slave. If Sarah was not careful, there was a good chance she would lose her child, if not her life.

Eventually, Charlotte managed to get Sarah into bed. The girl was asleep in an instant. Then Charlotte pulled up a chair and waited for John and Alan to return, furious indignation rising in her chest.

The sun was nearly set, only a sliver of burnt red and orange still peeking over the distant hills, when John and Alan finally made their way back to the cabin. Charlotte heard their boots crunching on the rocks and scrabble before they came into sight. She chose to meet them outside, fearful that what she was about to say and do might wake Sarah from her needed sleep.

Charlotte went right at Alan without hesitation, her finger in his face, pressing close despite the stench of liquor that covered him.

"How dare you, you worthless old fool!" she yelled, her seething anger finally breaking loose.

Alan recoiled from her, snorting in surprise. While he was clearly not as drunk as he had been when she'd arrived, his vision was still blurry.

"What in the hell?" He stumbled, nearly falling back on his rump as he stepped away from her.

"Charlotte?" John asked, equally taken aback. "What's gotten into you? Did somethin' happen?"

As far as Charlotte was concerned, it was as if John Grant weren't even there, so intent was she on Alan Beck. "Now you listen to me and you listen well, you lazy sot," she snapped, her voice as sharp as a knife. "That daughter of yours wasn't put on this earth to wait on you hand and foot, you good-for-nothing, no matter what you might believe otherwise!"

"Wait just a minute here—"

"I don't know if you've taken your head out of a bottle long enough to notice," she kept on, not wanting to allow him a word in edgewise until she had finished her piece, "but that young girl is well into her pregnancy and she deserves much better treatment than what you're giving her!"

Charlotte couldn't really believe the way that she was speaking to Alan; it was almost as if she were watching someone else administer a tongue-lashing. She had spent a long time in the cabin fuming about Sarah, and there was nothing to do but let it all out.

"Who in the hell do you think you are talkin' to me that way?" Alan bellowed, somehow managing to find his footing under the weight of Charlotte's onslaught. Crimson red color rose up his neck and spittle flew from his yellow teeth. He had the same look in his eyes as the night he had accosted her in the rain. Before he had frightened her, but now seeing him this way only served to make her angrier.

"I'm the woman who's not going to let you treat her the way you have been for even one more day! Right now she's in that cabin, sleeping from exhaustion, all because you force her to do the cooking, cleaning, and waiting on you day in and day out!"

"She's lyin'," Alan replied defensively, looking at John.

"Don't look at him," Charlotte demanded. "He's not going to help you."

Out of the corner of her eye, she could see John take a step back, the slightest hint of a smile curling at the edges of his mouth.

"Starting today you're going to become the father that girl has needed you to be for far too long. You will be there for her when she needs you; you're going to stop drinking, and you're going to do far more than your share of the household work. She needs regular meals, rest, affection, and plenty of peace and quiet. Do you understand me?"

Alan hesitated, clearly upset that he was being chastised by this slip of a girl. The age lines cut into his face seemed to grow deeper as he said, "This weren't the way it was supposed to be. She weren't supposed to be carryin' a kid . . . she's too young."

Charlotte reached out and grabbed a handful of the man's shirt. He had recoiled a bit when she moved toward him, but it hadn't stopped her.

"It's too late for excuses or to want for something else. Your daughter is going to be a mother and you are going to be a grandfather. This is the way it is going to be from now on. Starting today! She needs her family. Without a mother, her father should be the one to stand by her and see her through this."

Someway, somehow, Charlotte's words slowly cut through the years of neglect and alcohol that clouded Alan Beck's life: his eyes were downcast as they turned away from her, no longer able to hold her gaze; his shoulders slumped a bit, the confrontation bleeding out of him. When he spoke, his voice cracked with emotion. The fight seemed utterly drained from him.

"I guess I done failed that girl..."

"Then don't fail her anymore," Charlotte encouraged. She hadn't expected to be able to reach him; the best she hoped for was to be able to vent her frustration and anger and that maybe John would do something to change the Becks' situation. But now a flicker of hope flared in her chest. Maybe Alan could actually change. Maybe Sarah and her child wouldn't be all alone in the world after all.

Alan still held the liquor bottle he'd clutched when they had first arrived at the cabin; when he let it go, it fell to the ground, breaking against the rocks, the brown fluid that was left spilling out and soaking into the dry earth.

That's a good start...

"I don't want her to hate me..."

"Then walk in that door and give her a reason not to."

Alan nodded slowly and left them to walk toward the cabin, not looking back once until he had reached the door.

"I aims to do better," he said simply.

Those were the first words he had spoken that Charlotte believed.

Chapter Twenty

SATURDAY BROUGHT RAIN, a gentle tapping pitter-patter that woke Charlotte early, pulling her from a pleasant remembrance of her childhood, a dream of running beside Lake Washington, her loyal dog Jasper at her heels. Outside, the squall seemed destined for a short life; when she went to the window, blue skies were already breaking apart the overcast, dirty grey clouds in the east, the sun occasionally flashing into her eyes.

Charlotte brushed the sleep from her eyes, washing herself from her basin and dressing in the near-darkness. By the time she headed down the stairs, breakfast was already well under way. Plates full of pancakes, fried eggs, and sweet-smelling ham were set out beside cups of steaming coffee and pans of golden biscuits. Chairs creaked, silverware clinked against the heavy plates, and good humor abounded.

"—best get that done 'fore it gets out of hand..."

"That stubborn thing ain't gonna get the best of me today!"

"Bright-eyed and bushy-tailed as usual!"

Charlotte went into the kitchen and offered to help with whatever work still remained, but Amelia shooed her out, smiling brightly even though she must have been working for hours.

Hale held forth throughout the entire meal. Laughter filled the room, none louder than Hale's, but Charlotte noticed that his attention kept wandering to where Owen sat at the other end of the table, as if he expected to see a container of kerosene in the man's lap. Charlotte couldn't fault him; her attention kept being drawn in the same direction; she was rewarded with a wink when Owen seemed certain that no one else at the table would notice. But like Hale, her attention was also moving around the table. John Grant sat at the head of the table, his expression giving no indication of any unpleasantness.

"I can't imagine that sleeping out in the rain could be any worse than listening to your bellowing," Hannah teased Hale, her barb enough to still his tongue.

Once the meal had finished, the workingmen trudged out to start their day, while the women set about washing and drying the dishes. Charlotte kept an eye on Hannah, and when she started to head back to the cabin she shared with her brother Charlotte hurried along behind her.

During breakfast, the day had taken a considerable turn

for the better. The dewdrops that clung to blades of grass, panes of glass, and even the cobwebs woven between the wire fence sparkled in the sunlight. At her feet, purple locoweed flowers spread their petals skyward, somehow managing to avoid being stomped in the hustle and bustle all around them. The breeze was pleasant, rustling Charlotte's blond curls.

"I can hear you back there," Hannah singsonged over her shoulder.

"I wasn't trying to hide from you."

"You weren't?" she said with a playful grin. "You could have fooled me."

Up close, Charlotte was startled as always by how closely Hannah resembled Owen, though she shouldn't have been surprised; they were twins after all. But where Owen's face was rugged, his sister's similar looks, from the curve of her jawline to the small creases in the corners of her eyes, were softer, alluring, and enticing. There wasn't much doubt why Hale was so smitten.

"I wanted to talk to you but thought that I should wait until we could be alone."

"Is it a secret?" Hannah asked hopefully.

"Sort of," Charlotte answered. "Owen and I were wondering if you wanted to come with us to the roller-skating rink tonight."

"You and *Owen* were wondering?" she asked, a curious smile blossoming across her face, her eyes sparkling mischievously.

Charlotte nodded. Ever since she and Owen had shared their first kiss, she had wondered what, if anything, he would tell his sister. In the time since Charlotte had arrived at the ranch, she and Hannah had grown close, a friendship she was happy to have. She wouldn't have been embarrassed to have Hannah know about their relationship, but clearly Owen had chosen to remain silent.

"I thought that my brother was doing his best to drive you crazy, with all of the teasing and whatnot."

"He still teases me sometimes," Charlotte admitted, "but then there are other times when..." She couldn't say more and blushed instead.

"Did he tell you...about us?" Hannah asked hesitantly.

"He told me the reason why you came to Oklahoma. He told me what he believes happened to your mother."

Hannah nodded. "I don't agree with everything Owen has done." His sister sighed. "I'm still not used to having a different name. I keep expecting to blurt out 'Wallace' and give the whole thing away."

"I imagine it would be hard."

"Even with my job at the lawyer's office, I'm always frightened that my snooping will be found out and I'll be fired. Thankfully Barnaby is quite messy, so he has enough trouble sorting through the papers covering his desk, he doesn't notice when a file isn't just where it's supposed to be."

Charlotte wanted to press further, to learn whether

Hannah saw the same things her brother did in the scant evidence she had found in the lawyer's office, but she couldn't bring herself to press.

"Going skating *does* seem like it would be fun," Hannah admitted. "Certainly better than my usual nights."

Charlotte brightened. "What we're proposing is a break from your everyday work and worries. It's a chance to take a night out on the town, do something different, and have fun."

Hannah's smile grew brighter. "But what I don't understand is why you would want me to come along with the two of you. When a couple wants some time together, especially if they're in the mood for romance, the last thing they need is another person tagging along."

"It's not like that between Owen and me."

"Why ever not?"

"The reason that we were asking you," Charlotte explained, ignoring Hannah's teasing, "was because that first day we drove into town together, the day they were putting in the rink, you seemed so excited about it that it wouldn't seem right for us to go without you. Besides, I was hoping that..."

"Hoping what?" Hannah asked, hands on her hips.

Charlotte paused; it was ironic that, when the moment arrived to tell Hannah of her intentions, she ended up as flustered as Hale, unable to say what she wanted. She wondered if this was what he always went through, a tongue-tied, nervous feeling that he just couldn't shake.

"I thought...I thought that maybe...you'd like to go skating with Hale."

"Hale McCoy?"

A sickening feeling of disappointment spread in Charlotte's gut at the realization that there was no way that Hannah would accept. She felt like a fool. She could only hope that Hannah wouldn't choose to tease Hale even more than she did, lording his offer over him in mean-spirited humor. But then Hannah's expression softened, if only a fraction.

"Did he put you up to this?"

"Not at all," she answered truthfully...depending on how you chose to look at it.

"I hope that you don't think I'm a fool, Charlotte."

"I would never think such a thing."

"Because you would have to be deaf, blind, dumb, and likely dead to not realize how smitten Hale is with me," Hannah explained. "From the first time I ever met him, not an hour off the train from Colorado, I could see that he was more than an enormous ox of a man with a voice louder than thunder but also a bashful, bumbling boy unable to string five words together without blushing like a beet.

"But I'd also have to be without any of my senses not to see that he's a good man with a heart that's almost always in the right place. I always figured that someday he'd screw up enough courage to start talking to me.

"I suppose I've tortured him long enough. I can't say

that I haven't had my fun." Hannah sighed, and then gave a quick laugh. "All right, I'll go."

Charlotte was delighted. Besides her hope that Hale and Hannah might finally be able to spend some time together, she also wanted Hale to see Owen in a different light, to know him better and to realize that he was not capable of fouling the well with kerosene. Now, there would at least be the chance.

"Hale really didn't put you up to this?" Hannah asked. "He wasn't so shy that he couldn't do it himself?"

"It's not like that at all! Honest, it's not!"

"Then that must mean that he doesn't know you've asked me."

"I didn't want to say anything to him until after I'd had a chance to talk to you first," Charlotte explained. "There didn't seem to be any point in getting his hopes up if you didn't want to go."

"That makes sense," she agreed, "although I would give just about anything to see his face when you tell him that he's going on a date with me. I hope that you don't expect me to stop teasing him just because I agreed to this."

"Not in the least."

"Good." Hannah laughed. "Because I wouldn't even if you did!"

They made plans for when to be ready out in front of the main house for the drive into town. Charlotte had just begun to walk away, to go tell Hale the surprising and exciting news, when Hannah called to her.

"When you talk to Hale, you might want to step back from him a little ways."

"What for?"

"Because he's going to do one of two things," she explained. "He's going to either pass out or throw up on your shoes."

For a minute, Charlotte thought one of Hannah's predictions was going to come true; Hale wobbled, his knees suddenly going slack, eyeballs bulging out of his head, jaw hanging open. He looked as if he were drunk. Odds were that he would have collapsed at her feet had it not been for the conveniently close fence post that he clung to.

"Hale?" she asked, concerned. "Are you going to be all right?"

"We're goin' roller-skatin'?" Charlotte would have thought that Hale would have been over the moon with excitement at the prospect of going out for the evening with Hannah, but instead he looked sick.

"Take a deep breath."

He tried to oblige.

Charlotte had found him standing alone beside the largest of the ranch's horse corrals. Within the fenced enclosure, there was not a single horse to be seen; it had been emptied because the ranch was scheduled to receive twenty new horses later that afternoon, wrangled by Dave Powell and a couple of the other men, from Willingston, a town a few miles to the north. The ranch hands had been busy preparing for them for days. Owen had been among a group of men when she had arrived, and though he hadn't acknowledged her, she felt his eyes upon her, unwavering.

Hale had been happy to see her...until she started talking. Wide-eyed, he had listened as she recounted most of her conversation with Hannah; she thought it wise to leave out the parts where Hannah had known about his infatuation from the beginning, as well as the fact that she enjoyed mercilessly teasing him; if Hannah wanted to tell him all of that, it would be up to her to do so. The effect of her words was almost instantaneous.

"I...I can't believe you did that!" Hale exclaimed. "I just can't believe it!"

"But she said that she would go with you," Charlotte argued. "How can that possibly make you so upset?"

"Don't you understand? Now I gotta come up with somethin' for us to talk about, figure out what sorts of compliments I can give her, and even find me some clean clothes," he explained. "I can't rightfully take out a girl like Hannah with work stains up and down my shirt and britches!"

"It's not that bad!"

"That don't even take into 'count that I smell like a horse stall!"

Charlotte could barely suppress a smile. Hannah was certainly right about one thing: Hale's heart was definitely in the right place.

"You'll have plenty of time to get cleaned up," she

explained. "All the way until seven o'clock. That's when Owen and I will meet the two of you at the ranch house and from there we can drive to town."

"You and Owen?"

This was the one part of the story that Charlotte had neglected to tell him, choosing instead to focus on the fact that Hannah had agreed to accompany him to the roller-skating rink.

"We're all going to go together," she explained cheerfully.

Hale frowned. "I don't know about that, Charlotte."

"Are you telling me that you would give up a date with Hannah, the girl you have been pining away for from the first day she arrived here, all because you're unsettled by the idea of being around Owen, who, I might add, is the girl-of-your-dreams' brother?"

"It ain't that simple . . ."

"Do tell!"

"I ain't tryin' to upset you, but I got me a responsibility to John Grant and the ranch to make sure all's well. Just like I already told you, far as I'm concerned, Owen's the one most likely to have ruined that well, regardless of the fact that he's Hannah's brother."

Ever since she had seen Hale at the breakfast table, Charlotte had been hoping that he had found a reason to absolve Owen, some evidence that was contrary to his earlier accusation of guilt. She was disappointed that Hale was as suspicious as ever.

"I told you before that I thought you were looking at the wrong man," she reminded him, straightening her back in a clear indication that she meant to stand her ground. "I just think that if you spent some time with Owen, if you really let yourself get to know him a bit, you'd soon realize that he couldn't possibly be responsible for what you're accusing him of."

"I know you think kindly on him," Hale said, looking down on her with eyes that were filled with confusion, "maybe even a bit more strongly than that, least from where I'm standin', but I think you should be careful. I've come to care for you an awful lot since you've been here, like a brother would a sister," he hastily added out of fear she might take it the wrong way, "so I'm gonna do my best to look out for you."

"Then come to the roller-skating rink. What better way to ensure that Owen doesn't make any untoward advances?"

Hale sighed heavily, realizing that he was never going to be allowed to win the argument. "All right, you win." He threw up his hands. "But don't think that I ain't gonna be watchin' you like a hawk."

"If you can manage to take your eyes off Hannah long enough!"

Charlotte found Hale's overprotectiveness flattering and rose up on her tiptoes to give him a kiss on the cheek; she wondered if Owen was still watching them and if what she was doing made him nervous.

Before Hale could so much as mumble a form of reply, a shout rose up from somewhere close by; all heads turned to see Dave Powell leading the ranch's latest batch of horses to their new home. It was quite the sight to behold; dozens upon dozens of hooves pounded the earth as the horses, their ears pricked high and whinnies rumbling in their throats, came toward her and Hale. Dave and the other men kept circling the horses tightly, not allowing them much room to maneuver. Charlotte's breath caught in her throat. To see so many beautiful creatures together was a sight she was thankful to behold.

"Hold 'um, men!" Hale bellowed, springing into action.

The ranch yard was alive with activity. Men worked furiously at a multitude of tasks, whistling and shouting, pulling open gates, whirling coils of rope over their heads, and waving their hats this way and that. Owen stood opposite her, he and another man ready to funnel a number of the horses into the largest corral. John Grant supervised them nearby with Del, the two of them enjoying the spectacle.

And on the horses came...

Large and majestic, taut muscles straining at their forequarters, the horses surged forward. Charlotte marveled at their many colors: dirty white and tan, coal black, mottled grey, earthy brown, and every shade in between. Though she had been at the ranch for several weeks, she hadn't managed to lose her sense of wonder when she saw them and she had never seen this many at one time.

Stepping up on the bottom rung of the nearest corral fence, Charlotte strained to survey all the activity. The lead horses, just behind Dave Powell's saddled mare, entered into the narrow space between the first two corrals. Now the task was to move them into the corrals.

From where Charlotte stood, she could see nearly to the end of the train of horses. She found herself smiling uncontrollably, but just as she was thinking how wonderful it would be for Christina to see something like this, she caught sight of something troubling at the rear of the procession.

A ranch hand she didn't recognize, slightly older and with a large stomach that overhung his pants, leaned against a gate as if he didn't have a care in the world. That was what drew her attention to him; his lack of activity was so obviously different from that of the other men.

Then he picked up a board that, from a distance, looked as if it had a couple of nails driven through it. He looked around carefully, as if he wanted to see if there were any eyes on him. He never looked in Charlotte's direction.

What is that man doing?

Without warning, the man swung the board hard, driving it into the rump of one of the last horses in the procession. The black horse screamed in pain, rearing up on its back legs, huge eyes wide and rolling, before finally hurtling headlong into the group of animals just in front of it. Its panic caused a chain reaction; it was like watching a boulder as it began to roll down a hillside or a tree just cut as it crashed to the ground, each picking up speed as it went. One wild horse collided with a second who struck a third, which barreled into a fourth and fifth, and so on until what was once an orderly group became a riot, a calamity that instantly roared out of control.

There was nothing that anyone could do fast enough to stop it. It was a stampede, and it was coming right at the men.

Chapter Twenty-one

CHARLOTTE COULDN'T SHAKE the feeling that the scene unfolding before her wasn't actually real; it was as if she were watching an adventure serial or a newsreel at the theater. Panicked horses churned up the earth, the previously pleasant clopping replaced with a threatening thunder that shook the ground. Eyes bulged and manes twitched as the situation grew deadly serious. The fear was so thick in the air that she felt as if she could reach out and touch it.

With the horses trapped between the wooden fences of the corrals, there was nowhere for them to go but forward; they raced that way in a state of frenzy. Dave Powell tried to turn his horse toward the ruckus behind him, but it caught up to him so quickly that there was nothing he could do. The muscles on his forearms strained as he desperately tried to maintain control of his horse, but his mount was determined to bolt and he found himself swept up in the melee.

Ahead of her, Charlotte could see Hale's mouth opening and closing, as he shouted instructions, but she couldn't hear a sound save for the charging horses and the incessant beating of her own heart.

Someone was going to get killed...

The situation was growing worse by the second. One of the ranch hands was unlucky enough to be caught in the passageway between the corrals; the man was too close to the onrushing horses to have time to squeeze through the fence to safety. The first horse struck, smashing him into the railing with impressive force before sending him crashing to the ground in a heap. The horse barreled on. Charlotte feared that the man had been killed. Then she was relieved to see him curl up his body and cover his head with his arms.

While most of the stampeding horses raced straight forward, several of the more panicked animals tried to find other ways to get away; a black horse with a white spot high between its eyes leaped into the air, bringing its hooves crashing into a section of fence, intent on getting either over it or through it. The force of the horse's blow buckled the wood, but the fence held. The screams the horses made spoke of their terror.

Snippets of conversation floated to where Charlotte stood, incomplete and unfinished.

"... get to the gate before..."

"Watch out for that..."

"Charlie needs..."

"Luke! Be careful of that..."

Charlotte felt that she should do something, but she had no idea what. As on the day of the fire, she knew that nothing was expected of her, but that didn't mean that she didn't want to help. She would never be content to stand by while others worked.

Before she could decide on a course of action, a horse collided flush with the fence of the corral on which she stood. Its powerful body sent such strong reverberations down the length of the rails that Charlotte's hands were unable to maintain their grip and she was flung off and onto the ground, landing painfully hard on her hip.

Quick as she could, Charlotte righted herself. Only moments before, she had felt that the events unfolding around her were straight out of the motion pictures, but now they seemed unbearably real. While the danger of the fire had pressed her from all sides, she had not known the fear she felt now.

Thankfully, the terrorized horses were not racing forward in a steady group, but straggling along. Just next to her, a tan and white horse hurtled past, a few feet from where she sat, frothy spittle flying from its lips, the wind of its passing strong enough to tug at her clothes. In front of her, horses continued to collide with one another, into the railings, everywhere they could possibly go; a pair of them even managed to make their way into the main corral as had been intended. The chaos was everywhere, overpowering.

You've got to move ... you've got to go now or you'll be trampled!

Desperately, Charlotte looked around for help; it was then that she saw Owen. He was opposite her, halfway through the fence, his eyes on her as he gauged their surroundings. Suddenly, he raced into the gap between two horses, waved his arms at the deadly approach of another, before diving headlong to his left, landing on the ground and rolling until he reached her. Without a word, he covered her with his body, shielding her as another horse pounded past, its powerful hooves missing his leg by scant inches.

"We can't stay here!" he said in her ear.

"You don't need to tell me that!" she murmured in confusion. "What?"

"Now isn't the time to ask questions! Go! Go! Get to your feet and run!"

Unsteadily, Charlotte did as Owen told her, rising to her feet and stumbling forward, paying no attention to the charging horses as she desperately tried to make her way to the fence railing. Safety lay beyond, so she focused on it. Her hip hurt from where she had landed on the ground, but she ignored it as best she could. The fence was so close, only a matter of feet, but it seemed miles.

Without warning, Owen shoved her hard from behind, sending her sprawling into the loose dirt, her chin striking the ground. She never thought to pause and wonder what had happened, choosing instead to crawl and scramble, one handful of dirt following another, inch by painful inch. She was just about to the bottom rail of the fence, about to crawl under to safety, when a sound reached her ears that stopped her cold, freezing the blood in her veins.

Behind her, Owen yelled in agony.

The force of the collision lifted Owen from his feet as easily as if he had been a rag doll, tossing him into the air without effort. The blow from the horse's thick body was tremendous, sending brilliant chards of pain running wildly down the length of Owen's body. It brought an agony unlike anything he had ever felt before. For a long moment, everything went blacker than the deepest night. His head incessantly rang like a church bell on the day of a wedding. All the air in his lungs was driven out by the force of the impact, leaving him gasping for air; he winced painfully from the effort and wondered if he hadn't cracked a rib. When he hit the ground, he was so dazed that he thought he must have banged his head against a rock or a fence post. Desperately, he struggled against the urge to sleep, to close his eyes and let the pain simply fade away.

When the stampede began, he'd been standing beside Pete, preparing the corral for the horses' imminent arrival. The stampede had happened so quickly, so unexpectedly, that Owen had stood frozen in those first seconds, in disbelief. Then his concern for Charlotte easily overrode his surprise.

Charlie! he shouted silently.

Owen found her on the fence rail and had hoped that she had enough good sense to climb over and run to safety. But then she had fallen and he'd begun to run. Facing down the onrush of terrified horses, he'd proceeded without regard for his own life; it was irrelevant, unnecessary. Nothing mattered except getting Charlotte out of the corral.

Once he'd managed to make it to where she lay, Owen had been glad but hardly relieved; they were still in the corral with the frenzied horses. Once he'd gotten Charlie moving, a horse turned directly toward her. Owen acted without thought, pushing her out of the way even though it had placed him right in the path of the charging animal. He'd closed his eyes an instant before he'd been struck.

And damn! It hurt!

Now he lay on his back, blinking the confusion from his eyes. Everything seemed muted, dull. Blackness crept over his vision and the pounding of the horses' hooves, their panicked whinnying, sounded like it was happening far away. Somehow, he managed to turn his head to see Charlotte just out of his reach. She was shouting at him, but he couldn't hear a word she said. Deep down he knew that he needed to get to her.

With great effort, Owen rolled over onto his side, then to his knees. For all he knew, another horse might be barreling toward him, intent on finishing the job the first had started, but he hadn't the energy to look. He kept his eyes locked on Charlotte, even if he couldn't see her clearly, and never wavered.

"You can make it, Owen!" he heard her shout.

I hope you're right, Charlie...

A horse's hoof landed so close to Owen's foot that, he knew in his befuddled mind, when it rose to take another step it would strike his boot. At any moment he could be severely injured, perhaps killed. All he could do to prevent it was keep going...

Suddenly, a huge shape loomed up before him, blocking out Charlotte. He couldn't tell if it was on her side of the fence or his, but it surprised him so much that he quit moving.

"Give me your hand, damn it!" a man's voice shouted.

Owen heard it as clearly as if his head were submerged in the horses' water trough, but the meaning wasn't lost on him. Straining his sore muscles until his shoulder hurt from the effort, he reached out, wriggling his fingers, hoping to find purchase. Like a vise, a hand clamped down on him, pulling him roughly across the ground and through the fence.

"You're hurt!" Charlotte cried, her hands touching his face.

"It isn't...that bad," Owen wheezed. "Just...every bone in...my body..."

"Just lie there. Don't move."

"Don't think...I got much choice in the matter..."

The last of the traumatized horses raced past heading down the remaining length of the passageway. Men ran after them, shouting, yelling, and whistling more to one another than to get the horses' attention. The whole thing hadn't lasted longer than a few minutes, maybe two or three, but that had been more than enough time for significant damage to be done.

Owen lay still, hoping that the world around him would finally stop spinning. It was just beginning to slow a bit when a man's face leaned down toward him. He recognized him immediately; even as dazed as Owen was, it was impossible to miss a man Hale's size.

"I reckon that...I got you to thank for pulling me out of the way..."

"You would've done the same for me, wouldn't you?" Hale asked, a hint of a smile poking through his rough exterior.

"Maybe," Owen answered. "Don't know if I'd be strong enough...to pull you out, though..."

Hale chuckled, the humor a pleasant break from the wreckage the stampede had wrought. "You done right good today."

"He saved my life!" Charlotte exclaimed.

"And for that I'm grateful." Hale nodded. "But now ain't the time for us to be thankin' each other. Now's the time to figure out what the hell just happened."

Charlotte started to say something, but it was lost to

Owen. The urge to close his eyes had become too great to ignore, so instead of continuing to fight it, he gave in and let the blackness wash over him.

Charlotte sat on a pile of hay bales that had been tossed beside the open doors of the tack barn. She was glad to be out of the afternoon sun but annoyed when she had to occasionally swat at insistent flies buzzing about her head; they seemed utterly absorbed with nipping at her, even after she managed to kill a couple of them.

A couple of hours had passed since the stampede that had nearly cost her and Owen their lives. Her heart still hadn't managed to settle down. Every loud noise, the sound of a hammer being tossed aside or one of Salt's barks, set her off, certain that another calamity was about to take place.

Owen had been taken up to the main house just as soon as the horses were rounded up and safely put away in their corrals. A couple of other men were hurt even more seriously than Owen. Charlotte had followed the procession, fretting every step of the way, holding on to Owen's hand so tightly that their fingers had gone white. Once he was placed in a room, the tears she'd been holding back burst free. Owen tried to assure her that there was nothing to worry about; he even promised that he would be well enough for them to go roller-skating later in the week. Amelia had come in and shooed her away, explaining that there was nothing she could do for him besides worrying herself sick.

And that's exactly what I've done ever since…

Del had comforted her for a while, trying to explain to her that these sorts of things happened from time to time, part of living on a ranch, and that there was nothing that could have been done to prevent it, but he was soon called away to help with the repairs to the broken fence posts.

"I hear that you had something of a close call."

Charlotte looked up to see John Grant's smiling face; she couldn't tell if it was the shadows thrown by the barn, but he looked older all of a sudden, as if the events of the day had prematurely aged him.

"I could have been killed. Owen too."

"Speakin' for all of us, I'm mighty happy to see the two of you still with us."

"The only reason that I am here is Owen," Charlotte told him, eager to provide another example of how utterly mistaken everyone at the Grant Ranch was about Owen. "I was frozen in place. I wanted to move, but looking at those horses barreling toward me, I just couldn't will myself forward. Owen came to me. If it wasn't for him…"

"Hale told me all 'bout it. Don't think that it's gonna go unrewarded."

"He's a good man."

"Even more than I gave him credit for, it seems."

Charlotte couldn't help but read into what John was

telling her; he had such an easygoing nature, grandfatherly and warm, that he was nearly impossible to figure out. She knew that she could go crazy trying to unravel all of the mysteries she had encountered in Oklahoma and, quite frankly, she was too tired to try tonight.

"Been a long time since we had horses get so out of control," John said. "Usually it's only one or two that get out of sorts. Today must've reminded you of the days you can't control them kids at school."

Charlotte struggled to fix a smile on her face. Ever since the stampede at the corral, all she'd been able to think about was the shocking sight of the heavyset ranch hand violently swinging a board into the horse's rump. It seemed so impossible that she began to wonder if she'd imagined it or it was a misunderstanding. He'd been quite a ways away from her, down on the far end of the procession of horses, but she'd been looking right at him. Surely, he couldn't have done what she thought he had?

From somewhere deep inside her, Charlotte thought it might be a huge mistake to tell John what she had seen. Likely, he would think she was traumatized from nearly being trampled. If he *did* believe her, he'd want as many details as she could give him; maybe he would even walk her about the ranch, expecting her to pick out the man she had accused. The worst would be if he thought she was lying. Her growing relationship with Owen would cloud any claim she might make; after all, wouldn't she say anything to remove suspicion from the man she had become romantically involved with?

Before she did anything, she needed to talk to Owen. They needed to be united before any decision was made.

"Let's just hope that there isn't a next time," she said weakly.

"Amen to that."

As John walked away, Charlotte swore to herself that she would talk to Owen and they would get to the bottom of what was happening on the ranch. From the fire, to the well, and now to the stampede of horses, it seemed as if the ranch was cursed. If someone was behind all that had happened he needed to be stopped before something worse happened.

Chapter Twenty-two

THE TRUCK'S HEADLIGHTS cut through the thick darkness that blanketed the countryside outside of Sawyer. Owen, Charlotte, Hannah, and Hale drove into town to the roller-skating rink. The chirp of crickets and cicadas pierced the night, a keening that rose and fell, sharp to the ear. The moon hung just above the hilltops; only a few stars were bright enough to compete with its brilliant light. The night was much cooler than the evenings that had preceded it, and a low hanging fog clung to the air above the creek that ran parallel to the road.

"Aren't you cold with the window open?" Charlotte asked Hannah, wedged between her and Owen in the truck's cab.

"It's not so bad," she answered, her hair drifting in the breeze flowing from outside.

Charlotte shivered. "It's cooler than it has been."

"Must mean there may be a storm on the way," Owen observed. "Since we've been in Oklahoma, it seems that once the temperature drops, a day or two later there's one heck of a storm."

"I don't like it." Charlotte frowned as she rubbed her arms for warmth.

"I wonder if Hale is cold," Hannah said worriedly.

Hale bounced around in the bed of the truck as it made its way down the dirt road. It was impossible for all four of them to ride in the cab. With his hair slicked flat over his head, Hale was dressed in his finest clothes; Hannah whispered that it was the outfit he always wore to church. Charlotte thought that Owen's sister was flattered she rated so high. But then they were all dressed up for the night out. Charlotte wished she had thought to bring a jacket.

"Are you doing all right back there?" Hannah shouted out the window.

"What?" Hale bellowed, tapping his ear.

"I said, are you doing—?"

"He can't hear a word you're saying," Owen said.

Instead of continuing to holler, Hannah turned around and blew Hale a kiss. His face instantly flushed deep red.

"I still don't think it was such a good idea that you came along," Charlotte said to Owen. "A good night's sleep is what you need."

"There's nothing wrong with me."

"Oh, really," Charlotte said as she lightly brushed her fingers against his ribs.

"Ouch!" Owen winced, the truck weaving enough for Hale to rap his huge hand against the window out of concern. "Knock it off!"

"That's what I thought."

"You'd flinch, too, if I pushed that hard against your ribs!"

"I barely touched you!"

"It didn't feel like it."

"It's too bad that he didn't get hit in the head." Hannah smiled, leaning across Charlotte to give her brother a sly, mischievous grin. "With all the rocks he keeps in it, he wouldn't have felt a thing."

"Very funny," Owen said sarcastically.

"I'm starting to feel sorry for him," Charlotte added, getting in on the act.

"Why's that?"

"Do you remember what you said the first time we saw them putting up the roller-skating rink tent? You said that you've never been on skates before."

"So what?" He frowned. "Why?"

"Skating is a lot harder than it looks. There are a lot of people who aren't particularly graceful on their own feet, so you can imagine what it's like when they strap four wheels beneath each foot. It takes a while to get used to skates. Most people who have never been on them before tend to fall down a lot. Now, imagine what it would be like for a person already hurt. Falling over and over onto the wooden floor doesn't sound like a fun evening to me."

Owen said nothing, staring silently forward, his jaw set firm.

"You better watch it." Hannah laughed. "If you keep that up, he might turn the truck around and take us back to the ranch!"

Only the two women in the cab laughed.

Sawyer soon came into view; only a few lights shone from the houses on the town's outskirts, more faintly than the street lamps that lined Main Street. For a Saturday night, the town was quiet, although there seemed to be more activity at the tavern farther up the road. A few cars and trucks were parked near the entrance to the roller-skating rink tent. Colored flags lolled lazily at the tops of the tent poles, stirred by the scant breeze. When Owen parked, organ music floated through the truck's open window.

"This is going to be great!" Hannah declared. Whipping open the door, she jumped outside, spreading her arms in the fresh night air. "C'mon, Hale!"

"Okay."

"No point in wasting time!" she shouted, not waiting. Hale leaped out of the truck bed and hurried along behind, following her like a loyal puppy.

Owen smiled. "It looks like fun."

"Are you sure that you can do this?" Charlotte asked in earnest. "I was teasing you earlier, but you probably will fall down quite a bit. We can always come back some other night and skate."

"I'll be fine, but if you're so worried about me, then I guess you're gonna have to stay close to me to make sure I stay on my feet."

Charlotte stared at Owen suspiciously. "If I didn't know better, I'd swear that was your intention all along."

"I like being close to you, Charlie, but even I'm not dumb enough to let a horse run me over just so I can get your attention!"

After Owen paid the man at the entrance, they passed through a wooden gate and stepped out onto the floor of the roller-skating rink. Three tent poles rose up from the floor, high into the air, supporting an enormous blue canvas tent. The floor was larger than she had expected, shining brightly under the glare of the lights that had been strung down the middle of the tent and around the edges. Waltz music played on a record, broadcast over a loudspeaker hung in the corner, the needle occasionally skipping a beat. People of all ages skated around and around in circles, the well dressed and shabby alike, both old and young, some as couples and others with friends, all laughing and smiling as they rolled past, some of them struggling to keep their balance. Others stopped to rest on benches that had been set out along the edges of the floor. Charlotte caught sight of Paige Spratt as she skated past, arm in arm with her husband; he was as rail thin and awkward looking as his wife. Charlotte's fellow teacher gave her a dismissive look, her nose raised high in disdain. Charlotte stifled a laugh; tonight, of all nights, she wouldn't let anything mar her time with Owen.

"Oh, that looks like such fun!" Charlotte exclaimed.

"Sure does," Owen agreed, though his hand went to favor his bruised ribs.

Over in the corner just inside the entrance, an older man stood behind a tall counter. They gave him their shoe sizes; he bent down and came back up with skates for them to clamp onto their shoes. They sat down on nearby benches to put them on.

"You slip that through there and then you—" Charlotte said when it looked as if Owen was struggling with his skates.

"I know what I'm doing." He frowned. "I'm not totally worthless, you know!"

"You could have fooled me!"

Charlotte had come to love the playfulness between them. Though Owen was undeniably rough around the edges, there was much more to him than she would ever have guessed after their first drive into town. It was comforting to have him with her, sharing a laugh, giving her guff. But it was when she remembered what he had done for her earlier in the week, how he had nearly been killed saving her from the slashing hooves, that she realized how special what they had together was becoming. That he had insisted on coming skating was proof of his interest in her. Taking his hand in hers, she expected him to make some wise comment, something like *What are you doing that for?*, but instead he only smiled.

"What's taking you so long?" Hannah asked as she whizzed by, proving to be a natural on her skates.

"We're coming," Charlotte answered.

"Isn't this just what you were wishing for, Hale?" Owen's sister shouted over her shoulder at her date.

Hale looked as uncomfortable on skates as one of his beloved horses might look in a dress. His huge arms flailed at his sides as he desperately tried to maintain his balance, sweat dripping down his face. Rather than letting his skates glide over the wooden floor, he lifted them high before putting them down, as if he were simply walking down the street. All of the other skaters smiled at him as they went by, steering wide of him out of fear that if he went down he might take them with him.

"This...this is harder...than it looks..." he mumbled.

Hannah turned around and headed right back toward Hale. When he saw her coming, he stumbled, crashing down onto his backside with such a thud that it seemed the whole rink shook.

"Don't think for one second that I'm going to try to pick you back up." Hannah smiled. "You're on your own!"

Sheepishly, Hale rolled over onto his side and achingly, painstakingly struggled back to his feet; the only thing that he seemed to have wounded was his pride.

"The next song will be all skate," a man's voice announced over the loudspeaker. "Everybody skate." The scratch of a record needle was heard, followed by the sound of pleasant organ music. Many of the people who had been content to sit on the benches set up along the side rose to their feet and began skating, crowding the floor.

"Are you ready?" Charlotte asked Owen.

"I don't suppose you'd wait for me if I wasn't," he answered.

"I would."

"I know." Owen smiled, and then pushed off onto the floor.

Charlotte was pleasantly surprised to find that Owen was better on roller skates than she had expected. He took things slow, grabbing onto her arm now and again when his balance wavered, and fell only once, an awkward landing that caused him to wince dramatically, his teeth bared in pain. Around and around the rink they went, their hands clasped, troubles momentarily forgotten, and both of them happy. Hannah and Hale occasionally glided past, Hale desperately trying to keep up, but they didn't notice, keeping the evening to themselves.

"All right now," the man's voice said on the loudspeaker after a number of records had ended, "it's time for couples only. Couples only for 'The Skaters' Waltz.' Couples only."

More than half of the people who were on the floor retreated to the benches, leaving pairs of men and women for the next dance. Charlotte was happy to see that Hannah and Hale remained. Hale was so happy to have Hannah's hands in his own that he blushed as red as a tomato.

Maybe there's hope for them yet…

"I suppose that a couples' dance would mean us," Owen said softly into Charlotte's ear.

"It does," she answered, losing herself in his eyes for an instant.

Charlotte took the lead, taking one of his hands in her own and placing her other on his shoulder; Owen followed with a hand on her waist. As the music played, a soft medley that reminded Charlotte of a song her grandmother had been fond of, they skated together, side by side at first, then, to Owen's surprise, with Charlotte turned so that she was skating backward.

"You're pretty good at this," Owen said, impressed.

"I grew up in Minnesota, remember?"

"Where your father must have made a fortune in the roller-skating business."

Charlotte laughed loudly. "No, silly." She playfully pinched him. "The winters freeze the lakes hard enough to ice-skate on for months. Being on roller skates isn't *that* different from being on ice skates."

"I'm having enough trouble staying off the floor on these." Owen shrugged. "I don't have any urge to try anything else. But I suppose we're not going to find many frozen lakes here in Oklahoma."

They skated along together, Charlotte enjoying the way he looked at her, at least when he wasn't glancing down at his feet. It was then, her hand in his, the music reaching a crescendo, the lights flashing by as their skates hummed against the floor, that Charlotte realized she had completely fallen for Owen Wallace. He wasn't what she had expected to find in a man, but she had found him nonetheless. He'd saved her life, sweetly picked her up from work, gently kissed her, and even been a pain in her backside. She'd fallen for him for all of those things. She wondered what her sister, Christina, would think of him. She even liked the idea that put them out on the roller-skating rink floor, that they were a couple. There was no telling where they would go, but she hoped that they would go together.

Just as she was about to tell Owen what she was feeling, a loud ruckus at the entrance to the rink caused every head to turn in that direction. Three men had pushed their way inside without paying, shoving past the ticket seller. Each of them looked to be drunk, eyes wild and bodies swaying. The one in front, a mean-looking sort with a thin scar running the length of one side of his jawline, pulled a pack of cigarettes from his pocket and brazenly lit up, staring holes in all those who skated past him, seeming to dare him to leave. His two companions elbowed each other, pointing and laughing, their voices loud over the music. When the ticket seller tried to insist that they pay, the man with the cigarette pushed him to the ground, causing a few gasps to rise from the crowd.

Without a word, Owen knelt to the floor and began to take off his skates.

Charlotte put her hand on his shoulder. "Owen?"

"I have to," he said simply.

But she wasn't trying to stop him; she knew that he was the kind of man who would not stand by and let someone pick on another person who was weaker; it was one of the reasons she had fallen for him.

"Be careful. Please be careful."

"I'm not the one you should be worried about." He gave her a look full of determination before heading to the entrance.

Owen hated drunkards who only found their courage in the bottom of a bottle and when they had plenty of friends at their side. He'd fought them outside taverns, argued with them in the middle of the street, and even bled on one while on the steps of a church. Most of them folded soon after the first punch, unable to back up their mouths with their fists, but occasionally there would be a fight.

I wonder which one this will be...

The first one through the gate, the mean-looking one with the cigarette dangling from his lips, eyed Owen closely as he approached, the hint of a smile curling his lips, revealing tobacco-stained teeth.

"Who in the hell're you supposed to be?" he snarled.

"These folks are here trying to have a good time," Owen answered, ignoring the man's question while he tried not to ball his fists for the confrontation he already knew he couldn't avoid. "You're welcome to join us, but you'll need to pay first, same as all of us have done."

"And what if we don't want to?" the larger of the other

two men asked menacingly, crossing his thick arms over his broad chest, the taut muscles of his biceps straining hard against the fabric of his shirt.

"Then we're going to have a problem, I reckon."

"Are we now?" the one with the cigarette said, and the three men all laughed. Owen could smell the alcohol as it wafted off them, the fuel that had brought them all to this crossroads, intent on ruining a simple night of roller skating for as many people as possible.

Without warning, the group's leader, the man who had been smoking, flicked his still-burning cigarette toward Owen, striking him in the chest. It hadn't hurt him at all, hadn't startled him, either, but before the cigarette had even bounced to the ground, Owen was already throwing a punch, slamming his fist into the man's nose, so that blood spurted down his chin, and a squeal of pain shot from between his teeth.

"You son of a bitch!" the large one shouted.

Owen ignored him, turning his attention to the third man. He had remained silent thus far, something that made Owen believe he would be particularly dangerous, but now he let his fists do his talking. Owen blocked his punch, slipping a left under the man's guard and into his ribs, making his knees wobble. He meant to follow up, to press his advantage and thin their numbers as quickly as possible, but it was not meant to be. Agonizing pain shot down his side as the huge man decided to enter the fray and pounded Owen's already damaged ribs. He fell to one knee, desperately fighting to stay conscious, stars dancing in front of his eyes.

"Owen!" he heard Charlotte shout.

Now, clutching his hurting ribs, Owen supposed that he had bitten off more than he could chew. But as painful as it was, he knew that he couldn't have acted differently; he'd just have to take his lumps.

He'd expected his beating to be delivered promptly, but when it didn't come as he'd expected, he looked up, wondering. It was then that he found that a beating *was* being administered, just not the one he had expected.

Hale had already knocked one of the men, the silent one, unconscious on the floor, where blood poured from his mouth. The bigger man, the one who had struck Owen such a painful blow, now cowered, his hands up in surrender against a foe even larger than he was. Hale showed him no mercy, driving his fist, a hand used to maneuvering horses around easily, into the man's breadbasket. With a whoosh, he crumpled to the ground, gasping for breath.

"Next time," Hale growled, "why don't you start by picking on someone your own size?"

Even as Owen smiled at Hale's words, he saw that his fellow ranch hand was in danger; the rowdy with the cigarette had regained his senses and had flicked open a switchblade; the rink's lighting glinted off its steel. He meant to shove it into Hale's undefended back.

Get to your feet, Owen!

Struggling upright, Owen somehow managed to find

his bearings long enough to rush forward and, at the last instant, grab the man by the shoulder. The knife slashed with hard intentions and Owen managed to avoid it only by an inch, before he responded by landing another punch to the man's face, striking him flush on his scarred jaw. This time Owen put his weight into it and sent the bully back to the floor; this time the man lay unmoving.

For a moment, both Owen and Hale stood there, breathing hard.

"What the hell took you so long to help me?" Owen smiled.

"I had to take my skates off." Hale shrugged. "If I hadn't, I'd still be on the other side of the rink."

"Then I suppose I should be glad you did." He extended his hand and with no hesitation Hale took it, shaking it vigorously.

Before either of them could say another word, almost all of the roller-skating rink's patrons began clapping. Only one person, a woman he faintly remembered being at the school when he went to pick up Charlotte, seemed unhappy; her arms were folded over her chest and her face screwed up in displeasure. Owen didn't pause to wonder why. When his eyes found Charlotte, he was convinced that no one was cheering louder than she was.

Chapter Twenty-three

ARE YOU ALL RIGHT, Owen?"

Charlotte sat beside him in the truck as they drove back to the ranch. The moon was brushing the treetops as it set. They were alone; after Hale's show of bravery when he came to Owen's rescue and helped him dispatch the troublemakers, Hannah had considered him a hero and chosen to ride with him in the back of the truck. Even now, she was held tightly in his arms. Charlotte wasn't sure of if it was out of a need for warmth or affection, but she hoped it was the latter.

"I'm fine, Charlie," Owen answered her. "I didn't fall on the skates as many times as I thought I would. The fight was nothing."

"You didn't fall because I was holding you up," she teased.

"I'm sure that was it."

"But I am glad that Hale took his attention off Hannah for a minute."

"Not as glad as I am."

Charlotte hoped the relationship between Hale and Owen had changed as a result of the fight; it would have been almost impossible for Hale not to reconsider his opinion of Owen, for tackling that bully to help the rink owner. Now Hale couldn't continue to believe that Owen was capable of fouling the well or any other mischief. It looked as if they might now become friends. It was too bad that Owen had needed the fight to accomplish it.

When Owen had walked over to the men, Charlotte had known that there would be a fight, but she had done nothing but try to stay out of the way. A part of her had wanted to join him. There had been no silencing the shout that had escaped her lips when he had been knocked down.

The police came soon after the fight had ended, rounding up the three drunkards and hauling them off to jail. After Hale and Owen were thanked profusely by the owner of the rink, the two couples had skated to a few more records, but Charlotte had found it hard to concentrate on anything other than Owen. Her heart still fluttering as they clasped hands and glided across the floor . . .

"A fight wasn't what I was expecting on our first date," she said with a sly smile.

"Just wait and see what I've got planned for the next one." He laughed. "It'll make tonight look like 'ring-around-the-rosy.'"

"I can't wait."

The ranch house came into view. They crossed the creek and reached home faster than Charlotte would have liked. It was silent and still, the clock nearly ready to strike midnight, and only a single light shone deep in the house. The steady ticking of the cooling engine sounded loudly in the night.

Hannah and Hale headed off toward the cabins, arm in arm, Hale laughing beside her so easily that it was hard to imagine he had ever been so terrified simply to be around her. Dew dripped from blades of grass, bats dived hungrily from their hiding places in search of unwary bugs, and somewhere in the far distance a coyote let loose a lonely howl, but neither Charlotte nor Owen moved to part from each other.

"I'm not ready for this night to end," Charlotte admitted.

"Me either."

"So what do we do about it?"

"Well," Owen said, scratching at the whiskers on his jaw, "I still need to feed Cinnamon. You're welcome to come along if you'd like."

"I would like."

Walking toward the horse barn, they held hands, and contentment filled Charlotte. Somewhere in the back of her mind, she knew where this night was headed and knew that she could put a stop to it, could go to her room in the main house and be content with their date as it was, but that was not what she *wanted*. She wasn't naïve, wasn't ignorant about what paths romance could take. Owen wasn't just taking her to a destination; they were walking toward their future. Her heart fluttered with every step.

They saw no one as they walked along together and heard little more; through the open window of a cabin came the sudden snippet of large voices and raucous laughter. A variety show was on the radio, originating from a studio many hundreds of miles away, coming through the air around them, zipping past the moon and stars.

As Owen pulled open the doors to the horse barn, their hinges creaked. Without the starry sky to provide illumination, the inside was pitch-black. With the surety of a blind man who had grown used to his surroundings, Owen found an oil lamp on a table that was invisible to Charlotte's eyes, and brought it to life with a match. Though deep shadows danced wildly and often before her, she felt secure and unafraid because she was with Owen.

Cinnamon was happy to see them; she pawed at the ground as they approached, shaking her dark mane. Owen slipped a feed bag over the horse's head and she ate contentedly as they cleaned out her stall. Charlotte was happy, content to work beside him, and after Owen had run a wet brush across Cinnamon's back and sides they stood for a long while, neither of them saying a word, but both felt an undercurrent of expectation.

"Do you remember the last time we were here?" Charlotte asked.

"How could I possibly forget?"

"That moment is often the first thing I think about when I wake up and the last thought I have before I go to sleep."

"Our kiss...?"

"Mmmm," she murmured in acknowledgment.

Owen turned to look at her then, tipping his hat back on his head, the flickering flames of the oil lamp dancing in his eyes. His big hand moved into the space between her shoulder blades. "I can't say that memory hasn't crossed my mind a time or two," he said. "To say otherwise would make me one hell of a liar."

"I'm sure you've shared plenty of kisses with other women," she teased, "kisses that were much more memorable than ours."

"Not a one, Charlie," he answered quickly, his tone suddenly serious as he released her and looked into her eyes. "No kiss I've ever had could compare with the one I shared with you."

Charlotte was not so naïve that she didn't know a man as handsome as Owen had attracted other women. Some doubtlessly wanted him desperately. She was certainly not the first to taste his kisses, but the strength of Owen's declaration, the power contained in his words, told her all she wanted to know. She went willingly, eagerly, although a touch nervously into his arms.

"I've never expected to feel this way, Owen," she confessed. "I thought this happened only in the movies or in books, that it existed only in fantasies that lonely women told themselves to make up for the life they were living, but not the life they wanted. But then I met you."

"So what do you think now?" he asked, holding her closer, his thumbs tracing a gentle path over her bare skin.

This was Charlotte's moment of truth. Should she dare to reveal her true feelings, to climb out on a limb, vulnerable, allowing herself to be hurt if Owen did not return her affection? It was daunting, but she had never been the sort of woman who was afraid to take a chance or who would run from something because it was difficult.

"I think, no, I'm sure I'm falling in love with you," she said, taking the chance.

Her honesty momentarily took Owen aback, her words were a commitment, and he must decide if he wished to match it.

"I hope that I can be worthy of your love," he said.

"In the end, that's for me to decide."

Owen nodded. "I understand that it was hard for you to say right out," he said, pausing before adding, "because I've had to make a few hard choices in my life."

"What are you saying?"

"Love is something that I don't make any claims to understand. Horses," he said with a grin, "now them I know. But growing up as Hannah and I did, never knowing my father and having to struggle every step of the way, meant love was a luxury that I couldn't afford to even think about."

"You loved your mother and I can tell you love your sister from the way you take care of her."

"You're right," Owen said, his voice soft. "But I've not been able to consider love, real love, with a woman."

"Don't you want a woman of your own, Owen?"

"Are you applying for the job?" he teased. "After all, you're the perfect candidate."

Giving her no time to respond, Owen gathered her into his arms as his lips hungrily found her own. She rose on her tiptoes to meet him, settling her arms behind his neck, her fingers burying into his thick hair.

Charlotte held her eyes shut as she allowed herself to be carried away by the moment, as if looking on what they were sharing might cause it to suddenly vanish like a dream that was too good to be true. She had kissed boys before, nothing more than school ground flirtations, but kissing Owen, kissing the *man* who had won her heart, was an experience she didn't want to end. When his tongue entered her mouth, she wasn't repulsed but captivated and playfully nibbled on his lips in return and entwined her fingers into his hair so tightly that he gasped.

"I want you to love me," she said breathlessly, the words a surprise even to herself.

"Charlotte," he moaned into her open mouth. "You have to know what you're saying...what that means..."

"I wouldn't have said it if I didn't mean it. I love you..."

"...and I care more for you than any woman I've ever known..."

Without another word, Owen pulled a blanket from a cot, effortlessly lifted Charlotte, and carried her into the shadowy depths of the horse barn, the lantern left behind. He pushed open the gate of an empty horse stall and spread the blanket to lay her down into a thick bed of fresh hay. Impatiently, he tugged his shirt open and off, tossing it aside, before joining her. He pressed down on her, his flesh electric under her hands, his mouth again finding hers.

Tenderly, Charlotte ran her hands over his skin, starting at his hips, rising up over his ribs, and stopping as he hissed through clenched teeth.

"Does it hurt when I do that?" she asked, worried.

"Not at all," he lied.

"I'll be careful."

"If it means being here with you, I don't give a damn how rough you are." Even in the scant light, she could see him smile.

Drawing her blouse from her skirt, he ran his warm fingers across her bare skin. That touch, such a simple thing compared to all of the physical connections they had already shared, dissolved whatever restraint Charlotte still felt. It was gone in an instant. Her hands found his belt and tugged hard, trying to get it undone as fast as she could, and began to explore his body as Owen's hands caressed her breasts. The roughness of his fingers against the tender skin of the underside of her breasts sent flashes racing before her eyes. When he first touched her nipple, her breath caught in her chest and she flinched.

"Did that hurt you?" he asked, and she loved him for asking.

"Not one bit," she gasped.

The next few minutes passed as a blur as each helped the other shed clothes; blouse, jeans, shoes, skirt, and undergarments were tossed aside.

Charlotte lay naked on the blanket, her blond curls fanned out behind her, watching Owen's face as he lay down beside her. She could see that even though his passion threatened to consume him, he remained reluctant to act.

"There's something I want to ask you, but before I do, I want you to listen to me for a moment, all right?" he said.

"Yes, Owen."

"I want you to be sure that what we are about to do is what you want," he explained. "I don't want there to be any doubts, because the thought that you might regret making love to me is more than I could bear. I want this to be the beginning of our life together, not a night you would hope to forget."

"Then both of us want the same thing."

Tenderly, Charlotte lifted her lips to Owen's, softly kissing him. But as the seconds passed and their passion grew, his kisses became more frantic.

Urgently, Owen now slid his hand down Charlotte's hip, dallied on her thigh, and finally, gently as he could, ventured between her legs. To help him, she spread her knees. Immediately, his fingers found the centers of her pleasure, already moist and aroused by all that had come before, sending shivers racing throughout her body.

When Owen rose up on his arms, muscles tight from supporting his weight, and positioned himself above Charlotte, she lifted her body to his.

"I'm yours, Owen." She sighed into his ear. "I'll always be yours and you will be mine."

"Together," he answered breathlessly. "We'll always be together...you and I, so tell me. I want to hear you say it."

She did, over and over.

Gently, Owen moved forward, starting to push himself inside her. Charlotte gasped; it was a pain that she expected and one that she resolved to get past.

"Charlotte..." he began in worry.

"It's fine," she answered. "Trust me...when I say that it's fine..."

Once he was completely inside her, Owen waited for a moment allowing her to adjust to the feel of him, as he softly kissed her parted lips. When he felt certain she was ready, he began to move, slowly at first, but then almost imperceptibly faster. Soon, the pleasure rose and the discomfort subsided and Charlotte began to let herself ride with the moment, relishing what they were sharing.

Giving herself to Owen wasn't something she had entered into lightly, but now that it was happening, she knew that her choice had been right. Memories of their relationship drifted back to her: that first smile in the dining room on the night of her arrival, their kiss in the very horse barn in which they now lay, his visit outside the school and the surprise of the country pond, and their trip to the roller-skating rink only hours earlier. But what excited Charlotte now, as their bodies became one, was imagining what wonderful moments lay in their future. Whatever they were, she couldn't wait to discover them.

The pleasure mounted with every thrust, and both of them began to sweat and breathe harder.

"I never...dreamed it would be this wonderful..." Owen whispered.

"I love you, Owen Wallace," Charlotte answered. "I love you."

When the moment arrived for the climax of their lovemaking, both of them had reached their limit, unable to restrain themselves a minute longer. Charlotte held Owen so tightly that her fingers dug into the hard flesh of his back, her face nuzzled into the sweaty crevice of his neck and shoulder. Her body spasmed uncontrollably as he shuddered, filling her with warmth and happiness. And then they were spent, collapsing together, bodies still joined and entwined. Never in her wildest imagination would Charlotte have thought it would have been so fulfilling, so wonderful. She didn't want the night to end.

She just wanted to lie together with Owen, in his arms, forever.

Carter Herrick slumped in a chair before the fireplace of his ranch house's great room. He was beside himself with frustration. No matter how many glasses of whiskey he downed, no matter how many cigars he smoked, nothing seemed to settle his dissatisfaction. When the grandfather clock struck midnight, he knew sleep would never catch him that night.

Clyde had reported what had happened on Grant's ranch, and while he was pleased to learn that there had been some damages and a few injuries, the stampede had fallen far short of his lofty expectations. He'd envisioned Grant ground to a bloody pulp under the pounding hooves of his own horses or, at the very least, that he would have to put down half of his animals and rebuild much of his ranch.

But that wasn't what had happened at all...

Futilely, Herrick wished for it to be a different time. He had a burning desire to hold Caroline Wallace in his arms, to feel the press of her lips against his own. He desperately needed to speak with his son again, to ask him about his day as he had often failed to do during the boy's short life. He would have traded anything to be a young man again, to feel strength coursing through his ravaged body, not to have to rely on the actions of others to accomplish what he wanted done. But he might as well have wished for the moon for all the chance he had for his desires to come true.

Upstairs, the pistol still lay on his desk, waiting. In his darkest moments, Carter Herrick could swear that it was calling out to him. Either way, there wasn't much time left before he would no longer be able to resist the pull to use it. With a simple pull of the trigger, he would go be with his beloved son and be forever rid of the specter of loss that hung around his neck. But he still clung to the thinning hopes that he would not go into the ground alone. In fact, that night Clyde had argued for a different plan, a more aggressive one, a plan he had not been able to reject outright.

With another gulp of whiskey slowly burning its way down his throat, Carter Herrick managed to smile.

Chapter Twenty-four

Aɴᴅ... ᴀɴᴅ ᴛʜᴇɴ the... boy clim... climbed the lad... der to the... top of the wall... and then ju... jumped down to the... ott... other side...'" Sarah struggled, holding the book in both hands and staring hard at the words. "'What he... found there was... ma... ma...'"

"'Magical,'" Charlotte encouraged.

"'Magical,'" the girl repeated, rolling the word around, liking the sound of it, before adding, "That's a hard one!"

"It certainly is."

A gust of wind rattled the glass in the window, periodically tugging at the loose dirt on the ground and the branches of the few trees that dotted the landscape. Heavy clouds hung low in the sky, threatening. It was so dark outside that the middle of the afternoon seemed like early evening. In the distance, thunder rumbled.

As Sarah worked at reading her book and Charlotte

struggled to pay attention, her mind wandered to the night before, when she and Owen had made love. Words were unable to describe her emotions at that time. Afterwards, each had been content to lie in the straw beside the other, sweaty skin touching, breathing ragged. When they had dressed and parted, their long kiss was a seal and a promise. Back in her room, Charlotte had been unable to sleep, remembering.

Regardless of her own emotional state, it was hard for Charlotte not to notice the change in Sarah. When she and John had arrived, the cabin was as clean as she had ever seen it and Alan had been outside chopping wood, his scrawny body drenched in sweat. Sarah was well rested and cheerful. The most pleasant surprise was that there weren't any empty liquor bottles lying around. Clearly, Alan had taken Charlotte's tongue-lashing to heart and had begun to change his ways. A transformation had occurred.

Sarah finished the book and looked expectantly at Charlotte.

"That was much better, Sarah."

"I've been tryin' to read when you ain't here," she said, and beamed. "What you said 'bout sounding out the words, it really helps when I get stuck. I just keep at it until I get it, no matter how long it takes. My pa's been sittin' with me when I read at night, and even though he can't understand a lick of it, he's been noddin' and 'couragin' me some."

"It looks like he's been helping more around the cabin."

"He even helped me do the cookin' last night," Sarah said, her voice lowering a bit as she added, "Don't tell him I told you, but he's no good at it! He thinks he should use salt the way you would flour. I couldn't eat a bite, though it was awful nice of him to try."

"Once the baby comes," Charlotte said, "it'll get harder for the both of you."

"My pa's been sayin' the same thing."

"He's right."

Sarah's eyes drifted toward the windows as a burst of needling rain lashed against the glass, followed by another rumble of thunder. "I hope I'll know how to take care of it." She frowned, looking much older than her age.

"I know he's grown-up and can take care of himself. But a baby can't do that. He'll be needin' me to do everything for him and I worry I ain't gonna be up to the task. What if I do somethin' wrong? What if I ain't as good a mother as I wanna be, as my mother was to me? At least she had Pa to help. He wasn't drinkin' then . . . I ain't got nobody but him."

"I told you this the first day that we sat down and worked on your lessons," Charlotte reassured. "You're not alone."

"Sometimes it seems I am. It's gonna be so hard."

"Times *will* be tougher than you imagine they will be, but you will not have to go through them all by yourself. Besides, your father has already been through it. You said it yourself: he helped to raise you. Surely he can't have forgotten what to do."

"I don't know," Sarah murmured.

"I don't think people ever forget." Charlotte smiled. "Your baby will be his grandchild."

"Grandson," she corrected.

"Are you still so sure that you're having a boy?"

"Maybe not as much as I used to be," she admitted, "but even if I'm wrong and I have a girl, I'll love her just as much, that's for sure."

Charlotte knew that Sarah's heart was in the right place, but she would be a child raising a child. She had no idea what she was in for. Once the baby arrived, Sarah would grow up fast, but the whole experience would be much harder for her than if she were older, if she were married and had the child's father by her side. She and her father were living off John Grant's charity, and there was no assurance how long that would last. If only her life were more stable . . . But it was too late for such thinking. The baby would be coming soon.

"Do you know how far along you are with the baby?" Charlotte asked.

"Can't say for certain. It would have been last fall when I got pregnant, but I ain't too sure which month."

From the size of Sarah's belly, Charlotte knew that the time of the baby's birth was approaching. It wasn't really possible to say for certain where Sarah was in her pregnancy, since some women showed more than others, some had smaller babies than others, but Charlotte thought that there still might be a month, maybe a month and a half, to go. All the time she had spent with Rachel and her grandmother, both experienced in the birthing of babies, had given her enough insight to make an educated guess. Decisions would have to be made soon. A doctor or midwife needed to be called. If Sarah were to give birth in this cabin, still dirty, though cleaner than it had been, and something were to go wrong...

Charlotte was living proof of what could go wrong during childbirth. Her own mother's delivery had been difficult, though not impossible, but all it took for disaster to strike was Alice Tucker's unwillingness to live. Sarah showed no signs of abandoning her child in its first hours of life, but she also had no idea how difficult bringing another person into the world could be. What would happen if her labor were to last for hours? Would she have the fortitude to fight through it or would she surrender, allowing herself or her child to die?

Outside, the rain began to fall harder and the clouds darkened further, as if the weather meant to mirror the ominous trend of Charlotte's thoughts.

"Do you wanna be a mother someday?" Sarah asked.

Charlotte took a good long look at her young student, the question momentarily taking her by surprise. No one had ever asked her before, but there was only one answer that could possibly be given. "I do," she said simply, smiling.

"Do you have a fella?"

"You're asking an awful lot of questions."

"I just want to know." Sarah shrugged. "What could it hurt to say?"

"I didn't when I first arrived in Oklahoma, but then I met someone," Charlotte admitted.

"Would you wanna have a baby with him?"

The bluntness of Sarah's questions was becoming difficult for Charlotte to deal with. Her relationship with Owen was something she hadn't shared with anyone; she hadn't told Hannah much or written about it in great detail to Christina. Discretion held her tongue and she changed the subject, asking, "Have you picked out a name yet?"

"Oh, yeah." Sarah smiled. "But I ain't tellin' no one till after the baby's here."

"Not even your teacher?"

"Nope," she said.

"Not even if I traded you the name of my fella," she kept on, teasing. "Would that be enough to get it out of you?"

Sarah seemed to think about, but blurted, "Still not enough!" and they both laughed, covering the sounds of the growing storm.

Occasional flashes of lightning pierced the gloom of the afternoon storm, punctuated by the deep bass of thunder, as Charlotte and John drove back to the ranch after Sarah's lesson. Oppressively dark clouds pressed down. Insistent gusts of wind pushed at the vehicle's frame, forcing John to keep both his hands on the wheel to hold the truck on the road. The rain came down in huge, sporadic drops that struck the truck's metal body with the hard sound of hail.

"This weather don't look good," John remarked, his forehead wrinkled, as he peered out the window.

"What do you mean?" Charlotte asked.

"Sometimes the weather here in Oklahoma gets a bit wilder than what you might be used to back in Minnesota," he explained. "Storms come rollin' in off the plains with intentions meaner than a horse that's set on not bein' broke. Difference is there ain't any way to tame a storm. Wind comes howlin' hard 'nough to pull all the tin off a roof, nails and all. Rain fallin' so hard and fast that there ain't no time for it to sink down into the dry ground, so it goes a floodin' every which way and you got to just hope it ain't in the direction you're standin'."

"Is this serious?" Charlotte asked, staring out the window and suddenly concerned about their predicament. There were storms back in Carlson that felled trees, overran rivers and creeks, and blizzards that buried them under enormous piles of snow, but something about the way John spoke unsettled her, the unknown potential of the storm making her feel vulnerable.

"Could be," he said simply. "But at least we can be home before the brunt of it gets here. I feared it'd come while you was givin' Sarah her lesson. We can be thankful it waited."

The mention of Sarah brought Charlotte's thoughts back to the moment when John and Alan arrived back

in the cabin. John's gaze had wandered again and again
toward the pregnant girl. His concern for Sarah's well-
being was obvious, but Charlotte couldn't help but question his motive. Nor could she stop wondering about what
was to come next...

"What will happen once Sarah has her baby?" she asked
after another peal of thunder rattled the truck.

"She'll be a mother, of course." John smiled, glancing
over at her as he pushed the wiper lever back and forth in
an effort to clear the windshield so he could see. "There'll
be plenty of feedin's, lots of diaper changin', and probably
not a lot of sleep."

"I'm not joking, John," Charlotte replied with a seriousness she hoped he would find impossible to ignore. No longer was she willing to play along with the charade. "Once
that baby arrives, Sarah is going to need a lot more help
than you're currently giving her. Groceries and firewood
are no substitute for having someone there to help. Alan is
doing better, but we both know he won't be enough, and
that's if he doesn't go back to his drunken ways, which is
a possibility I don't even want to imagine."

"There's no need to worry. I'll make sure they get whatever they need."

"But what if Sarah needs a doctor or a woman to stay
and help her care for a sick or difficult baby?" Charlotte
pressed, a sliver of anger sliding into her voice. "I've done
as you asked. I've been willing to be her teacher, but I don't
know if I'm up to the task of being her mother."

"No one has asked you to do that," he said gruffly.

"That doesn't change the fact that she might need one."

"These are all bridges that we'll cross when we get to 'em," John said dismissively. "There're folks in town who I know can keep quiet if I need 'em to go out and check on Sarah and the baby."

"Then what happens when winter comes?" she argued, refusing to accept John's easily given answers. "I know that the weather here in January isn't like the winters we have back in Minnesota, but it must get cold at night, too cold for a newborn to be expected to live in a ramshackle cabin on the edge of your property. Surely you don't intend for the Becks to live there forever?"

"We'll take care of it."

"Tell me the truth, John," she demanded, the dam blocking her frustration with a situation she had never fully understood finally breaking and her pent-up emotions finally running free. "Why are you doing all of this for them? Be honest with me: who are the Becks to you?"

For a long while, the only sounds in the truck's cab came from the savage storm; though they had not been on the road long, the weather appeared to have significantly worsened. The rain began to hammer them relentlessly, smashing into the truck as if it were hell-bent on breaking its way inside. Charlotte thought John was remaining silent because he was otherwise concerned with keeping them on the road, his jaw set hard and his knuckles white on the steering wheel. When he finally spoke, he surprised her.

"The last time you asked me 'bout Sarah and them, I told you that my life holds its fair share of regrets," he said.

"You did."

"Maybe someday, when you're as old as me, you'll understand that you can encounter a situation, something that can remind you of times past, moments you'd like to forget but can't, no matter how hard you try." John took a deep breath, pausing as he maneuvered the truck around a bend and the ranch came into view in front of them. Charlotte looked out and was instantly reminded of the day they had raced back to confront the fire, another time that had filled her with dread and foreboding. "You wish you could change things," he finally added, "but the past is the past for a goddamn reason."

"John?" she bravely asked. "Does your past have to do with Sarah?"

"There was a girl I knew back 'fore you would have been born, I reckon. A girl I loved. She was the sweetest thing you could ever set eyes on. Smart, funny, full of life. I was gonna make her mine, marry her, you know, but then..."

Try as she might, Charlotte couldn't bring herself to push John Grant for the answers she so desperately wanted. She knew that the only way to get him to talk was to force the issue; that was a course of action that seemed particularly cruel, especially since she already knew the answer from Owen: John had gotten Caroline Wallace pregnant and she had left Sawyer forever.

"Does Amelia know?" she asked.

"About Sarah? No ... I haven't told her a thing. She was round back then, watchin' as I fell in love. If she knew I was keepin' them out at the cabin, she'd understand in a second why I was doin' it."

"So what *are* you going to do after the baby is born?"

"If I was bein' honest," he said, looking at her in such a way that she knew he was, "I don't rightly know."

The truck followed the path that wound through the horse corrals toward the main house. Their headlights cut through the gloom of the storm, but the going was awfully slow. Just as they were about to pass the horse barn where Charlotte and Owen had been together the night before, she was startled to see Owen rushing from the doors and frantically waving his arms for them to stop. John tromped down on the brakes and the truck skidded to a halt in the growing mud.

"What's happenin' here?" John asked.

Charlotte got out of the truck, shielding her head from the rain, although it showed her no mercy, instantly soaking her blouse.

"What's wrong?" She shouted to be heard.

"Come into the barn right now! Both of you!" Owen yelled back. "Hurry!"

Neither John nor Charlotte hesitated, following Owen

as he ran into the barn. The meager light of the thunderstorm was enough to poorly illuminate the building's interior, but Charlotte could see no sign of anything the matter.

She was just about to ask Owen another question when he did something that made her blood run cold as ice; the man whom she loved, the man who had captured her heart, drove his fist into John Grant's jaw with all the strength he could muster, his face screwed up in a mask of rage. The sound of the blow was as startling as a crack of thunder. John never saw the punch coming; he dropped at his attacker's feet as solidly as if he were a bag of feed. Charlotte could only stare.

Chapter Twenty-five

OWEN STOOD OVER John Grant, his fist throbbing, a sharp ache from where it had struck the older rancher's jaw. His heart thundered even louder than the storm just outside the barn door. Unknown to him, his shoulders shook slightly, the tremors running down the length of his arms, he was so enraged, staring holes through the man whom he believed to be his father. Though Owen had come to Oklahoma for the purpose of making John Grant pay for what he had done to his mother, this was the first moment when his rage threatened to consume him and he struggled to resist it.

When he had risen that morning, his sole thought had been of his night with Charlotte. Happiness gripped him so tightly that he never wanted it to let him go. All he had desired was to hold her in his arms, kiss her, and make her promise that what they had would last forever. After he finished the morning chores, he'd hurried to find her.

But when he had, he'd watched as she'd left the main house with John Grant and gotten in the truck and driven away. It was a sight he'd seen many times before but had never asked her about; at first, he had supposed that Grant was showing her around, acclimating her to her new home, but then he kept seeing them together, again and again. Still, he never asked Charlotte for an explanation; if there was something untoward about it, she would have told him, he was sure. But on this day, for a reason he could not explain or even fully understand, he decided that his ignorance was no longer enough and that he needed answers. He determined to follow them.

Once the truck was out of sight, Owen had saddled up Cinnamon and set out after them. The weather had been threatening, growing worse with each passing second, but he hadn't given a damn if he got caught in a downpour. The truck was much faster than his horse, even without a head start, so he'd had to be content to follow along behind, hurrying in the direction they'd been headed. He pushed Cinnamon hard.

Where were they going?

He'd known he was taking a risk, both with John and with Charlotte, but he hadn't wavered in his resolve. If he was found out, he'd simply say that he was out on a ride, stretching his beloved horse's legs. He would have hated to lie to Charlotte. In the end, he needn't have worried; he'd never seen a soul.

Soon, Owen had climbed a low rise and found a cabin he'd not known was located on the ranch property. It wasn't much, decrepit and shoddy looking, with smoke drifting from its dented stack. John Grant's truck sat outside. Owen had tied Cinnamon to a felled tree trunk, made his way to a spot where he felt confident he couldn't be seen, and waited. Long minutes passed, but he saw no sign of them. They had to be inside.

Owen's curiosity had eventually gotten the better of him. Painstakingly, he had inched his way down to the cabin. With every rock that clicked off his boots, louder to his ears than the thunder that pounded in the distance, he expected to be found out, but no one came out of the cabin's door. With sweat streaming down his face, he made it to the cracked window. When he looked inside, his heart had wanted to leap from his chest.

Charlotte sat at a table opposite a young girl. To Owen's eyes, she couldn't have been more than fifteen or sixteen, little more than a child. But her age was not what sickened him; it was her obviously pregnant belly. He'd looked away quickly, the sight too much for him to bear. All he could see was his mother, made to suffer and lose all that she had, simply because she was unmarried and with child. Charlotte was there because of John Grant, because he had brought her there. The pregnant girl was obviously connected to him as well.

Desperately, Owen had fought against the urge to kick in the front door and demand answers, but his love for Charlotte made him pause; she might never forgive him for it. There was also no doubt that such an entrance would terrify the girl, and that was something he would not do. In the end, he'd decided that he would be better off hurrying back to the ranch and waiting for them to return.

Furiously pushing Cinnamon, Owen had beaten the rain and settled into the horse barn, steeling himself for what needed to be done. When he had finally seen the truck's headlights, he'd waved them down and lured them into the barn. It was then he had begun to take his revenge.

And this is only the beginning...

To Charlotte's eyes, time seemed to stand still. Outside, the raging storm paused. The blustery wind died as if it ran on electricity, its current snapped shut. Even a fork of lightning froze in the sky as if it were nothing more than a child's drawing, its forks twisting here and there, up and ultimately down, but never striking, never producing its telltale thunder.

Inside the barn, the same held true. No one moved, no one breathed, the very dust motes hanging in the air like snowflakes. Owen remained perched over John, the furious rage never leaving his twisted face, his fists never unclenching. Everything around Charlotte was pregnant with violence.

"You worthless son of a bitch!" Owen bellowed, his

brutality finally breaking the spell that held Charlotte's world temporarily still. His voice echoed, rolling as if *it* were thunder. "You're going to pay for all that you've done! I'll make you pay!"

"Owen!" Charlotte shouted, tears springing to her eyes. "Don't do this, Owen!"

"I saw you, Charlotte!" He turned toward her, irate, barely resembling the man who had held her in that very barn only the night before. "I saw where he took you, who he took you to see!" His attention returned to John, who was sitting upright, one hand rubbing his aching jaw, suddenly looking much older than his years. "Wasn't ruining one pregnant girl's life enough for you? Why would you destroy another? Answer me, damn you!"

"I don't know what you're talkin' 'bout," John murmured.

"The hell you don't!" Owen shouted. Viciously, he kicked John square in the chest with his booted foot, driving the man flat onto his back, forcing the air out from his lungs. Owen was over him, dropping his weight down onto the man's chest, a fist raised and ready to be thrown.

But before Owen could punch John as he lay defenseless beneath him, Charlotte rushed across the distance between them and grabbed him by the arm, struggling to hold him. "No, Owen! This isn't right!"

"What's right is that he pay for what he's done! For what he did to Caroline Wallace! For what he did to my mother!"

Owen's words roused John from the cobwebs blanketing his head. He had been dazed, teetering on the verge of losing consciousness, but the mention of Caroline's name appeared to stir something in him, like embers in a dying fire, and he began to struggle, blood smearing the corners of his mouth.

"What... what did you...?" he asked. "Whose name... did you say?"

"Caroline Wallace, you bastard!" Owen raged, renewing his desire to beat John to death, nearly pulling his hand free from Charlotte's grasp. "The woman you got pregnant and chased away because you were too much of a damn coward to take responsibility for what you'd done! The woman whose life you ruined, who died alone!"

"But I... but I didn't... but I loved her..." John stammered.

Throughout their exchange, Charlotte kept trying to force Owen off John. He fought against her every second, far stronger than she, but his attention was much more focused on his opponent than on her. She strained hard, desperate to keep Owen from doing something she felt certain he would come to regret, and, through constant struggle, she finally managed to topple them both to the floor.

"Get off me!" he shouted.

"This is not the way to do this!" she insisted, "This isn't what your mother would have wanted!"

"Don't tell me what she would have—"

"Stop! Just...just stop!" John suddenly shouted, the authority in his shaken voice enough to silence the bickering between Charlotte and Owen; outside, a peal of thunder served as punctuation for his demand. "Just stop for a minute," he repeated, but now his voice had lost all of its strength, a balloon that suddenly found itself without any air.

For a moment, everything returned to the instant just after Owen had struck John and the world had gone still. No one moved or made a sound. But unlike what had come before, when she had wondered at the frozen world, Charlotte knew that it would regain its natural state, and that was what scared her.

"You're...you said that...Caroline Wallace is your mother...?" John managed to ask, stumbling over the words.

"She *was*," Owen spat. "She *was* my mother."

"And Hannah is your sister...your twin sister..." John said, finally putting together all of the pieces as the strength of the storm intensified.

"And you are our bastard of a father!"

"No," John said, his eyes finding Owen for the first time since he and Charlotte had entered the barn; what could be seen there was best described as pity mixed with sadness. "No, I am not."

"Liar!"

"Listen to me, Owen," John protested. "As...difficult as it is for me to hear...that you and Hannah are Caroline's children, it is not because I ain't man enough to accept responsibility. I have been many things in my time on this here earth, even a coward like you're cussin' me, but a liar I have never been. You need to listen good to what I'm sayin' to you. I'm tellin' you the truth."

"My mother had a letter with your name on it when she died! I read it! It said that you were the love she never forgot, that she could never have!"

"And she was right," John agreed, "but the reason we couldn't be together wasn't 'cause of my choice, but 'cause of hers."

Charlotte was floored with disbelief. She found herself captured by John's words, rapt with attention and desperate to know more. But there was no pleasure in knowing that she was right, that there was much more to Caroline Wallace's story than Owen had ever been willing to accept. It was hard not to believe John, but it was clear that Owen would not be easy to convince.

"I don't believe you!"

"I loved your mother more than anything in this world." For an instant, John's eyes searched Charlotte's and she remembered the things he had told her in the truck. "There was nothing I wanted more than to make her my wife, to father her children, to spend every day and night content by her side, makin' our way in this world."

"You're lying!" Owen said, angrily shaking his head. "You're trying to trick me, to protect yourself!"

"Goddamn it, Owen! Listen to me!" John thundered,

asserting himself and demanding that he be heard. "Your mother was the finest woman I've ever met and she weren't the sort that would be happy knowin' any son of hers wasn't willin' to listen to a man explainin' himself! At least give her that respect!"

Owen was silenced for a moment, uncertain of how he was supposed to react. Charlotte could see that he was thinking it over, trying to make it work in his head, to make it fit against all of the hate he had been carrying for so long.

"If you loved her like you say you did," Owen said, losing much of his fury, "if you wanted a family with her so badly, tell me why she left here and died alone."

"I...I wish I were your father, Owen...I wish to God..." His voice trailed off.

"Tell him," Charlotte said, the first words that had been spoken between them since they had entered the barn.

John sighed deeply, nodding. "The first time I set eyes on Caroline Wallace, I knew I wanted her to be my wife more than I wanted to draw my next breath. She had other suitors, men who had a hell of a lot more to offer than I ever did, but somehow she saw through my rough exterior for the man I was inside, and gave me her heart. When she made her choice, the other fellas was surely disappointed, but they understood and let us be. But there was one man who never let it go.

"Carter Herrick...he was a bastard even when we was boys, not far from our daddies' knees. He never could 'cept losin', even when it come to marbles or some other such, so it shouldn't been no surprise that he wouldn't come to grips with losin' a woman he thought belonged to him. In his own way, he loved Caroline, too. Lookin' back on it now, we weren't nothin' but kids, all of us, even Carter, older than Sarah and 'bout the same age as the two of you. But that ain't no excuse for what happened.

"One night when Caroline was headin' home from this here ranch, walkin' when she shouldn't never have been allowed to be alone, she was attacked by a fella come out of the side of the road. He dragged her..." John faltered, his voice thick with emotion. "Dragged her...into the bushes...and raped her..."

"Oh, my God!" Charlotte exclaimed.

Owen remained silent, his breathing ragged and fierce.

"No matter how much she fought, no matter how much she screamed, no one heard her or come to help...and her attacker never stopped..."

Charlotte recoiled in horror; to even imagine a man forcing himself on her against her will made her sick to her stomach. That it had happened to Owen's mother was just as bad, but she knew that worse was to come; if what John was telling them was true, then...

"Caroline never told anyone what happened, not even me, not at first," John continued, tears in his eyes. "When she found out she was pregnant, knowing that it had happened the night she was raped, that was when she told me...

"She'd known from the moment he come out into the moonlight that it was Carter Herrick that done it. Said he talked to her the whole time he was havin' his way with her, tellin' her that if he couldn't have her, that he'd make sure she was ruined for anyone else, meanin' me. When he'd left her there, broken and cryin', the last thing he'd said was that he loved her, but she hadn't given him no other choice to make."

"Is Carter Herrick still alive?" Owen asked, his lip snarling.

John slowly nodded. "He is."

"Why?" Owen shook. "Why wouldn't you have made sure the man who raped the woman you loved was dead before the next morning sun?"

"Because of Caroline. Because she knew that I was little more than a boy, hotheaded enough to go off half-cocked and do something that I would pay for for the rest of my life," he explained. "Carter's family was better off than any in Sawyer. Makin' him pay would've torn our lives in two. She didn't want that for me, would not even hear of it. So she made me promise, made me swear on my love for her that I wouldn't take revenge on the son of a bitch that had forced himself on her. I didn't want to do it, but I couldn't deny her; I just couldn't." Tears flowed freely down John Grant's face. "She did it 'cause she wanted to protect me, to make sure I was safe, all 'cause I failed to protect her, to make up for the moment I wasn't there when she needed me."

Charlotte knew that John was telling them the truth; there was no way that he was capable of lying so brazenly. The story he was recounting had been locked away for a long time, hidden from the world in which he lived. In among the tears, there may even have been some relief for finally being able to release his burden.

"And then she left Sawyer," Charlotte suggested.

"I could've lived with it," John struggled, unable to look at either of them so instead he looked down at his shaking hands. "I could have raised her child as if it were my own, but Caroline decided that the shame of her rape was her burden to bear alone. She figured that every time I was lookin' at the child, I'd be remindin' myself of what had happened, but I wouldn't have . . .

"One day she was just gone, leavin' her family and disappearin' into the countryside. She left me a note that I have to this day. If you still don't believe me, you can read it."

Looking at Owen, Charlotte could see that there would be no need for further proof; though his fists were still balled and there was tension in his shoulders, his eyes had softened; his intent was no longer violence . . . at least not toward John Grant.

"Why didn't you go after her?" he asked.

"I tried, Owen. I really did. Pert near spent every cent I had trackin' all around the Southwest, even down to the border of Mexico, but I could never find her, 'specially when she didn't want to be found," he said, clearly still pained. "In the end, I found a new life with Amelia. She'd known 'bout Caroline, has always accepted that my heart lies with another, but what we have is worth carin' for, worth fightin' for.

"All these years, I wondered whatever 'came of Caroline's child...and I guess now I know..."

Outside, the storm kept raging, the wind rising to tug at the barn's open door, pushing it back into the wall with a crash. But no one moved until Owen rose up to his feet, pain in his face.

"So my mother...was raped...by Carter Herrick...?" he asked.

John nodded.

"And that...makes him my father...?"

"It does," John said, but quickly added, "but that doesn't mean that—"

"Tell me where he lives, John," Owen cut him off. "Tell me where to find him so I can murder that rapist bastard!"

From the depths of the barn, deep in the shadows that the storm's illumination failed to reach, there came the sound of a gun cocking, followed by an unknown man's voice.

"I ain't gonna let you do that."

Chapter Twenty-six

CHARLOTTE HELD HER BREATH, horrified by what she saw; a man stepped from the rear of the barn, a pistol in his hand. His oversize nose, grey-streaked hair, and enormous belly that hung over his waistline were all features that she immediately recognized; it was the same man whom she had witnessed striking a horse with a studded board, starting the stampede. In that instant, she knew that she had made a huge mistake by allowing herself to believe she had imagined seeing him, and a bigger one by not saying anything to Owen. Now, with the man grinning ear-to-ear, his gun pointed at them, it was far too late.

"Clyde Drake." John scowled, unintentionally answering Charlotte's unspoken question. "What in the hell are you doin' here?"

"Protectin' my own hide, that's what I'm doin'." Clyde laughed, setting his huge belly to rumbling. "'Long with threatenin' yours, you damn old fool! Just imagine my surprise to be headin' this way, tryin' to get outta the rain, when I see you pullin' up to the barn. I just come in the back way, kept my big mouth shut, and started listenin'. Amazin' what you can hear when no one knows you're there. I been plannin' on payin' you a visit, somethin' private 'tween the two of us, but what you done said made it so now's got to be the time."

"What you heard was none of your business."

"But it was so entertainin'," Clyde said sarcastically. "That there was a hell of a story you told, Grant. A real teary story if I ever heard one. Good 'nough for the movies. But if you ask me, the bitch got what she deserved."

Owen snarled, looking as if he wanted to tear the man limb from limb.

"Hold it right there, boy," Clyde answered, clearly understanding Owen's intention to jump him. "If you think I won't plug you for even lookin' at me the wrong way, you're dumber than a stump. Unless you don't wanna live a bit longer, I'd stay still if I were you."

"You're the one who started the stampede," Charlotte said.

"Nice to see you got yourself a brain in that pretty little head of yours, darlin'. Done a pretty good job of it, too, even if I wished it had gone a bit better." He laughed, his eyes roaming over her in such a way as to make Charlotte uncomfortable. "Had my hands in settin' the wildfire and foulin' the well, too. There's some fellas who're good at findin' trouble, but I'm a little different. See, I'm the guy you hire when you want trouble to find someone else."

With Clyde's admission of guilt, all the problems that had beleaguered the ranch over the last couple of weeks were explained. Even the theory she and Owen had concocted, that the fire had been intentionally set, had proven true. Though she was frightened, there was one thing that relieved Charlotte: now it was clear that Owen had been wrongly accused. While she had never once doubted him, she knew that John and Hale had. Since they had been in the barn, more than one misconception had been cleared up.

"Carter Herrick hired you to do this," John said, getting to his feet and dusting off his pants.

"Reason 'nough for me."

"You'd even kill a man in cold blood?"

"If the occasion calls for it and I was paid enough," the man replied, smug because he stood on the right side of the gun. "See, money goes an awful long way in my book. Lots of things a man will do to put coin in his pocket. Liquor and women don't find their way to you without handing over some money. Course, that ain't the only reason a fella will follow orders of a man the likes of Mr. Herrick."

"What in the hell are you getting at?" Owen growled.

"From the way you're all lookin' at me, I bet you figured I've been workin' here alone, didn't you? Wreckin', burnin', and ruinin' all by my lonesome, but you'd be wrong 'bout that." Clyde Drake grinned broadly through tobacco-stained teeth, enjoying his position of power. Over his shoulder he shouted, "Why don't you come on out here and show 'em!"

For as surprised as Charlotte had been when she recognized Clyde Drake as the man responsible for starting the stampede, it was absolutely nothing when compared to the shock she felt when the man's accomplice stepped out from the depths of the barn to join him, pointing another pistol at them.

It was Del Grissom.

Owen couldn't believe what he was seeing. Of all the men who could have conspired against John Grant, who could have done all of the despicable, destructive things that had been done to the ranch, Del Grissom would have been the last person he'd have expected. From the first day he and Hannah had arrived in Sawyer, it was Del who had gone to great pains to make sure they were settled. Kind and considerate, he'd driven Hannah into town to help her get whatever she had needed. As a boss, he was honest, fair, and hardworking, the sort of man you wouldn't mind busting your tail to help. Hell, when Owen had discovered the fouled well, Del was the first person he considered telling, even before John or Hale. Never in his wildest dreams could Owen have imagined this moment.

And from the look on John Grant's face, neither could he . . .

"What . . . what in the hell is this, Del?" John asked, all

of the color immediately draining from his skin, his knees suddenly weak enough for him to take a step back before steadying himself. "Why are you here? Why do you have that gun? Don't tell me you're workin' with this man!"

"I'm awfully sorry 'bout what's happenin', Mr. Grant," Del answered, his eyes never once able to meet those of the man he had worked beside for seven long years.

"You ain't got no reason to apologize to him none," Clyde admonished.

"The hell he doesn't!" Owen snapped.

"I'm sorry all the same," Del said simply.

"What sort of leverage does Herrick have on you, Del?" John pressed, ignoring Clyde's disregard for all of the long years they had spent together, working side by side on the ranch. "I've known Carter all my life and, without question, he's the biggest snake I ever met. Why, he'd blackmail his own mother if he thought he could get away with it."

Clyde Drake's pistol bucked in his hand, the slug pounding into the ground just in front of where John Grant stood. Dirt kicked up as the retort of the shot reverberated around the barn. Owen struggled to steady his heartbeat, his eyes never leaving the bastard with the gun; Charlotte standing beside him was silent but wide-eyed.

"What the hell did you do that for?" Del hissed. "Damn it all! You go shootin' off that gun, someone's gonna hear it and come running!"

"Ain't no one gonna hear nothin' in this here storm," Clyde contradicted his partner. "If they did, they'd just reckon they heard a bolt of lightnin' or roll of thunder or the wind blowin' a door shut. Besides, even if they was curious, they ain't gonna go out in this weather to check."

"You're pushin' your luck!"

"I'll decide that!"

With a sickening feeling in his gut, Owen knew that they were running out of time. If Clyde was so unconcerned about shooting his gun, it was because he felt confident he could do whatever he wanted without fear of discovery. The truth was that the bastard was right; no one would hear them over the din of the storm. Everyone on the ranch would be taking shelter, in either the main house, the cottages, or another barn. Even if they were to yell and scream at the top of their lungs, it would be useless, a futile gesture that would only serve to get them killed.

That didn't leave them with many options. With Charlotte at Owen's side, there was no way he could try to escape; if she were to hesitate, lag behind him, he would be signing her death warrant. And after what John had told him, a story he could not help but believe, he didn't want to get him killed, either. That meant his only option was to overpower them, but how could he if there were two of them? Would he really have to attack Del? Having just discovered the happiness of Charlotte's love, he had no intention of giving up easily.

I won't let them hurt you, Charlie! I swear it, I won't!

"Just tell me why, Del," John prodded again; Owen

couldn't help but admire the rancher's courage, unshaken after having a gun fired in his direction.

"You got stones, old man; I'll give you that." Clyde chuckled. "You know, I suppose there really ain't no harm in you knowin' why the man you trusted all these years suddenly stabs you in the back; you got a right to know why."

"Hold your tongue," Del hissed.

Clyde paid him no mind. "Del here got in too deep at the card table and now he owes more money than he could ever hope to repay. Herrick was the only one capable of pullin' him out of the hole he dug."

"I would have helped you had you asked," John said to his friend. "I would have made sure that your debts were paid."

"It's too damn late to help with the problems Del's got."

"Shut up, Drake!"

"There ain't no shame in it, Grissom! Gamblin' has ruined a far better man than you, believe me."

"I said shut up!"

"Now don't go gettin' all mouthy 'bout it," Clyde said defensively. "Some folks gamble too much; some prefer drink; others eat more than their share." He demonstrated by slapping his enormous stomach. "Anyone can overdo anythin'. I bet even the girl"—he waved the gun at Charlotte—"has got vices she can't barely keep under control. How 'bout it, little lady? I bet you like liftin' your skirts on the sly, don't you? Take any fella you can for a roll in the hay!"

"Watch your damn mouth!" Owen barked, taking a step in Clyde's direction.

"Now, now, now!" Clyde warned, leveling the gun so that it was pointed right at Owen's face. "What did I tell you 'bout wantin' to live? I'm beginnin' to think you want me to put you out of your misery."

"Leave him be!" Charlotte warned, unable to hold her tongue.

"Watch it, girlie," Clyde warned, swinging the gun until it was now pointed at Charlotte's head, "unless you want the same."

Owen decided that he had to take a chance, that he had to risk being able to wrestle the gun from Clyde Drake's hand before the man could pull the trigger. By threatening Charlotte, the bastard had gone too far. Owen was just about to spring, to try to protect the woman he loved, when the door on the side of the barn suddenly burst open, and Hale and Hannah ran inside.

Charlotte could instantly see that neither Hale nor Hannah had any idea what they were rushing into. Both were drenched to the skin, and were simply trying to get in out of the rain. Since Owen had led Charlotte and John inside, the storm had grown in velocity. Another growl of menacing thunder rolled in, closer than before.

"I told you that we shouldn't have gone so far down the creek!" Hannah complained.

"It's only rain," Hale argued.

"Well, you're not the one who catches cold easily!"

It was while Hannah was shouting at him that Hale noticed that they had entered a barn already full of people, some of them waving guns. At first, he stared at Del with disbelief, but Charlotte was amazed by how easily he took it all in, never showing surprise or fear, only slowly raising his arms and stepping back.

"What the heck's gotten into you, Hale?" Hannah asked, still unaware of how dangerous their choice of shelter really was.

"Quiet now," he said softly.

"Why on earth should I be quiet—"

"Shut your mouth, Hannah!" Owen barked, causing his sister to jump as if she'd seen a ghost.

"What's going on here?" she yelped when she saw the guns, her hands shooting up fast. "What are you doing, Del?"

"Get over next to them others," Clyde ordered, and both of the newcomers did as they were told. Though he and Del still held the weapons and were in control of the situation, the arrival of Hale and Hannah seemed to unsettle Carter Herrick's henchman. "This makes things more complicated."

"What are you talkin' 'bout?" Del asked.

"'Fore these two showed up, the way to deal with Grant

and the others was easy," he explained. "Shoot all three of 'em and say that we come 'cross the bodies. Blamin' it on the kid would've been a breeze."

"Have you lost your mind?" Del argued, panicked and enraged at the same time. Droplets of sweat glistened on his forehead as his nerves started to get the better of him. "This wasn't part of the deal! You never said nothin' 'bout killin' anyone! Not one damn word!"

"How else did you expect us to get out of here?" Clyde looked at his partner as if he were insane. "Herrick and I figured it would come to this. They know we done all the damage we been asked to do, so lettin' 'em live ain't no option no more!"

"We could tie 'em up..."

"And the sheriff would have us 'fore the sun rose tomorrow mornin'! No, the only answer is to just finish every one of 'em..."

"But—"

Charlotte knew that there wasn't much time to do something, anything to get out of the barn alive. Whether it was intentional or not, Del's worrying was delaying Clyde acting on his decision, one that looked increasingly like he wanted to murder them all. Time was running out.

But then Owen caught her eye. He was looking right at her, willing her to notice him. When she did, he smiled weakly, but it was enough to uplift her, to hope beyond hope that it wasn't too late for their fate to be changed. She thought about how happy he made her, how meeting him had changed her life, how handsome he was, even when their lives were threatened, about what it felt like to envision her future at his side. She wanted Owen to meet her family, to celebrate Christmas with her, to make love to her again, to laugh and sing and tease and...

"I love you, Charlotte," he said, his voice little more than a whisper, unheard by the bickering men. At first she found it endearing, but then she knew, *she knew* why he had said it and her heart nearly quit beating.

He's going to do something.

"No, Owen!" she protested. "Don't do it!"

But it was already too late.

Owen sprang forward when he felt Clyde's and Del's attention was squarely focused on each other and not on him. He moved quickly, hoping that even if he was noticed, they wouldn't be able to react fast enough to stop him. His focus was on Clyde, hoping that Del would be more reluctant to fire on a man who had worked beside him. He'd get Clyde away from his gun or die trying. Either way, once he had moved, the chance had been taken.

If he were to die here, gunned down by these devious men, he could only hope Charlotte had the good sense to run, to try to save herself. If it meant sacrificing himself so that she could live, that was good enough for him. He'd told her that he loved her, words that couldn't possibly be truer. Protecting her was all that mattered now.

"What in the hell!" was all that Clyde managed before

Owen slammed into him, his shoulder ramming him in the midsection, barreling into him with such overwhelming force that the both of them were carried hard to the floor, grunting as they struck.

"Owen!" Charlotte shouted from somewhere behind him.

Run, damn it! Run!

Pushing himself up on his hands, Owen readied himself to again attack Clyde, to beat him senseless for what he had done to the ranch, for what he had said about his mother, but especially for threatening Charlotte. But he was instantly disappointed; Clyde had crashed to the ground as Owen had intended, but he had somehow managed to hold on to his gun.

"Goddamn it all to hell!" he bellowed, and began firing his gun while lying on his side.

Fortunately, from the moment Owen had gone after the two men, everyone else in the barn had begun moving, so Clyde's bullets had more difficult targets to hit. The first slammed into the barn wall, opening a hole out into the storm in a shower of splinters. The second ricocheted off a saw blade, shooting sparks into the dark afternoon before finally thudding into a bale of hay.

But the third . . .

When all hell had broken loose, Hale had grabbed hold of Hannah and shielded her with his enormous body. The bullet struck him in the meat of his shoulder, blasting through skin, muscle, and bone. Blood instantly drenched his shirt. Hale shouted in pain, but he never went down, refusing to expose Hannah to danger.

"Hale!" Hannah cried.

"I'll kill you all!" Clyde shouted. "Every last—"

Another gun blast echoed around the barn, but this time the bullet had not been shot from Clyde's gun; smoke drifted from the barrel of Del's pistol. The bullet tore into the ample flesh of Clyde's midsection, the impact of the collision forcing the weapon from the man's grip and sending it flying across the ground. Dark red blood poured from the wound, the pain so great, the fact that he was going to die from the wound so obvious, that Clyde made no move to staunch its flow.

"Enough of this," Del said, dropping his gun at his feet. "Enough..."

Clyde coughed, a mist of blood painting his face. "You're...you're...you're finished...Grissom..."

"I was finished the moment I agreed to work for a bastard like Carter Herrick."

"See...see you...in Hell..." Clyde managed to curse before he died.

Charlotte ran to Owen's side, threw her arms around his neck, and held him close. "It's over, Owen! It's over!"

But even as he comforted her, Owen knew better. Carter Herrick had raped his mother, chased her off to Colorado, and ruined her life. Herrick had taken away the family he and Hannah could have had, leading them across the country in a misguided desire for revenge. He had sent men to ruin John Grant's life, to destroy his ranch, because Caroline Wallace had dared to choose to love him. Owen wondered if there had ever been another man who deserved to be punished more. He would never rest, *could* never rest, until Herrick had gotten what he deserved.

Carter Herrick was going to pay for his crimes.

Chapter Twenty-seven

CHARLOTTE STEPPED OUT of the doors of the horse barn and into the afternoon. The weather had changed dramatically. The rain and wind that had lashed the countryside had disappeared, replaced by a calmness the likes of which she had not seen before. The air had taken on an almost greenish tinge; she seemed to be viewing the world through a thin, colored cloth. Everything was deathly still, no branches swinging, no birds flying, as if the world had momentarily stopped turning.

"This is gonna be bad," John said, stepping up beside her and peering out over his land. The gun Del had used to kill Clyde Drake, the one he had dropped on the ground afterwards, was tucked into the waistband of John's pants. In the immediate aftermath of what had happened, Del had resigned himself to his fate; he had vowed to go with John to Sawyer and tell the sheriff all that he knew about Carter

Herrick's plan. For his part, John had already appeared to have forgiven Del, but he held on to the gun all the same.

"What's going to be bad?" Charlotte asked.

"The weather."

"But the storm is lifting," she replied.

"No, it ain't. I've been livin' in these parts long enough to know when a storm is in the air, and now is one of them times. This is the calm before the real storm. This is the sort of weather where folks get killed. There's a cyclone or one of them tornado's is a-comin'."

As if to validate John's words, a wall of wind came rushing toward them; Charlotte could *see* it coming, a shift in the clouds, rain falling in the distance, followed by the scraggly grasses dramatically bending until they nearly touched the ground. When it hit them, a howling keen that whistled hard in their ears, slamming the barn doors back with a tremendous crash, Charlotte had to struggle to maintain her balance, to prevent being blown off her feet.

"We've got to get to the storm cellar!" John shouted to be heard. "Go now!"

In the aftermath of Clyde Drake's assault, all their senses had been thrown out of kilter. Back inside the barn, Hannah was tending to Hale's wound, the bullet still painfully lodged in his huge body. He hadn't complained much, though it was obvious he was in agony. That he had saved her life, taking the bullet meant for her, was a fact that was not lost on the woman he loved.

"Get to the cellar!" John shouted at them.

"Hale can't make it!" Hannah answered.

"I can so," Hale disagreed, although it was obvious he was struggling to stay conscious.

"You're gonna make it, son," John reassured them. "Del, you get on the other side of Hale and give him some help! With you supportin' him, he can walk, if only for a short ways. Take him and go to the storm cellar. You'll be safe there."

Without hesitation, Del did as he was told and, with Hannah doing her best to support Hale's other side, they started to limp back toward the main house.

Owen stood just inside the door, his eyes never wandering from the truck. Ever since she had embraced him just after Del had shot Clyde, Owen hadn't said a word, keeping to himself. At first, Charlotte had wondered if he had been hurt in his attempt to stop Carter Herrick's hired gun, but she slowly began to understand that he had learned an awful lot about his origins in a very short time: what horrible tragedy had befallen his mother, as well as who was responsible. But when she ran to him, he never even glanced at her.

"Owen!" she shouted. "We have to go! We have to get to the cellar!"

"I'm not going," he said simply, his voice nearly swallowed by the wind.

Charlotte couldn't believe what she had heard; she hoped that it had been a trick of the ever-increasing gale. It was just as John had said; what she had seen was the lull before the true fury of the heavens could be unleashed. The air was thick with dirt and whatever else could be swept up in the storm's path; brush, leaves, and even a man's hat sailed by in front of them.

"The weather's getting worse!" she shouted again. "We have to get to the main house before it's too late!"

"You don't want to be out here any more'n you have to," John added. "There ain't no tellin' how much worse this'll get."

"I'm not going," Owen said more firmly, turning so that they could see the resolve in his eyes, his determination to do what he wanted.

"But we—"

"Listen to me," Owen snapped, not allowing Charlotte to protest further. "I've waited my whole life for this day, have spent years looking for the man who was responsible for ruining my mother's life. For most of it, I blamed an innocent man," he said as he looked at John, "but now I know the truth and I'm not waiting a moment longer before making sure he gets what's coming to him."

"Carter Herrick can wait," John said.

"He's already enjoyed far more time than he deserves."

"Owen," Charlotte said. "Please don't go."

"I have to."

It seemed ridiculous to Charlotte that Owen was fixated on getting his revenge at a time like this. They had all been threatened; Hale had been shot. The storm had escalated to a point she could not have imagined, and John thought it would only get worse. To go out there in search of Carter Herrick, a vindictive man who had sent his thugs to try to kill them, would be risking his life. Yet Charlotte could see that he was serious, that he was intent on doing right by his dead mother. She had trouble understanding it; revenge was an emotion with which she had no personal experience.

"You can't go out in this weather, son," John argued. "Anyone caught out is gonna be swept away faster than they'll know what hit 'em. Goin' out there now is riskin' your life."

John's warning pushed through the dense fog that had enveloped her ever since the moment Owen had lured them inside the barn. It lifted in an instant, her heart thundering.

"Sarah!" she shouted into the wind. "Sarah is out there!"

"Oh, Lord!" John exclaimed. "If this storm comes anywhere close to that old cabin, they'll be findin' pieces of it a couple of towns away!"

Charlotte imagined the meager belongings the Becks possessed being scattered to the winds as the tin roof was peeled off, the cracked windows gave up what remained of their resistance, and the thin walls were flattened. Even the cast-iron stove would be pushed and prodded, moved until it plunged down a hill, forever destroyed. Sarah's picture of her mother would be lost, along with all trace of its owner, who would surely die.

"We have to go for them!" Charlotte pleaded, her face searching both John's and Owen's for some sign that they agreed with her. "We have to get the Becks out of that shack before it's too late!"

"It might already be," John answered gravely.

"No!" Charlotte shouted, running toward the truck. The wind was so fierce that every step felt as if she were trying to make her way through water, its current tugging and yanking at her. Grit and sand pecked at her face, stinging her skin and forcing her to keep her eyes nearly closed, daring to take a look only when she felt she might be heading in the wrong direction, her hands extended in front of her in case she were to run into an unexpected obstacle. She couldn't say if John or Owen had shouted for her to stop, since the incessant roaring of the wind was the only sound she could hear. Though the truck was only a matter of feet away when she started, it felt as if the journey covered miles.

When she finally managed to reach the truck, Charlotte desperately pulled at the door, but she couldn't open it. Over and over she tried, her anger and fear rising with every failed attempt, but still the door remained shut. Tears began to race down her face as she struggled to stay upright. Her mind was filled with the imagined horrors that would strike Sarah Beck if she were unable to reach the pregnant girl in time.

Strong hands grabbed her, holding her upright just as she felt herself falling. Owen held her close, turning her to his chest so that she might be shielded from the storm. John stood beside him.

"We have to go to her," she pleaded. "We have to help her."

"I'll go with you," John offered, extending his arm toward the truck's door.

"No," Owen answered him.

"Damn it all! It might be a fool's errand, but we gotta try!"

"And we will," he said calmly, "but I'll be the one going."

"You don't know the way!" John protested.

"But Charlotte does. Besides, if this storm is going to be as bad as you think, you'll be needed here at the ranch. You know it better than anyone. The folks here will be depending on you."

John looked like he wanted to argue the point further, but finally nodded and said, "I reckon you're right, but if you're gonna go, you best hurry. There ain't much time."

They'd only just left John behind, Charlotte watching through the rear window as he struggled to make his way toward the ranch house, the truck's old engine sputtering loudly to life, when the rain began to fall in earnest. Sheets of heavy raindrops were whipped horizontal to the ground by the wind, slamming into the truck with abandon. Huge drops pelted the windshield.

"Can't see a damn thing," Owen muttered, peering into the gloom.

"Be careful," Charlotte said as the tires slipped in the mud, her breath catching in her throat.

"There isn't time for careful."

Even though they were driving into a storm, possibly even heading to their deaths, Charlotte couldn't help but be glad Owen was with her. She knew that it must have been hard for him to set aside his desire to go for Carter Herrick. But that was what he had done, he had made a choice, and she knew it had been to be with her. While she wouldn't have wavered in accompanying John Grant to the Becks' cottage, she was glad that it was Owen sitting beside her.

"How much farther?" Owen asked, his face knit deep in concentration.

"I'm not sure," Charlotte answered. She had been out to the shack many times, familiarized herself with the quirky landmarks that dotted the way, but with the weather as bad as it was, she wasn't certain where they were or how long it had been since they left.

The truck turned sharply to the left, then back to the right. They dropped down into a depression, making Charlotte's stomach sicken, before rising rapidly. The road was so narrow, so bumpy, that she was thankful that it would eventually end at the Becks' cabin.

"That's twice today we've put our necks on the line," Owen observed.

"It's not something that I want to make a habit of doing."

"Me neither."

"When the storm is over and everybody is safe," Charlotte said, stressing the positive outcome of their journey, "I want to go back to the pond, just the two of us, and take a swim."

"It'll be a lake by the time this storm is over."

They both laughed, the sound strange in the cramped interior of the truck's cab. But their grim laughter was suddenly cut short; just ahead of them on the road, barely visible through the rain-streaked window, a tree that had been felled lay in their path. It wasn't much, not a bit larger than a young stripling in Charlotte's Minnesota, but if the truck was to hit it . . .

"Watch out!" Charlotte screamed.

Owen yanked the wheel hard to the side and the truck lurched off the road and down a sharp decline. Charlotte's hands gripped the dashboard. The truck's tires bounced off large rocks, slid in the slick mud, and finally splashed through the water of a creek that had been formed by the runoff from the storm. The effect was jarring for the truck's passengers.

"Hold on!" Owen shouted, and Charlotte did her best to oblige.

Just as fast as the truck had gone down a hill, Owen straightened the wheel so that it would climb another. With the engine straining hard, whining as it struggled to maintain the uncertain footing beneath its tires, they slowly, surely picked up speed. When they crested the low hill, they were going so fast that the wheels left the ground and they hurtled into the air. They landed with a thud, a bone-jarring knock that bounced Charlotte around the cab. By some miracle or out of blind luck, they had landed back on the road.

For a moment, neither of them could make a sound save for the raggedness of their breath. Charlotte was so frightened that she could barely focus her eyes and her temples throbbed.

Then, up ahead of the rapidly diminishing road, she suddenly spied the cabin that Sarah Beck shared with her father. While the afternoon had definitely darkened as a result of the storm, Charlotte could see its distinct form outlined against the persistent gloom. Relief welled in her heart to find that it was still, miraculously, standing, though a portion of its tin roof had been peeled back by the relentless wind. Light shone through the cracked window. The cabin looked even smaller than normal in the face of the storm.

"Stop the car!" she shouted. "I see it! I see the cabin!"

Owen jammed down hard on the brakes and the truck began to slowly skid, listing to its side for so long that Charlotte began to worry that they would be unable to stop, that they might drop down into yet another depression or, worse, they might flip over. But somehow the truck held, the wheels locking.

"We need to be fast," Owen said. "Let me go in and get them."

"I'm coming with you," she cut him off defiantly.

"We don't have time to argue!"

"So don't!"

Charlotte knew that Owen wanted her to stay behind so that he would know where she was, know that she was safe. But she couldn't allow him to take all the risk. Her teaching Sarah had created a bond between the two of them. Charlotte felt a responsibility to the pregnant girl and wanted to go to the cabin to make sure that she hadn't been hurt.

"All right," Owen agreed, "but you get out on my side of the truck and hold on to my hand. I don't want the wind blowing you away leaving me unable to find you."

"All right."

"Whatever you do, don't let go."

Charlotte was thankful that Owen insisted she take his hand. The weather had worsened dramatically. Rain pelted her mercilessly with every step, drenching her blouse and plastering her hair to her head. The wind was considerably stronger than it had been back at the ranch. It roared with such ferocity that Charlotte could hardly hear herself think.

Owen was shaking her hand furiously; at first she thought it was because he was trying to make sure she was close, but it soon dawned on her that he was trying to get her attention. Shielding her eyes, she looked at him. His face was white with terror. With his other hand, he pointed, and when she followed, she too felt as if their world were surely about to end.

Oh, my God...

In the distance, over the roof of the Becks' dilapidated cabin, was the black spiraling cone of a tornado.

Chapter Twenty-eight

THE TORNADO STRETCHED DOWN from the dark heavens as if it were the finger of God himself. Immensely broad at its top, it narrowed as it reached toward the ground, a churning engine of destruction. Debris of every size and shape roiled in its cylinder, to be jettisoned as more was pulled up to take its place. The tornado looked to be miles across, with an appetite for destruction that could not be sated. Charlotte was awed by the sheer force of the wind; the gusts that buffeted them were nearly enough to lift her from her feet. If she weren't so frightened, a part of her would have found the tornado beautiful, something to fill her with wonder.

I don't want that thing to be the death of me...

Still holding tight to her hand, Owen half-dragged Charlotte to the door of the cabin and began to pound on it furiously. Over and over he smashed his closed fist against the wood; with the roar of the approaching tornado, Charlotte wondered if the Becks could even hear his effort. She was surprised that the door hadn't been torn open, but the Becks must have barricaded it shut to keep the wind from ripping it off its hinges.

"Sarah!" she shouted, scarcely able to hear her own voice.

Finally, the door opened a crack. Alan Beck's alcohol-ravaged and wrinkled face peered out at them through the gap. Owen made no effort to identify himself, shouldering open the door and pushing back the table and chairs that had been blocking their entry. Charlotte rushed inside.

Sarah sat on her bed back in the far corner, cradling her stomach with one hand, her mother's picture in the other. The poor girl looked scared out of her wits, but brightened at seeing Charlotte. An oil lamp sat on the apple crate, its burning wick the source of the light they had seen from the road.

"How'd you get out here?" Sarah asked nervously. "It sounds bad, like this cabin is gonna fall down."

"Shush now, Sarah," Charlotte quieted her as she rushed over and began helping her to rise from the bed, mindful of her belly. "There isn't time to talk about it now! We have to go! Go right this instant!"

"It's a twister, ain't it?" Alan asked, staring out into the storm he had exposed by opening the door.

"It is," Owen answered. "I can't say for certain, but I think it's heading right for us. If we don't leave fast, we're *never* going to get to safety."

"We'll go in the truck," Charlotte explained, hoping that her encouragement would calm Sarah's panic. "We can outrun it and make it back to the ranch."

"Ain't no chance in hell of doin' that," Alan disagreed. "I seen my share of these damn things when I was a boy and they're faster than you'd ever believe 'em to be, I say. Ruthless as killers . . . like a rabid dog that done got its first taste of blood . . . ain't likely to stop till it's got its fill."

"I can drive fast," Owen insisted.

"You ain't faster than nature, boy." Alan shook his head.

At the finality of her father's words, Sarah began to cry, sobbing into Charlotte's shoulder. Outside the door, the tornado sounded as if it were a locomotive barreling down toward them, its whistle shrill. As if to demonstrate its potential, the tornado's winds shattered the already broken window. Sarah screamed in terror.

"We can't stay here," Charlotte pleaded, looking at the flimsy walls. "If we do, this cabin will be our coffin!"

"If it's too late to take the truck, where can we go?" Owen asked Alan, realizing that the older man was right and there was no chance for them to outrun the storm.

"Down the back of the hill opposite this here cabin, there's a small cave. It ain't much, no more than a couple a feet dug into the side of the hill, but it's carved outta rock 'stead of earth. Stumbled 'cross it when I was drinkin' one night 'bout a month back. I can't say it'll be safe, but it's safer than here."

"Take us there!" Owen shouted.

"I'm scared," Sarah cried.

"I'll be with you," Charlotte said as confidently as she could.

Alan Beck led the way from the cabin, Charlotte and Sarah behind him, with Owen bringing up the rear. Even in the short time Charlotte and Owen had been inside, the storm's rampaging intensity had increased; lashing bursts of wind snatched at his legs, trying their best to entangle him. Occasional flashes of lightning exploded before their eyes. Rain drenched them in seconds. But the most unbearable part of the storm was the noise; Owen couldn't imagine a more ferocious, unstoppable sound. He covered his ears, but even had he packed them with cotton, it would be useless. He never looked back, did not want to know how much closer the funnel had come. The tornado was a rampaging animal, and it was after them.

Ahead, he saw Charlotte stop, struggling beside Sarah, the poor girl awash in tears and panic on both of their faces. Charlotte screamed, her voice a wandering whisper that barely caught his ear. "Owen! I need you to take Sarah! I can't...I can't in this wind...and she—"

Without speaking his answer, Owen scooped Sarah into his arms as carefully as he could, cradling her close to his chest. He was surprised by how light she was, especially given how far along she was in her pregnancy. Though he could feel her shoulders shivering from either fear or the rain, he could not hear her sobbing.

"Stay close," he shouted to Charlotte, "but don't stop running!"

Alan rushed past the truck and stopped at the scant shrubs and stunted trees that marked the edge of the hill that led down and away from the cabin. He looked back, waiting, frantically waving his arms for them to follow.

He yelled something, but no one could hear.

Even as he passed the truck, Owen had to fight the urge to leap inside and take his chances outrunning the tornado. He knew that Alan was right, that it was a pointless gesture that would only get them all killed.

"We gots to go down this here hill!" Alan shouted in his ear as another round of lightning lit up the sky. "The cave is near the bottom!" And then he was gone into the darkening afternoon, over the ridge, his footprints in the fresh mud the only sign of his passing.

"Follow him!" Owen screamed at Charlotte. "We'll come on just behind!"

Going down the incline was harder than Owen had expected. From the top, the path would have looked steep and treacherous in the best of conditions, but with all of the furious rain loosening the ground, turning it into mud, he met a constant challenge to stay upright, a task made all the more difficult by his carrying a pregnant girl. Because he could not see his feet, he shuffled them carefully as they awkwardly descended, hoping that he would know when he met an obstacle.

Then suddenly a gust of wind made his wishes worthless, unbalancing him and sweeping his feet out from under him. When he knew that he was falling, Owen leaned backward as far as he could and absorbed the rough collision with his back, protecting Sarah as they half-slid down the embankment. Though his throbbing ribs screamed, still sore from being struck by a stampeding horse, he gritted his teeth and bore his agony silently, worrying more about ensuring Sarah's safety.

Mercifully, the descent was short. Once Owen struggled back to his feet, he followed as Alan led them around a stone outcropping, stopping before a low hole cut into the rock wall, half-covered by brush. It wasn't much, Owen even wondered if he would have noticed the cave if he had not been looking for it, but it would have to do.

"Put her in there!" Alan shouted.

Owen ducked down at the cave's entrance and pushed his way through the dead shrubs, their sharp nettles clinging to his shirt and scratching against his skin. He discovered that they had been shepherded into more of a depression than a cave; the solid rock wall met him mere feet past the opening. Owen's feet stumbled over empty liquor bottles, undoubtedly left over from one of Alan's benders.

How in the hell are we all going to fit in here? Owen thought.

Blindly, he felt along in the dark, his hand against the smooth, cold stone. Thankfully, he found that there was a small opening that rounded to the left, barely deeper than a closet. He was relieved to find that it offered some protection from the incessant wind. Owen gently set Sarah down on her feet and then hurried Charlotte to join her.

"Hold Sarah close!" he shouted. "Stay around this corner and don't move! I'll be just behind you both!"

Seconds passed, Owen's arms wrapped around Charlotte in the darkness, before he became aware that there were only three of them in the cave.

"Stay here and don't move!" he bellowed in Charlotte's ear. He could feel her turn to question him, but he was already too far away to hear.

Owen found Alan outside the entrance, his face turned up into the rain, watching the calamity breaking all around them. He had no idea what Sarah's father thought he was doing, but he wasn't willing to ask.

Grabbing him by the shirt, Owen made to drag Alan back to the safety of the cave, but he was astonished to have the man shake off his grasp.

"What in the hell are you doing?" he shouted.

"There ain't room for all of us to fit in there!" Alan answered. "I'm stayin' here!"

"That's crazy talk!"

"You know I'm right!"

"I won't let you do this!" Owen yelled, frustrated. When

he reached to grab Alan again, the man just moved farther away.

"You got your whole life 'head of you! Get back in there 'fore it's too late!"

"But your daughter...!"

"I ain't never done right by that girl a once in her life! Ever since the day her momma died, I expected her to do all the cleanin', cookin', and maintainin' of the house without ever thinkin' of what was best for her! Well, now I am! I'm doin' my part to keep her alive! You just tell her that her father loved her!"

By the end, Owen could barely hear the words coming from Alan Beck's mouth, so near had the tornado come. Even with his feet planted as hard as he could, the wind grabbed at him, trying to pull him to his death. There was no more time for arguing. Sarah's father had made up his mind, and there would be no convincing him otherwise. A part of Owen understood his decision; he would have gladly sacrificed his own life so that Charlotte might live.

Owen nodded once to Alan, then hurried back into the cave.

"I'm here!" he shouted into Charlotte's ear.

"Where's Alan?" she asked, but he pretended that he hadn't heard her.

Huddling as close to Charlotte and Sarah as he could, Owen strained to maintain his position inside the cave. Outside, the roar of the tornado escalated, its winds annihilating everything in its path as it moved ever forward. For the first time since he was a child, Owen gave a silent prayer, a plea that they would survive this encounter with the wrath of nature. He also gave a prayer for Alan, who had undoubtedly already been absorbed by the storm, hopefully already dead so that he might be spared the agony of enduring the tornado's wrath.

Heaven help anyone unlucky enough to fall into the tornado's path...

Carter Herrick sat behind his desk, sipping whiskey and smoking a cigar. Outside, the storm roared like a wild beast, but inside his home all was silent save for the ticking of a clock. With the advance of the rampaging storm, all the men who worked for him on his ranch had fled for safety, barricading themselves in shelters and holes in the earth, desperately trying to save their own hides. But Carter didn't share their desire to live; when he saw the tornado outside his window, he decided just to stay and watch.

Caroline Wallace returned to his thoughts, the memory of her pretty face a stark reminder of all that he had risked and lost throughout his life. There had been no pleasure to take from forcing himself on her all those many years ago. Recalling her horrifying cries had wakened him from his dreams on many a night, but he had refused to let her denial of his advances be the final word, could not allow her to belong to someone like John Grant.

"Why couldn't you have accepted me, Caroline?" he asked into the gloom.

Would he be sitting here now if she had? Carter doubted it. He would never have married that waste of a woman in her place, would never have had to endure whatever sickness it was that finally felled her. Maybe he would have had a son strong enough, *man enough*, to replace him.

Instead, he remained alone.

Even his machinations to ruin John Grant had come to nothing. Whatever he asked Del Grissom and Clyde Drake to do, setting a wildfire, fouling the water supply, even starting a stampede of horses, resulted in little more than a temporary inconvenience. Grant had always been a resilient son of a bitch when they were young, a talent that served him well now. Carter supposed that if he really had wanted to end things between them, he should have gone up to the man and shot him himself.

Something heavy slammed into Carter's ranch house. Looking out the window, he could see the tornado begin to pull apart one of his outer buildings. It was fascinating, in a way, to watch the boards being lifted into the sky. He wondered what that force might do to a man.

Soon, he would be with his son. He'd stopped living when the boy died, a corpse who didn't have the common sense to know he shouldn't be drawing breath. Time would rectify that.

When the windows of his office broke, and the wood

was plied from his home by the wind, Carter Herrick sat back . . . and smiled.

Everywhere around them was destruction. Remnants of the Becks' cabin littered the ground, a piece of tin roof here, scattered boards there, and even a bit of bedding lodged in the boughs of a nearby tree. Running to the cave had saved their lives; staying behind would have ended them.

The truck had been pushed to the lip of the path they had followed and now lay upside down at its base, a spidery web of cracks spread across the windshield.

How is it possible that we are alive?

The answer was that they were indebted to Alan Beck. If it hadn't been for his knowledge of the land, his wouldn't be the only death. Charlotte couldn't imagine what it must have been like for the man, first to decide he should remain outside the cave and then to have to wait for the tornado to inevitably end his life. She and he had had their differences when she had begun teaching Sarah, but now she saw him in a new light, as a father who knew his final responsibility was to his child.

Owen settled Sarah onto a rock just outside the cave entrance. The poor girl appeared traumatized, in shock over what they had experienced. She still had not asked for her father, but Charlotte knew that moment would soon come.

"Are you all right?" Owen asked as he took her hands in his own.

"I don't know," she murmured, and laughed.

"Me either."

For a long moment, they stood surveying the carnage all around them, uncertain of what to say or how to start picking up the pieces.

"You saved my life," she said softly, the world suddenly so quiet after the cacophony of the tornado.

"Alan saved us all...we saved each other..."

Charlotte loved Owen Wallace; the choice she had made in giving him her heart had been the right one. Even now, in the face of such widespread destruction, she felt hope. They would build a life together, would build a family. She would help him to let go of his sorrow, his need for revenge, until there was no more darkness in his heart, just as the darkened sky above would someday clear. They would laugh, cry, shout, and everything in between. None of it would be easy, but standing together, there was nothing that they couldn't overcome.

They had just proven it.

Epilogue

Sawyer, Oklahoma—Christmas Eve, 1940

"...THAT GERMAN PLANES again struck the heart of London last night, sparking fires that raged out of control. Reports are that civilian casualties were limited due to the timely evacuation to subway tunnels. German chancellor Adolf Hitler went on state radio to declare the bombing a success."

Charlotte shut off the radio with a frown. They had listened to the war news all day. She had hoped to catch something lighter, perhaps listen to some music, maybe a variety show, but the war in Europe seemed to monopolize the airways. Right now she had to focus on the imminent arrival of her dinner guests.

For the fourth time in two hours, she reviewed her

checklist. Everything seemed to be as she wanted; the table had been set with their nicest dishes and silverware, a turkey was roasting in the oven, Owen was grumbling out back while cutting firewood for the night, and even all of the ornaments on their small Christmas tree were just as she wanted them.

"May·this be the best Christmas of all our lives," she murmured to herself.

So much had changed since that first summer she had arrived in Sawyer to become a teacher, far from her home and family in Minnesota. Looking back on those days, she was amazed at all that had happened. So many calamities had struck John Grant's ranch, culminating in the tornado that had nearly blown them all away, that there had never seemed a moment's peace.

But peace...and joy had come with Owen...

Owen and she married the following spring in a simple ceremony at Sawyer's church, an occasion that prompted a welcome visit from her family. Unfortunately, her grandmother had not felt well enough to attend, but Rachel and Mason Tucker came, along with Charlotte's sister, Christina. Charlotte and Owen expected the weather to be tumultuous, much like their courtship and the adversity they had faced, but when a gorgeous day dawned they considered it an omen, predicting a glorious future.

They moved to a house closer to the school, one that needed a little fixing up, but they enjoyed doing the work together; Owen repaired the columns on their porch and Charlotte came along behind, applying a fresh coat of paint. Slowly, they built something to be proud of.

In other places, lives needed to be rebuilt.

When the tornado rampaged through the Oklahoma countryside, lives had been forever altered. John Grant was fortunate in that his ranch was spared any significant damage; a couple of outlying buildings had been destroyed, a large amount of fence had been felled, and roads and creeks had been choked with debris. Immediately, the men of the Grant Ranch set about repairing and restoring.

But for others, the damage was beyond fixing. Carter Herrick's ranch had been directly in the line of the tornado's path and had paid a tremendous price. Practically every structure had been annihilated, scattered over an area of many miles. Fortunately, most of the men and women who worked there had managed to find shelter before the storm arrived, all except Carter Herrick himself; he was found dead in the wreckage.

When Owen learned of Carter's death, his reaction had been muted. Charlotte had expected him to feel cheated that he hadn't been able to confront the man who had raped his mother and sent her life into a spiral, the man who was his father, but Owen had surprised her.

"Good," he'd said when he learned of Carter's death, but nothing more.

The relationship between Owen and John Grant had improved in the time since the revelation of the true identity of Owen's father. Owen continued to work on the ranch beside John and Hale, and Charlotte was happy to see them laughing together, in a way becoming the family her husband had always needed.

Del's betrayal had undeniably wounded John. Though he never requested that Del go to the sheriff and confess to what he had done in the service of Carter Herrick, living with his guilt was more than Del could bear to accept. One night, while all of the ranch slept, he packed up his belongings and left, never to be seen again. His responsibilities were given to Hale, who then passed more and more of his duties on to Owen. Charlotte worried about the war, about the likelihood that the United States could be dragged into it and the nation's men sent off to fight, but if it were to happen, she knew Owen would do his duty. Her father had gone to Europe and returned, although it had taken years. Owen might need to go as well.

Charlotte hurried into the kitchen and checked the turkey; it was a golden brown as it cooked in its succulent juices. She smiled broadly; she desperately wanted tonight to be as special as she hoped.

This was to be the first night out for Hannah and Hale as a married couple. After a courtship that seemed to go on forever, much to Owen's sister's consternation, Hale had finally summoned enough courage to ask his beloved Hannah to be his bride.

"What took you so long?" she asked in place of a simple "yes."

Their wedding had been quite the sight, Hale perspiring and stuttering over his pledge to love and honor, so uncomfortable it looked as if he were being forced into matrimony against his will. Hannah smiled through it all, confident in Hale's undying love.

As the other person whose life had been irreversibly changed the day of the tornado, Sarah Beck had managed to do well. Though she had lost her father in the cataclysmic weather, she had moved forward with her head held high, and a few weeks later she gave birth to a boy just as she had always predicted, and named him Ethan. Charlotte had continued teaching Sarah's lessons, now in her room in the ranch's main house, and she had shown real improvement; there was even talk that she would go to public high school in the following year. Amelia had taken a particularly strong liking to the girl and their closeness had created a sense of family among the two of them and John. Though Caroline had been taken from him, in Owen and Hannah, John had discovered what it meant to be a parent.

"This better be enough wood," Owen said as he burst in the back door with an armload of cut oak.

"If it isn't, you can just go out and get some more."

"Next year, I'm going to show *you* how to swing an axe," he grumbled, but kissed Charlotte on the cheek as he went past.

While Owen lit a fire in their wood stove, Charlotte found herself reflecting on the one person in her family she wished were with her for Christmas. Her sister, Christina, was finally old enough to leave their home in Carlson and to set out on her own. Charlotte remembered what it was like for herself, the excitement of a new beginning, the nervousness of a train ride into the unknown, and prayed that her little sister would find as much happiness as she had.

Owen came up behind her and laced his arms around her; even after their year together, Charlotte never tired of the feeling.

"Have I told you lately that I love you?" he whispered in her ear.

"A time or two," she teased. "But tell me again."

"You better watch out, Mrs. Wallace, or Santa won't bring you any presents."

"I've already got just what I wanted."

"And what was that?" He kissed the side of her face.

"You, my love," she whispered.